FAREWELL GESTURE

ONE

The first thing to do when I got out was obviously to settle my affairs with the family solicitor. Easy enough to decide but so very difficult to execute, I discovered. There was the question of persistence. A dozen times in the first week I pointed my nose in that direction and couldn't carry it through, unable to shake off a hollow feeling of disorientation and even a hint of fear. Although this was only a small market town, it seemed to me to have become a teeming metropolis. Traffic was confusing, and uniforms still repressed me. I found myself crossing the road to avoid traffic wardens. Hilliard, himself, was another aspect of authority, old and dusty, and an officer of the law. I didn't want to confront him.

It was getting along to the end of September, which was a bad time to come out, as there's no greenery in Gartree Prison and seasons mean nothing. Now I was in the middle of leaf-fall, and the trees were sad with their loss. I didn't need that. New life, that was what I was aching for, and I couldn't resurrect my past delight in the sun-shot red and gold.

I'd booked into a small hotel, and after a week my money was running short. Like it or not, I now had to nerve myself to face Hilliard, senior partner in Hilliard, Pouncey, and Pierce, family solicitors.

He wasn't pleased to see me, though he faked something of a crackly parchment smile. There was no offer of his brittle hand, and he called me Mr. Manson, not Paul, as it had always been before. I sat. He made a protracted performance of explaining the legal point, which I already knew, that I was fortunate in that my father had died before my mother, who'd lingered on for a fortnight.

"I trust you realise you could not have inherited from your father," he said heavily, his face creaking. "From your mother . . ." He cleared his throat. ". . . yes."

I nodded, not giving him anything, no self-justification and no explanations. Definitely no explanations.

The will had long ago been probated and the house sold, the

money sleeping in a bank and acquiring interest. Drily, he explained about the availability of credit cards, as though I'd been out of touch for forty years instead of four.

As I left he roused himself so far as to extend his arthritic hand. "And what do you intend to do now, Mr. Manson? I understand you were in America at the time . . ." He allowed that to fade away, clearing his throat, obviously hoping I would return there.

I could have explained that I had a lot of catching up to do, but he wouldn't have understood. In Gartree, you fared best if you suppressed most of your awareness, and allowed your emotions to slumber down almost to the level of coma. I hadn't yet risked a laugh, afraid of how it might emerge.

So I smiled. I said I would look around. This was not really as vague as it sounded. There was a life I might be able to save. I didn't know whether I'd be able to find her, or what I might do to intervene, but I had to try. It was at least an objective.

A young woman called Philomena Wise was due to die.

All I knew was that she had lived in a town called Killingham. I had never heard of it. I travelled there by train, my few bits in a kitbag, and found myself another dusty hotel, which wasn't going to frown at my old jeans and anorak, then I went out to explore the town.

My confidence was growing. I had now a definite intention, and I could dare to venture into my memory. Hadn't there been a sense of humour? That, surely, was worth digging deeply for.

Unfortunately, Killingham presented nothing to laugh at. It was a black Midlands town, dull and uninspiring, nursing its wounds from the dissolution of its industrial heart and putting on a brave front with a shining shopping area, where one in four shop fronts exhibited "for rent" signs. I scoured the pubs. Philomena. Surely the name would ring out, though people were more likely to call her Phil, I realised. There was nothing to go on, as I didn't know her social standing, whether backstreet dives would more likely attract her than clubhouses and hotel lounges. Or even no night life at all.

Carl Packer had done no more than approach me. Once I'd impressed on him that I wasn't interested in the contract, he'd said not another word. Stupid of me. I'd been appalled that he'd seen me as a possible hired killer. It would've been impossible to explain moral niceties to a lout such as Packer, but there's a big difference between a professional killing and a domestic one. I'd felt offended, and I'd made that clear, so he'd backed off.

Yet Carl Packer wanted her dead, and the Carl Packers of this world usually get what they want. I didn't know what he had against her. It didn't matter. He approached me a month before my release, and someone else, someone better equipped to do what he wanted, might be out at any time. Might already be out.

I spent a month on it, the impetus gradually dying. Now I was spending more time on considering my own motivation in this, and into a corner of my mind was edging the thought that I had uncompleted business in the U.S.A.

I decided to give it one more week, and, as fate usually decrees, I found her on the Tuesday.

This was in the Four Aces, a dim gambling club with no membership fee but a large entrance one. No black jackets and bow ties were on display, but suits and ties were, and that first evening I felt conspicuous in my jeans. All the same, they accepted my money. I was sitting at the roulette table, venturing an occasional one-pound chip on number seven, this being my lucky number—the sentence I'd been given. Then I heard her name. The croupier said, ". . . Ms. Wise."

I looked up. The young woman who smiled at him would have been in her mid-twenties, I thought, not much younger than me. She was wearing a severe black jacket over a white shirt, and a straggly black tie. That was all I could see across the table. She was older than I'd expected (though I couldn't recall how I'd got the impression she would be young), with dark hair and dark eyes, a thin, determined face, except when she smiled, and straight eyebrows that almost met above a long nose. She caught my eye, the smile still hovering there, and I inclined my head.

Then an older woman, sitting beside her, called her Phil. I played on, but seven didn't seem to want to come up. After half an hour I heard Phil Wise murmur to her companion, "I've had enough." So I rose to my feet as she did and was standing at her shoulder when she cashed in her chips. She was very much aware of this manoeuvre.

Now I could see that she was five feet eight inches or so, so that I topped her by five inches. She was wearing a skirt and semi-high heels, and hoisting a heavy shoulder-bag.

"May I get you a drink?" I asked. My social confidence was expanding.

I had not expected her response. Not acceptance nor rejection, it was at first a flickered grimace, then a calm consideration of me, as though I had to be measured. In her eyes there was certainly suspicion, then she tossed her head, dismissing it.

"Why not?" she said. "There's a bar in the back."

"Good. I didn't know that."

In this way we became acquainted. There was no more to it

than that, at first. I didn't understand enough of the background to be able to complete my business with the passing of a warning and leave it at that. I was tentative, and perhaps she sensed it. But I could hardly plunge in. She told me her name was Philomena Wise, and I told her mine was Paul Manson. She began to relax a little. I asked if I could meet her again, and if she'd backed off I'd have had to follow her home in order to keep in touch, but she simply told me she would be at the Four Aces every night.

"For a while, anyway."

I didn't know what she meant by that. We parted on the street. I assumed she had a car parked somewhere.

The following evening I was there again. After a week it became almost routine. We sat together at the tables, and we went for a drink or two afterwards. Phil and I could laugh together. I was finding it possible to laugh now, and she could be amusing, in a dry, cynical way. Sometimes she joined the woman I'd seen her with that first evening. Sometimes not, but she was never far from her.

By this time I'd been taken to her flat for a final drink. That was all. Friendly—no more. Emotionally, she was keeping me at a distance. She had one of four flats in a converted Georgian house four miles out of town, its rear overlooking a lake. The house was quiet and secluded, wrapped in subdued dignity. The door into the hall was inset with a stained-glass panel, the hall itself was floored with oak, and there was always a smell of furniture polish. The three other occupants were retired couples. Phil's flat was upstairs, Number 3. It was quiet and relaxing, and she seemed to become another person, softer and less on edge, once she was beyond her door. But there was no hint as to why her life should be threatened, and I was feeling that I'd be making a fool of myself by bringing it up.

"Nice place," I said, looking round, that first time.

She loved colour. The sitting room was light and airy, all pastels and scatter-cushioned, everything in a disarray. Tidy it for her, and she would never find anything again.

She made me welcome. But strangely I could not relax there. I felt the urge to tell her why I was there, if only to watch her expression change. But that was an impulsive thought, and I felt she would laugh at warnings.

She did not easily respond to implications, but between us I felt a growing awareness. We were very much alike in one respect; we were both loners. This seemed a strange reason to be drawn together.

For five evenings I visited, and left again. She seemed to realise our relationship was becoming unusual, because, on that fifth evening, she was restless.

"I work alone, Paul," she said suddenly, right in the middle of Dvořák's Sixth on her stereo. She said it as though that explained something.

I grinned at her. "Want a partner?"

"Not in this."

We listened for a while, then she got up and switched it off. She had come to a decision.

"Paul," she told me, "I'm an enquiry agent. I work alone, from here and from a little office I use. I'm good at it, but it's dreary work. I used to be in the police—detective sergeant—but I left after a disagreement. Don't ask me what it was. The fact is, I've been keeping an eye on a certain Mrs. Eugenie Thompson, whose husband thought she was out every evening with a man, but it's not so. She's at the gaming tables. So the job's coming to an end."

"I see." What I saw was just a hint of what might be behind any vague threats on her life.

"Do you, though?"

Or of course I could be getting my marching orders. No, it wasn't that—or so my ego said. I thought I understood her, being a loner too. But whereas I'd always been contented with my own company, she was alone in the sense of being withdrawn. Something had happened—a disagreement, she'd called it—but perhaps it'd been something much more important to her. Her career had been destroyed. If she'd been dedicated—and she seemed the sort of single-minded person who would be dedicated to the upholding of the law as a sacred trust—then the removal of it would have left her bereft and lost. To go private might have seemed a solution, and yet, the sense of aloneness would then have gone with the job, whereas in the force she'd been one of a team.

"I'm trying to tell you," she was saying, "that I shall be on an entirely different job next week. Surveillance. A factory, pilfering and the like. Night work. Oh, for heaven's sake, Paul, I'm a working woman."

Was she asking me to be patient, saying that she couldn't at that time fit me into her life? Now she watched me with her head tilted and her eyes huge, and in her expression something I couldn't understand, almost a tearful appeal. And perhaps distrust.

To dispel this, and remembering that I'd not been very open with her, I decided to tell her more about myself. But not all.

"I know what it's like," I assured her, "working on your own. I spent two years researching in the foothills and deserts to the west of the Rockies. From Montana to Idaho, through Wyoming and

Utah and Colorado, down into Arizona and New Mexico. Living in a tent or the back of the big Cherokee I used, or in a shack on some Indian reservation. I was studying the history of the Indians."

"But surely, the Americans will've drained it dry!"

"A fresh approach. An outsider's view. I was working for a Ph.D. in history. But it was interrupted."

"Oh? How's that?"

I could feel her interest. It was almost as though I was offering her something she was pleased to hear, and which gave her hope.

"A death in the family. I had to come home."

I had deliberately changed the sequence. My married sister had managed to contact me at the home of a friend in the university at Palo Alto, where I'd taken a break to bring my notes up-to-date. She had asked me to come home urgently. My father, who was something not quite legal in the city, had taken a wrong step, had gone half crazy with the pressure of his failure and his fears for the future, and had been making my mother's life hell. My sister feared for her safety, so I'd flown home at once, and arrived at the house at the climax of his outburst of frustration. He'd gone completely wild, was beating her in a blind fury, and I had to drag him off with my hands. I . . . well, I could match him, it seemed, in his fury. Certainly in his strength. Before I knew it, I'd got his throat in my fingers, and then he was falling to the floor, dead. My mother was very close to death when I turned to her, and died a fortnight later.

So I could honestly say that my studies had been interrupted, by four years in Gartree. I was not going to tell her the details, though.

"And you never got your Ph.D.?" she asked in sympathy.

"I might go back and take it up again."

"Might?"

"It's been a four-year gap. Too much, perhaps."

"Four years?"

"I've been otherwise occupied."

She said nothing, looking down at the drink in her hands. I couldn't read her expression. There was a distancing, though. She could, having been a policewoman, have been able to fill in a few gaps.

"When?" she asked suddenly, looking up. "When did you think you might go back?"

"Nothing's settled in my mind."

She was silent again. I wondered whether she'd have been more pleased if I'd said: at once.

But that could not be so. My plans were becoming entangled

with my emotions. I had not faced them squarely, yet sometime or other I had to sort them out. This encounter with her had been prompted partly by impulse, but subconsciously, I now realised, by something more powerful. It had seemed imperative to take some action to help Philomena Wise—but behind it there was something I didn't wish to face—my father's death. I had taken a life. Perhaps I would feel better about it if I could balance the slate by saving one.

And yet, I could not feel remorse for his death. I'd hated how he'd made his money and what he stood for, and he had despised my scholarly pretentions, as he called them. And I'd loved my mother. No, I did not regret his death. What appalled me—still did, and I couldn't shake it off—was the fact that for two or three minutes I, who had always prided myself on my control, had gone completely berserk. That was what I regretted, and I was desperately afraid that that feeling could return.

Yet already it was clear that I'd plunged into this like a white knight to the rescue of his flaxen-haired damsel, when in fact she had turned out to be more like the damsel's self-confident minder, with her own Ph.D. in unarmed combat.

I'd waited too long, and she had begun to venture into a new topic. Seized once more by one of the impulses I've never been able to control, I plunged in, afraid I'd never be able to recapture the mood between us.

"If I decide to go, would you like to come with me?"

Frowning, half laughing, she said, "What?"

"To America. I'll need another year there, at least. No strings. No commitments. Just come along for the ride."

This was a welcome sign that I was getting back to my former self. I'd always enjoyed slapping fate in the kisser. It was something to do with challenging; the white knight syndrome, if you like. And how better to remove her from the orbit of Carl Packer's enmity? This thought leapt at me, taking me by surprise.

"But I can't do that!" she burst out, her dark eyes wide and startled.

"Why not?"

"I've got"—she waved a hand vaguely—"ongoing investigations all over the place. And I couldn't afford—"

"As my guest. Share the driving, if you like."

"You're a big, damned fool, Paul Manson. You know nothing about me."

"We'd find out—in Arizona, say."

She gave a short laugh. "It's ridiculous."

I shrugged. It would've been quicker simply to tell her that I'd been in Gartree, and knew that Packer was trying to arrange her death. But something stopped me. It was too late for that—or too soon. It would explain my interest in her in an ambivalent way.

"You've got to give me time to think," she said at last. "Ask me again tomorrow."

This I did. In the evening. By that time I had it planned more fully in my mind, and could give the invitation more conviction.

"I'd need a week," she said, breathing quickly. "I'll have to go to Sumbury. There's a special case I'll have to clear up."

"A week." I nodded.

"Maybe less. You can move in here, Paul, so that I can get in touch. I'll phone you—yes or no."

"Yes or no," I agreed. I'd hoped it would simply be when.

She went there on a Monday, the last day of September. From the window of her flat I watched her drive away in her little red Fiat two-seater. I'd moved in, as she'd suggested, to be close to a phone, but this soon proved to be an encumbrance as I couldn't allow myself too long away from her flat. I played her records and her tapes, and had interminable hours in which to recapture mentally the trend of my research. I couldn't wait to get back to it. If she phoned and said "no," then I would simply give her my warning and leave.

The snag was that I was now seeing our trip together as a joint adventure, and alone it seemed to have lost some of its attraction. I had completely lost touch with the fact that if Carl Packer wanted her dead, there had to be a damned good reason.

In the meantime, I was trapped in her flat, apart from rapid excursions to the shops. But she didn't phone.

The week dragged along. I got tired of music, and left the radio on the talking programme. It was company. Saturday arrived, and by that time the announcer's voice had become a meaningless drone. It was the mention of Sumbury that jerked me into alertness. I dived for the volume control.

". . . Sumbury in Devon, where the body of a woman has been found strangled in woodland. She has been identified as Philomena Wise. Inspector Greaves stated . . ."

I heard no more. The words pounded through my head. ". . . has been identified as Philomena Wise."

Then I sat down and tried to control the impulse to run from the flat, anywhere that was away from the oppression of my feeling of responsibility. I found myself staring at the phone, willing it to ring. I told myself I was insane.

After a while I got up from the chair and systematically walked through the flat, doing things like packing my kitbag, switching things off where necessary, walking out of the flat, closing the door quietly, and double-locking it. Then I walked steadily to the railway station and asked about trains to Sumbury. I would have one change.

I arrived at Sumbury at 4:35 P.M. It was a dull day, with a wind bitter enough to penetrate my consciousness. I went straight to the police station. The policeman I asked for directions looked at me as though I might need his assistance to reach it. It was a quiet town, its police station small and only two storeys. There was a constable at the desk. When he realised what I wanted he phoned through, and a woman came to take me upstairs.

The man sitting behind the desk wasn't very responsive. A typical small-town copper, I thought, stolid and unimaginative. I should not have trusted first impressions. He introduced himself as Detective Inspector Greaves, and took down my name and address. Paul Manson, of no fixed abode.

"She's already been identified, sir," he said politely.

"I'd like to see her." To prove it . . .

"What's your interest?"

"We were . . . going away together. When she got back."

"Indeed?"

Now that I came to look at him, I decided he was trying to be kind, but he was decidedly uncertain about me. He was a large man with a heavy face, which kept moving around with a series of grimaces as though he was searching for an expression that fitted the circumstances. When he said, "Indeed?" the grimace happened to be one of distaste, his pouched eyes considering me morosely, his bushy eyebrows climbing almost to his hairline.

"There's no reason why I shouldn't see her, is there?" I challenged him, impatient with the protocol.

"No reason at all." His eyes switched to the woman who'd brought me there. "Sergeant Rice will take you." He smiled suddenly. "And bring you back, if that should be necessary."

I didn't like that smile, and I was having difficulty getting out of the chair, my legs suddenly going weak.

Sergeant Rice was a detective sergeant, apparently, as she was wearing a grey two-piece suit, skirt not slacks. She had large and compassionate eyes. I didn't want compassion.

"Leave your bag," she said, walking past it on the floor in reception, and making it imperative for me to return. "My car's round the back."

I slumped in the passenger's seat, paying no attention to the small, neat town centre as we drifted through it.

"Where're we going?"

"St Giles's. She's there."

"What happened? How did she die?" The words nearly choked me.

"She was strangled with a silk scarf. It was her birthday," she told me, her voice empty. "It was a birthday present."

Her birthday? A present? What the devil did she mean?

We drove round the back of the hospital, which turned out to be a long way from the town, and parked against a shadowed, tall wall. It was now dark. A single, opal lamp jutted from the brickwork above the door. The nameplate read: PATHOLOGY.

She led me inside. I can recall nothing but whiteness and the smell. It probably takes a strong smell to cover death. I followed her along corridors and through a door. The atmosphere was chill. Perhaps the inspector had phoned ahead, because we seemed to be expected.

"I'll wait outside," she said softly, touching my shoulder when I hesitated.

I was conducted across the room to a wall consisting of large cabinet doors with central handles. A label on the outside of one of them was neatly lettered: Philomena Wise. The drawer was slid open.

She was covered with a sheet. I had been desperately afraid that she would be lying there naked. To have looked upon her, dead and naked, would have seemed a foul treachery. But there was the sheet.

"Sir?" said the attendant quietly, and he drew back the top of the sheet.

I looked down at a face. Similar features, the sharp nose and the prominent cheekbones. Dark hair, very close to the colour of my Phil's. But this was a younger face, rounder, more softly modelled. Did they change in death? Did they become shorter? This one seemed not much more than five feet. No! No! I cried to myself.

She was not my Philomena.

I remember nothing more. They told me later that I fainted. If so, it was the first time in my life.

TWO

We were back in the cubicle that Inspector Greaves called his office. Apart from a metallic taste in my mouth and the fact that I couldn't prevent my hands from shaking, I was feeling better. She was alive, wasn't she! I tried not to think about the woman who wasn't.

My sergeant had looked after me, bringing me back to consciousness on a seat in someone's office, her serious face concerned, her gaze not leaving mine, switching from eye to eye as though to get the full perspective. She had driven me back to the station. This was necessary, in any event, if only for me to pick up my kitbag. But without hesitation she had taken me straight up to see Greaves.

So there we were, me perched on an upright chair facing the desk, and Sergeant Rice quietly sitting a yard to one side. She was not taking notes. When I glanced at her she gave me a small encouraging nod and a thin smile. I looked back to Greaves, who was arranging his blotter to his satisfaction, and deciding what face to present. When he looked up it was clearly his patient and long-suffering expression he'd selected.

The office was crowded, there being another man, whom I'd not seen, sitting to one side of the desk. Two beady and probing eyes homed in on me and settled on my face. As far as I could tell he did not glance away for one moment after that. The impression was of a sharp and lethal instrument pointed directly at me.

"So," said Inspector Greaves. "What have we here?"

I said nothing. It didn't seem to deserve an answer, and in any event I didn't know what we had. I was pleased to realise that my brain had started working again, as though the shock had flushed it clean. Everything in the room was sharp and clear, every intonation in Greaves's voice, every expression could be examined and analysed.

"This is Inspector Filey of Killingham," he introduced, as though that completely explained his presence. It did not. In fact, my first impression was that he'd been contacted because the dead woman had come from there. But the dead woman had not; my Philomena Wise had. This small confusion distracted me for a moment.

I glanced at Filey. He was a thin, aesthetic type with a wide brow tapering down to a sharp, questing chin. He was much younger than Greaves, in his mid-thirties I guessed, yet they were the same rank. But Killingham was a larger pool than Sumbury, so perhaps their fish grew bigger earlier. There was no revealing expression on his face. It had set into lines of contemptuous rejection, which was probably his professional attitude, masking the real Filey.

Greaves got into his stride, his voice uncompromising. "You came here, demanding to see the body of Miss Philomena Wise. Now you say she's not the person you expected to see."

I nodded. He still hadn't asked me anything.

"I don't go much for coincidences like this, Mr. Manson. Will you explain why you expected it to be."

Were they always so polite? "She told me she was coming here . . . to Sumbury. Her name is Philomena Wise. I heard of her death on the radio. Naturally, I jumped to the conclusion—"

"She came here from where?" he interrupted.

"Well . . . from Killingham. You must know that."

"Must I?"

"Why else is . . ." I gave Filey one of my glances. No reaction. "Why else is *he* here? From Killingham, you said."

"Do you mind if I ask the questions?"

"Not at all, unless you're intending to charge . . ." I stopped abruptly, realising with disgust that I was talking like an experienced criminal.

He wrinkled his eyebrows. "If so, I'd warn you, but there's no charge. I'm simply interested, put it like that. You'll have to admit that Philomena is an unusual name."

"I call her Phil."

"And there can't be many women around with the name of Philomena Wise. Certainly not in Sumbury. As far as I know, there's only one family in our little town with the name Wise, and they haven't been here for very long. And before you ask, they came here from Killingham. The Philomena Wise who now lies in the morgue is definitely their daughter, and they have no other children. Her father made the identification, though in the circumstances there could've been no doubt. What d'you have to say to that?"

I thought about it. I had to hang on to the fact that my Phil was

alive somewhere, and I wanted to be away from there and searching for her. There were questions urgently requiring answers.

"I can't argue with that," I said carefully, staring past his left ear.

He waited a few moments, and then went on, "Doesn't it seem
strange to you that your Philomena Wise came to Sumbury, where
a young woman of the same name was already living?"

"That's putting it mildly," I said.

"I'm assuming our Philomena was alive then, when yours came.
Exactly when did your Philomena come here?"

"Monday."

"And ours died on Friday. I wonder where yours has got to."

I took a deep breath. "You're suggesting there's a connection
between my Phil coming here and the other one's death?"

"I'm saying there must be a connection." Still there was no emphasis in his voice.

"You're as good as implying my Phil killed yours."

"Am I?" His mouth set in a tight, straight line. "You're jumping
the gun—a whole battery of them. All I'm saying is that there has
to be a connection."

He stared at me, daring me to take it further. I said nothing. He
leaned towards Filey and whispered something. Without taking
his eyes from me, Filey shrugged and gave a minimal shake of his
head. Greaves turned back to me. He became jovial, like a lion
contemplating his lunch.

"You'll be staying in town, Mr. Manson?"

"Yes."

"Let me know where, please, and I'll be obliged if you'll not
leave the district for a while."

He'd be obliged! He'd make damned-well sure. I nodded, and
guessing I'd been dismissed I got to my feet. At last Filey took his
eyes from me. They put their heads together. I turned and went
out.

Sergeant Rice was at my elbow going down the stairs and into
the reception office. My kitbag was where I'd left it. I hoisted it on
to my shoulder, and we went out to stand under the small portico.
The air smelt clean and fresh. I breathed in deeply.

"Have you got anywhere to stay?" she asked.

"I came straight here from the railway station. I'll find somewhere."

"There's the Victoria, but it's pricey."

"Not for me, then." I smiled, going along with her.

I realised I hadn't been taking much notice of her. Now I saw
that she was about five feet seven, a little solidly built but giving
an impression of poise and competence. Her hair wasn't quite

blond and was worn short. There was very little make-up on her face. But the main impression was of solemnity and placidity. Then I saw that there was a smile after all, but only in her eyes, large grey eyes that sparked at me. I suspected that behind the facade there was a fire cracker, waiting for a stray ember.

We moved out on to the pavement. "Have you known her for long?" she asked, apparently dismissing the question of my night's lodging.

"Who? Phil? Well no, not long. A fortnight or so. Why?"

"You said you were going away together, and you didn't mean for a holiday." One eyebrow lifted, creating a crooked wrinkle above her nose. "Didn't take long, did it?"

"I'm a creature of impulse."

"Dangerous, that is."

"I'm trying to control it," I assured her.

She turned to look at me directly, cocking her head. "And your present impulse is to get away from here as fast as possible?"

"On the contrary. There're things I'll need to find out."

She pouted, nodding. "Then we'll have to keep you in order, Mr. Manson, I can see that." Her eyes were mocking, but her mood switched abruptly. She became practical and professional, turning to point down the street.

"You can go along from here, and you'll go through a small square. Carry straight on. Elm Lane is on your left. Try The George. It's only a pub, but he's got a room or two to spare."

"You're sure of that?"

"Yes. His name *is* George. Tell him Lucy sent you. He's my brother."

"I'll find it. Is that where you send all your down-and-outs?"

The eyes glinted. "The inspector will want to know where you're staying, and this saves me tracking along with you."

"Thank you, Sergeant," I said gravely.

"He'll want to know more about you, I'm sure. Much more. With a bit of luck he'll give me the job," she confided gravely. She was too free with her confidences, throwing down her cards face upwards. But what about the joker she hadn't revealed? I was expected to know it was there, and be cautious.

"How d'you know I shan't let you down and simply disappear?" I asked, really wondering, probing too.

For a second she seemed to pout again, then I realised this was as much as I was going to get of her smile. "You'll be at George's when I want to contact you." She nodded. Heaven help me if I wasn't.

Because she was a police officer I kept it official by holding out my hand. Quietly she took it, and we shook hands.

I turned away, then hesitated. "How long's he been here?" I asked. "Filey," I amplified.

"He came on Wednesday."

"Wednesday." I pushed it around in my mind, but it still meant nothing.

"On some private business of his own, it seems. Isn't it strange? You'd almost think he was expecting something to happen." She put her fingertips together, hanging them like a cage at her waist. She looked almost demure. I decided she'd taken a dislike to Filey.

I went out on to the dark wet street and hunted out The George. From the water in the gutters, it must have been raining for some time. It was strange that I hadn't noticed it. There was very little traffic around, and the streets were poorly lit. It was a little town that slept with the dusk. They retired to rear rooms to watch the telly, observing even meaner streets and darker crimes than their own.

The George was just along the side lane called Elm, though there were no trees. It displayed a beckoning, cheerful flood of light from its tiny windows. I entered. George Rice was serving behind the bar. He noticed my kitbag when I dumped it beside me and ordered half of bitter. He didn't say he was expecting me, but he knew who I was. Lucy had phoned in, and no doubt he would report back that I'd arrived. I drank half of my beer before I spoke to him. He told me he had a room. What he asked for it barely covered the breakfast he promised, and for a moment I felt I was cheating him by not presenting myself at anywhere near my best. But George had his instructions, and Sergeant Lucy Rice didn't want me wandering off in search of cheaper lodgings.

It was getting close to George's closing time when I finished my beer. I didn't order another, but George offered me a sandwich and I went straight up to my room. I felt exhausted. There was just time to look round the room, small, tidy, and clean—what more could anybody want?—and realise it overlooked the railway line, then I fell into the bed, and if the trains were running they sneaked past behind my dreams.

In the morning I searched out the bathroom and cleared away the grime, and had a shave. The face that looked back at me was lean and thoughtful and a little battered, the eyes brown and the mouth not what I'd have chosen. My father's mouth, that was. I always searched it for signs of his viciousness, but of course I never saw my face reflected back at me in anger. That morning I was

angry, I decided. Phil had been far from honest with me. There
was even a virtual certainty that it was not her name.

But after all, I'd not been completely honest myself. There'd
been no mention of Gartree.

I fetched out my crumpled jacket and my slacks, deciding that a
slightly more sober appearance would get me further with what I
wanted to do. I had a clean shirt with a collar, but no tie. All the
same, the total effect wasn't bad, though the waist of the slacks
seemed a bit tight and the jacket was stretched across my chest.
How long since I'd worn them? More than four years.

I had breakfast in the empty bar. Cereal, two eggs and bacon,
and toast that was hot, which was more than I'd have been given
at an hotel. It was served by the plump and jovial woman I'd
noticed helping George the previous night. She turned out to be
Mrs. George.

She said, "If you're seeing a woman, you need that outfit press-
ing. If you'll take 'em off, I'll do it for you."

"I don't know who I'll be seeing."

"Whoever it is, you're not going to make a good impression. No
hurry, is there?"

I didn't know, so I smiled and said, "Thanks. I'll let you have
them."

So after breakfast I changed back into jeans and anorak, and
took a stroll around the town. Through it would be a better way of
putting it. There seemed to be no more than a main street, weaving and winding for no obvious reason, with cobbled side streets
jutting out at random angles. On one side they were very short,
seeming to peter out to nothing but scrub and shingle in a few
yards. On the other they were longer, but went nowhere, lined
with abrupt rows of cottages as though tossed down by a negligent
builder. Behind them were hills.

The rain of the previous night still lay on the narrow pavements,
though the sky was clearing. The wind was brisk. I walked past
the police station, and it was some while before I realised all the
shops were shut. Then I remembered it was Sunday. Only a rare
pedestrian padded the streets, with a dog on a lead. The occasional
car drifted through. Otherwise, there was no activity. I spotted a
café with dim lights in its interior. It might have been open, but I
suspected you'd get yesterday's teabags.

At the far end of the town, the houses left behind, the main road
turned away to the left, climbing into the hills. A minor road
continued onwards. It was signposted: Port Sumbury. Port? It was
then that I became aware of the seagulls. I hadn't realised I was so

close to the coast. Although the distance was marked as two miles, I set out to walk to Port Sumbury.

To my left the ground began to rise in terraces. Above me were expensive houses, well separated, smug in their elevation, with expensive cars glinting in the sunlight that was now bursting from behind a cloud. To my right the terrain was flat, with patchy woodland, sparse, with an occasional cottage set well back. The cries of the gulls were now impatient.

I rounded a bend to the right, and caught my first glimpse of the sea, grey and sombre, beyond the scrub and the vegetation. I walked on. There was another bend, this time to the left, and the sea receded. Ahead, the scrub became a patch of solid woodland, and I saw that there was activity along the edge of it. A police car and a dark van were pulled over on to the grass verge, and a section was taped off. I stopped abruptly.

This must have been where she'd died. Strangled, they'd said.

I had no wish to stand and gawp, nor even to walk past it, so I turned back sharply. A hundred yards behind me—but ahead now—there was a stretch where no cover existed on either side of the road. A man in dark clothes and a short raincoat turned at the same time, and began to walk rapidly away from me.

It wouldn't have been surprising if Inspector Greaves had put a man on to follow me, but he wasn't big enough to be a policeman. I'd caught a distant glimpse of his face, in that split second before he twisted on his heel, and there was something about the narrow, predatory features I thought I recognised. Now, watching his walk from behind, with that roll on the outsides of his feet and the straight, stiff back, I thought I knew that too. But for the moment I couldn't place him.

I allowed him to gain distance, as there was no point in mounting a chase. When I got back to where the town started, I was looking for something else.

Two hundred yards beyond the junction, where the Port Sumbury road joined the main one, there was a red phone box, and further along one of those new cubicle types outside the post office. But neither held what I wanted, a phone directory.

Mrs. Rice had one. She handed me my pressed jacket and slacks, and grinned wickedly when I said put it on the bill.

"What d'you want a directory for?" she asked.

"To look up an address."

"Whose?" She was clearly part of Sergeant Rice's team, helping to keep a rein on my movements.

"The name is Wise," I said. "I'm told there's only one around here."

"What's this then, Ada?" asked George, coming up behind me, stripped to braces and rolled shirt sleeves and looking as though he'd been priming his pumps in the cellar. The overhang of his belly hinted he'd been testing them.

"He wants to call on the Wise family," she explained. Turning to me, she admonished, "But it's Sunday!"

George took a seat at one of the tables and slapped it with his palm. Obediently, I sat opposite him.

"Now what's this, eh? The poor girl's been dead only a couple of days. They won't be wanting visitors, now will they?"

"Not wanting, perhaps. But I'm rather pushed for time." But was that true? Certainly there was a sense of urgency, though I couldn't have justified it.

He rubbed the end of his nose with his forefinger. "The police wouldn't want you messing around there."

"Hell, George, you know how it is. Your sister sent me here, so you must know I'm involved. And that inspector seemed mightily suspicious. I'm suspected of something, though I'm not sure what that is."

"Not of killing her." It was a statement, but he lifted his bushy eyebrows and turned it into a question. He had his sister's clear grey eyes, though they'd seen about fifteen more years of the world's failings. She'd been a last-chance baby.

"Heavens no!" I laughed, but it didn't sound right. "I was two hundred miles away when she died."

It was in saying this that I realised it meant nothing. I could claim I was in Killingham on Friday, but I couldn't prove it. From Monday to Friday I'd barely put my nose into fresh air.

"You can prove it?" His question was bland. He'd been reading my expression.

"No," I admitted. "No proof."

I must have sounded rueful. He laughed, and reached over to slap my shoulder. He had a large and beefy hand, and there was a lot of weight behind it. I thought it could be a warning, a suggestion to behave.

"Lucy said I was to look out for you," he told me. "Sounds like you need somebody to hold your hand. My advice is not to go and see Aubrey Wise."

"If I don't take it, do I get thrown out?" I'd intended to be flippant, but it came out all wrong and sounded challenging.

He got to his feet. "You going to be in for lunch?"

"It wasn't in our arrangement. Bed and breakfast, you said."

"Yes or no?"

"Yes. There seems to be only one café in town."

"Right. There's no need to rush this visit of yours. Three o'clock's about right, I'd say. So why don't you go and wander round the town." His voice was even. Now Lucy was clearly visible in his face, though his eyes were more penetrating. "Lucy'll want a report. Where you are and what trouble you're stirring up. So watch your step, laddie, she's terrible when roused."

He didn't laugh until he reached the bottom of his cellar steps.

So, with no intention of following George's instructions meekly, I nevertheless went for my second trip through the town. This time I had my own objective, as I'd now been able to set the man who'd been following me against the background where I'd met him. In Gartree. His name was Dougie French, Frenchie to the inmates. I'd encountered him briefly, and afterwards steered well clear. There, if anyone wanted one, was a natural killer. He could prickle the hair on your neck at fifty feet.

The obvious assumption, therefore, was that Carl Packer, having failed to interest me in the enterprise, had resorted to Frenchie, much the more reliable prospect. There were, though, one or two snags to that theory. If Frenchie had succeeded and killed Philomena Wise, then what more did he want? Why was he still hanging around here? Only a sure knowledge of his own innocence would give him that sort of confidence. He'd be all for a quick in-and-out job, here and gone before you'd felt the pain of his passing. And pain it would be, because Frenchie was a knife man. Yet Philomena had been strangled, another pointer towards Frenchie's innocence.

There seemed only one answer to his continuing presence in the district: it was me he was after.

I had come to this conclusion reluctantly; one cannot take pride in being a target. But it did seem that I had to see him before he saw me, because I wanted a word or two with Frenchie, and if he saw me first I wouldn't get out more than one. My trip through the town was therefore a complex scheme of lure and trap, but it got me nowhere. I was walking out of myself the energy I'd need if I met him.

But I caught no glimpse of him, and nervously circled back to George's place. Frenchie was naturally a night person. I decided he was no doubt sleeping the sleep of the unjust.

Lucy was there for lunch. I might have guessed—it had been set up. All right, that suited me fine. I might be able to get some information from her, and facts were something I desperately needed.

"There you are," she said, as though locating a mislaid treasure.
She was in the bar, which was packed. Where had they all come

from? I certainly hadn't seen many people on the streets. Perhaps the smuggler's caves and passages still existed, and they emerged in George's cellars.

"We're using George's snug," she said. "We can't talk here."

"We're going to talk, then?"

"I am. I don't know about you."

"You're on duty?"

"Always. Why ask?"

"I might have some questions of my own," I told her.

She eyed me quietly, rubbed her nose just like George, and said, "All right. They might give me some answers."

"Answers to what?"

"I shan't know, shall I, till I hear what the questions are. It's Ada's steak and kidney pie. Come on."

THREE

And snug it was, though lacking the *joie de vivre* of a medieval cell. There was one small and high window in the thick stone wall, and the clamour from the bar was muted by an oak door. Today she was wearing a dress, bright blue with a pleated skirt and a white collar. She didn't look like a police officer, more a secretary who was entertaining a visiting executive. But she ate heartily like a policeman, with a glass of bitter in front of her. The dress made her eyes glow.

"What's this I hear about visiting Aubrey Wise?" she asked. "Not a very good idea, is it?"

"It's your boss who's asked me to hang around, but I can't just sit and twiddle my fingers. I don't see why I shouldn't pay a social call. After all, I've got a personal interest in Philomena Wise."

"Not *his* Philomena, though. Somebody else's daughter."

I prodded out a portion of kidney and lifted it with triumph. "One of them is and one of them isn't. You've got to admit there's something very funny going on."

"Umm!" she said, chewing, her eyes on me.

"Well, there is. *My* Phil came to Sumbury. There's only one family called Wise. *My* Phil has gone missing."

"You're very possessive, aren't you!"

"The father—this Aubrey character—identified the dead one as his daughter. Who's to say he's not lying?" I was reaching for anything that would make sense of it.

She put down her knife and reached for her glass. "They've been here a couple of years. She was known in the town. She's always been his daughter." She said it crisply and decisively.

"Always said she was," I qualified.

"Stubborn, aren't you! All right, Mr. Paul Manson, you go and see him. Don't be surprised if you get tossed out on your ear. As you will, if you keep saying that."

I was experienced in pointing my nose at the unknown, and trusting in a lack of aggression to carry me through. I'd faced more daunting encounters than this Aubrey person, though I must admit that a rattlesnake isn't influenced by a friendly face.

"I'll be careful," I assured her gravely.

"I'm sure you will. All I'd ask you to remember is that his daughter was murdered two days ago. Strangled. You can't intrude in their distress. If he makes one phone call to complain he's being harassed, my chief'll have you inside before you can snap your fingers. Right—warning over. D'you want some lemon meringue pie?"

"Love it."

She punched a button on the wall. There was more emphasis in the gesture than there'd been in her voice.

Ada came in beaming, carrying two plates of pie. Lucy said, "Thank you, Ada. He hasn't attacked me yet."

"You know where the button is." Ada nodded at me. I nodded back. I was to believe that it was for me the button waited, in case Lucy scared me too much.

"Don't you think I ought to know more about this murder?" I asked, after Ada had gone. "If only so that I can avoid the wrong things. And why haven't you made an arrest, anyway?"

She lit a cigarette, offering me one. I shook my head. She blew a plume of smoke at the bell-push, so thick it was a wonder it didn't ring it. I guessed she'd been briefed as to how much she could tell me.

"Yes, I think you ought to know something about it, and for your information, we've had a young man in custody, for questioning, since Friday evening. In"—she glanced at her watch—"just six hours' time we'll have to let him go. No arrest. We can hold him so

long, then he's free, unless we charge him. Mr. Greaves doesn't
think he can, not on what we've got."

"Why not?"

She sighed, then rested an elbow on the table so that she could
cradle her chin in her palm and drown me with her eyes, the
cigarette fuming beside her ear.

"Because once he does, he's got to prepare his case for the public
prosecutor. And he doesn't think it can stick. Any defence lawyer
out of rompers could tear it apart. The whole thing's crazy. The
young fool's bright enough to have made it all up, but he's also
bright enough to have realised he could simply have made a bolt
for it."

"You're ahead of me. I know nothing."

"Perhaps it'd be best to leave it like that."

"I'd find out. Somehow. You'd simply save me time and effort."

She leaned back and contemplated me with her head on one
side, as though searching for something that wasn't there: an easy
compliance, lack of patience or persistence, a weakness, a temer-
ity. Apparently she saw none of these because she suddenly flickered a grin at me, quelling it at once.

"Sorry, I'm sure. You shall hear. His name's Arthur Torrance, Art
for short he tells us. Picture him." She gazed above my head, seeing him standing up there. "Five and a half feet of street-wise
layabout. No weight to him, no strength. Just his tongue. That's his
muscle. Clever-boy Torrance! He could talk his way out of a bear
trap. So . . . if he's so clever, why did he hang around? Why did
he go running to the house, of all places, if he'd killed her?"

"I don't know," I admitted. "Could I have it in sequence,
please?"

She grimaced. "I keep forgetting. This Aubrey Wise you're going
to see, he lives in one of those houses on the rise along the Port
Sumbury road, a quarter of a mile the other side of the woodland
where she died. He's a business consultant, which means he works
away from home, with his brain, and makes flying visits to exotic
places. And people visit him from afar. For the past month or two
he's had a young man over from Australia. Your age. Better-look-
ing, though. Anyway . . . this Australian was quite taken with
Philomena. Wanted to marry her and take her back to the thou-
sands of acres of sheep and the like his father owns. And that
suited our Philomena. Can you see her? Twenty-two on the day
she died, and never really grown up. Been playing the field, but
round here there's not much of a turn-out, and I reckon she was
bored. Perhaps the wilds of Queensland or wherever it is sounded
romantic. She'd have gone crazy with boredom, the silly creature."

She didn't seem to think much of Philomena Wise.

"But it would suit you?" I asked casually.

"What?" Then she was solemn again, considering it seriously. "Perhaps it would. Horseback all day and all that sky. I don't think I'd be bored. No. But I'd come out in freckles."

"Most attractive."

"Where was I?"

"This Aussie, wanting to take her away."

"Yes. It was about settled, and they were getting to the point of deciding whether the wedding was going to be here or there, and along comes this person, Arthur Torrance, an ex-boyfriend from years back."

"When did he come along?"

"Tuesday."

"The Tuesday before she died?"

"That one." She studied me impassively, waiting for it.

"And he'd known her in her Killingham days?"

"That's where he said he'd come from. He's been very open about everything. Too open. He said he'd heard she was going to leave the country. So he came. He hadn't seen her for over two years, and he came running. It's called an abiding passion," she informed me, nodding briefly.

"It's called a coincidence where I come from."

It was as though my Phil's visit here had triggered something. But I recalled she hadn't been happy about it, so maybe she'd expected something upsetting. Not so upsetting as murder, surely, but something.

Ada Rice brought in coffee. Lucy didn't take her eyes from me for a second. It was becoming disconcerting, that calm and placid stare. Perhaps she had her own methods, luring me into relaxation so that I would confide more than I intended.

"And didn't anybody ask him," I said, "how he suddenly heard, two hundred miles away, that his ex-girlfriend was thinking of getting married?"

"We did. Of course. He said he'd heard it in a pub."

"For heaven's sake! And you believed it?"

"Of course not." She pouted. "But he's been so open and forthcoming, and there's no reason he'd lie about that."

"More important things to lie about, perhaps."

"Plenty. This is what he's told us. He came here, knowing that Friday was her birthday, and he could give her a present instead of sending her a card. He claims he's always wanted to marry her, and he was going to make one last try. He used the term: shack up with her. A fat chance he'd got. At least, he managed to get her to

meet him. There was going to be a party at the house later that
evening, so they arranged the meeting for seven o'clock, to give
her time to get back and change. I suppose she saw it as a bit of a
giggle, seeing him that once, accepting his present, and dashing
back to the champagne and canapés." She wrinkled her nose. That
image of Miss Wise met with her disapproval.

I said nothing, keeping my mind open. She stared at her coffee,
then she continued.

"Seven o'clock it should've been, at this end of the coast road,
where it branches off for Port Sumbury. He was naturally there ten
minutes early. She left the house a few minutes before seven. Her
mother asked her where she was going, and she just said out. She
ought to have reached the meeting place by seven. There would be
no point in wasting time. See him and get it over, that'd be her
intention."

"Can I say something?"

"You may."

"It'd surely be dark along there at that time."

"Getting dark. Sunset was about six-thirty. It was a clear evening, but there was a low mist coming in from the sea."

"And she walked it alone? No car?"

"If she had a car, she didn't use it. It's possible she wanted him
to watch her walking away into the sunset."

"What romantic pictures you conjure up! Why don't you like
her?"

"I don't know. I never met her. I'm going by what's emerging."

"Ah yes. Carry on then."

She inclined her head in mocking thanks. "So there he was,
clutching his present and waiting. He'd bought it from Trafford's,
in town here. A fawn silk scarf. Gift wrapped, with a label tied to
the ribbon. Love from Art, in his own writing. But she didn't turn
up. He says. He waited. Seven-fifteen, and she still hadn't come. He
didn't know what to do. Go to meet her . . . or what? He thought
she couldn't possibly have stood him up, so he hurried back towards town to the nearest phone box, about two hundred yards
away. Phoned her house. Don't ask—he knew the number. How
else had he arranged the meeting? He got her mother, who said
she'd left before seven, and what was this about, so he ran back to
their meeting place, worried that she might've turned up and he'd
kept her waiting. And . . . this is the point. He says he left her
present in the phone box on the shelf, he was so agitated. And
when she still wasn't at the meeting place he ran all the way on to
her house and told them. So they phoned us. The call is timed at
seven thirty-five. As she must've gone missing somewhere be-

tween the house and the meeting place, and as there's only one place of concealment, that patch of woodland a quarter of a mile from the house, we found her in less than half an hour. Now—and this is where it all goes wrong—he insists he left the present in the phone box, and he won't budge. But the scarf was there, tied in a knot round her neck, and when we looked for it there was the torn wrapping, lying at the side of the road with the label still attached: Love from Art. Now tell me why he hasn't been arrested and charged. Go on, let's have a fresh mind on it."

I was intrigued that she assumed I had a mind at all, but in fact there's nothing as good as the study of history to train you in logic. I smiled at the thought.

"Let's see, then. To start with, if he'd killed her . . . imagine he walked to meet her, and did meet her, and she tore open her present and dropped the wrapping and told him to go lose himself, and then he strangled her with it. Then there'd be no possible reason why he shouldn't just trot off into the wide blue yonder, because he could assume nobody knew he was meeting her, and probably nobody knew he was in town except her. He could simply pick up the wrapping and walk away, after dragging her into the trees. She *was* dragged, I suppose?"

She nodded. "Umm!" Her eyes were steady, an unlit cigarette in her fingers. "Dragged by her legs. Her skirt—plain black—was rucked up round her waist, the jacket, with the buttons torn off and up her shoulders. She was wearing a crew-necked jumper. Pale blue. No hair covering. And she'd not been sexually assaulted."

I realised she was probing for how much I might already know, how clear my picture of it might be. It was clear enough now, and into my mind shot another image. I'd been staying on an Indian reservation for a while, talking, listening, taping, and a young Navajo girl I'd known had been raped and killed. By a white man, it turned out. Things became tricky, and, as a white man they thought they could trust, I'd acted as a kind of intermediary. So I didn't need a picture, and I'd managed to pick up quite a lot about police procedures at that time.

"Any skin or blood behind her nails?" I asked.

Her expression didn't change, except for a widening of the eyes. "It's early days, but we've had a verbal report from forensic. No. They found nothing."

"Then there'd be no marks on this young chap, Torrance. He could have been back in Killingham the next day, arranging an alibi with his mates, just in case. If he'd done it, that is. How'm I doing?"

"Fair to middling. Carry on."

"Right. Next point. That was what he oughto've done. But just think about what he did do. If he'd killed her, he'd have been absolutely crazy to leave the wrapping, with his name on it, and then go running to the house. And if he invented the story about leaving the present in the phone box, it did nothing to help him. It's contradictory. It makes it appear in two places at once. I suppose there *was* only one? They didn't sell two fawn scarves that week, by any chance?"

"They haven't sold two in six months. Carry on."

"Is there any more?"

"Of course there is. Mr. Greaves has taken it a lot further than that."

But he'd had more time. "Try this, then. If it wasn't him, then you have to assume he's telling the truth. Therefore, he did leave the scarf in the phone box. But she must've been dead before he did that—"

"She was," she cut in. "She was found quite quickly, so the ME got to her in good time. He says at seven, as near as damn it. So she was dead before Torrance even went to the phone box."

"Lovely! So she was dead. The present was in the phone box at a later time. I suppose her mother's confirmed the time he called?"

She gave a minimal nod. "Seven-twenty, she told us. It fits exactly with what Torrance said."

"It gets better and better. Even if you assume somebody could've been watching him, and saw him leave the scarf there, what a coincidence that it just happened to be somebody who wanted to kill her! And how the hell could anybody kill her with the scarf around twenty minutes before they could've got their hands on it!"

She sat back. I thought I could see the echo of a smile. "So there you are," she said with satisfaction. "Now you know why we haven't charged Arthur Torrance. I hope you can see why Mr. Greaves is moving very carefully."

"I can. And where is this wonder boy right now?"

"He's in digs, with Mrs. Druggett. When we let him out, he'll be asked not to leave the district."

"Like me? And with a bit of discreet surveillance, no doubt?"

"Exactly like you." She didn't answer the second question.

"You mean I'm a suspect?"

She showed emotion, her eyes snapping. "Of course you're a suspect. You come here to view a body, and then say it's not the right one! Oh, Lordy me! D'you know anything about criminal psychology? Anything at all?"

Only what I'd picked up inside. "It's not my subject."

"Then I'll tell you something. There're people—ghouls—who *enjoy* another look at the person they've killed."

"That doesn't sound like me," I said mildly. My stomach had turned at the thought.

"You say that. But d'you imagine murderers look like murderers? Evil eyes and drooling lips! Nonsense. They look ordinary. Like you. Ordinary Paul, that's you. But to explain yourself, you produce some fantastic story about another Philomena Wise it might have been, and it's not. So where is she, this friend of yours? Produce her. Let's have a look at her."

"I don't know where she is."

"You see. I'll bet you can't produce an alibi for last Friday."

I smiled at her. "You're right there."

"Then don't look so complacent about it."

"I'm not really pleased about it," I assured her. "I didn't know I'd need one."

"So where were you?"

"I was waiting in the flat at Killingham belonging to this imaginary Philomena Wise of mine."

"Waiting?" She eyed me with her head cocked sideways.

"For her to phone me."

"Which she didn't?"

I shook my head.

"Then don't you see, you complete idiot, that if this Philomena Wise of yours is real and not imaginary, and she came to Sumbury for a specific purpose, then it could've been in order to kill the real Philomena. If that's the case, then she's landed you with no alibi, and with a perfect motive for killing her yourself. Just you think about that."

I thought about it. She was making huge jumps in imagination. "So if I manage to produce her as proof that she exists, you'd take that as a good indication that she's your murderer?"

Her eyes flickered, but she refused to back down. "Yes, yes. Something like that, anyway."

I smiled at her. One of us had to do it, if only to break the tension. "Then perhaps—even to prove I've been telling the truth —I'd better not look for her."

Because her solemnity was habitual, it put her in some difficulty when she really wished to look solemn. It was like trying to improve the subtlety of the Mona Lisa smile. But she managed it.

"You're not taking this seriously at all, are you!" She shook her head stubbornly. "No, don't deny it. You're treating it all as a big joke. But, Paul . . ." She stopped, and bit her lip. There was something she'd not intended to say.

"Yes?"

For a moment more she hesitated, annoyed with her own impetuosity. "All right," she decided. "Motive. Let's think about that."

"For me? You mentioned that, but I thought you'd got carried away."

"I never get carried away."

"Of course not. But I don't see how I can have a motive for killing somebody I'd never heard of."

"But you had heard of her. Philomena Wise. Remember?"

"I haven't got a motive for killing either of them."

She made an annoyed little click with her tongue. I noticed that when she was angry one eyebrow went up. I hoped to be elsewhere if they both did it together. "Do you think we're country yokels?" she demanded in a tight little voice. "Just because we're tucked away . . . we can still contact the Police National Computer, the same as everybody else. We asked it if it knew you. It said it did. You are Paul Frederick Manson, aged twenty-nine. Two months ago you came out of Gartree Maximum Security Prison, having served four years of a seven-year sentence for murder. No, damn you, keep your mouth shut. You turn up here in Sumbury to identify the body of a young woman, whom you said you were involved with. She'd been strangled. On the computer print-out there are the words: manual strangulation." She took a deep breath. The effort had brought moisture to her eyes. "Well? Anything to say?"

"Was there evidence of manual strangulation in Miss Wise's death?" I asked quietly. "With the hands, the fingers, I mean. The forensic lot don't need much time to be able to tell you that. I wouldn't be surprised if they can pick fingerprints off skin, these days."

"That would take longer," she said quietly, primly. "And no, there were no signs of hands on her throat. A ligature bruise round her neck, a deeper bruise where the scarf was knotted. D'you want it *all*, damn you . . ."

"You accused me—"

"Not accused! Suggested. Call it what the hell you like. I can give you the scarf maker's name and address if you insist—"

"Now, don't take it too far. I've only ever strangled one person in my life, and that was my father." I stared down at my strangler's hands, lying quietly in front of me on the table. My fingers were shaking.

When I looked up she was pushing back her chair. There was anger in the gesture. Her face was stern and uninformative again, and she made her cage with her fingers, as though I might be trapped inside.

"I'll let my chief know what you say," she said in a firmly controlled voice.

"Yes." I scrambled to my feet. "Do that. It'll save me calling in." This interview had saved them from fetching me in.

She turned away, then paused. "Oh . . . it's called Seagulls."

"What is?"

"The house. Aubrey Wise. Watch what you say." It was a crisp command.

"Yes, ma'am," I said quietly, but she was going out of the door, and my words were engulfed in the sudden surge of noise from the bar.

Slowly I sat down again, furious that I'd betrayed myself into a flippant dismissal of my father's death. It had been an attempt to belittle it to myself, when already the memory of my anger at that time was dying, and therefore the pain of the incident was receding to where I might not be able to retrieve it. For some reason I needed to hold on to the fury, if only to recognise its onset as a warning in the future. But—lurking there in the shadows of my mind—was the concern, the certainty, that if I'd been able to control myself he might not have died.

I got myself to my feet, and went heavily up to my room to change into my finery for the visit, with not the slightest idea how I was going to approach it, nor what I hoped to achieve.

At two-thirty I left The George. All I had to do was keep walking, take the minor road to Port Sumbury, and keep my eyes open for a property called Seagulls.

But on the way I had to pass all the physical elements involved in Philomena's death. First, the red phone booth. It was here that Arthur Torrance had hurried back to phone the house. I looked in. There was the shelf on which, he claimed, he'd left the wrapped scarf. No phone directory, but he'd already known the number. I walked on to the junction where the Port Sumbury road started, leading on from the main road, which turned inland. Here he had waited for her from ten minutes to seven until seven-fifteen, at which time he'd hurried back to phone.

It was a logical place to arrange a meeting. There was a bus stop, with a small shelter, which would have provided cover in case it rained. It stood in stark isolation, the houses having dribbled away to nothing a hundred yards back. Beyond it was the expanse of open territory, rock-strewn and scattered with stunted trees, the sea not visible from there. It occurred to me that if he'd waited there for nearly half an hour on the evening of a weekday, he

would surely have been noticed. There was a bus timetable in the
shelter, so I checked that possibility, peering round and through
the scratched graffiti on the plastic.

There was no bus going through Sumbury between six and eight
on weekdays. It was that sort of bus service, single-deckers covering every hamlet in the county and occasionally making a dash
back to the coast. The route wound so tortuously that you could
probably catch one bus, get off at Stop 9, walk a mile across country, and get the previous bus at Stop 47.

I walked on. Arthur Torrance had run this way that evening, his
eyes searching for signs of her. Or so he said. The police presence
was no longer at the patch of woodland, and the ribboned barriers
had been removed. Their interest was now elsewhere. With me,
possibly.

A quarter of a mile further on was Seagulls, high on my left.
There were gateposts, but no gates. The drive was open and bare.
Perhaps nothing would grow, apart from a lawn, on the sandy soil
and in the wet, salty wind. The whole frontage was a series of rock
gardens, one above the other. The tarmacked drive curved away
and round, but even so the grade was steep. It had me breathing
heavily. At the top, where it levelled off, I stopped and looked
back over a low wall. It was high and open enough for me to be
able to check that I didn't seem to have been followed, and it gave
a brave and splendid view of the sea, with away to my left the
harbour at Port Sumbury, nodding the naked masts of its yachts at
me.

I turned back to face the house. I had been observed arriving.
The front door was open and a tall, gangling man stood waiting. So
I had time for no more than a glance at the house. Business consultant, Aubrey Wise called himself. One look at his home, and it was
evident that he'd managed to clutch to himself a considerable
amount of wealth, so the expectation would be that he could help
you to do the same.

But this man was not Wise. He was about my own age, athleti-
cally poised, giving the impression that a wrong word would provoke attack.

"You wanted something?" he asked in an expressionless Australian drawl. It was clear that he didn't care what I answered.

"I'd like to see Mr. Wise, if it's convenient."

"Can't say about that, but I'll ask. You wanna come inside?"

I nodded, gained access to the hall, and he left me there.

FOUR

The house was a huge shoebox with a fancy green pantile roof, its long side facing the drive and therefore the distant sea. You'd have thought they would want to take full advantage of the view. The hallway ran sideways, the complete width. You could certainly sit in there and admire the outlook, but it was impersonal, a long corridor as aseptic as a hospital, with bow windows at intervals to break up the line. Seats there were, but miserably uncomfortable, tables too, scattered with magazines of interest only to brain surgeons or computer wizards, on one of them a tossed headsquare in a Paisley pattern, blue against a background of yellow and brown.

I strolled along it, and back. Pictures broke up the blank facing wall, but they were no more than coloured shapes. The view behind me was more attractive. You could have skated along that hall, you could have practised your sprint, your long jump but not your high jump. What you couldn't do was relax. I wished I hadn't given up smoking.

The man who had appeared at the far end of the corridor might have been watching me for several seconds. I didn't know he was there until he spoke, quietly, but all the same I jumped.

"What is it you want?"

His voice had a deep timbre to it, and just a touch of some guttural accent. He was as tall as me, but broader, and more secure in his knowledge of his place in life. His face was lean, but his forehead wide, packed with brains. His hair was completely white, but the moustache and the neatly trimmed beard were a ginger colour speckled with white. He wore gold-rimmed spectacles, and here in his own home of a Sunday afternoon, when one might expect him to relax, he was neatly dressed in a grey suit, perfectly tailored, a white shirt and a striped tie, and brown shoes of a fine hand-lasted leather.

"I'm sorry to disturb you. I know it's not really the time—"

His gesture halted me. It rejected any condolences I might have been about to offer. There was no change in his expression. I saw no evidence of grief. Perhaps he was already reconciled to losing his daughter, perhaps not to death, but to Australia.

He reached up and touched his lips. "Please state your business."

"It's about your daughter."

"Yes?" The mention of her had not affected him. "You knew her?" He'd already become used to the past tense.

"I thought I did. Not as your daughter, of course. This was in Killingham—"

"Come with me," he commanded, swinging on his heel.

He walked away from me to the end of the corridor. We weaved a few corners and passed a large number of closed doors. He opened one of them and we entered a room. There were, I thought, two women sitting in its far shadows, side by side on a monstrous leather settee, with just the tops of their heads showing. I heard one of them whisper, ". . . such a shock . . ." and then we were through the room and out on a terrace overlooking a large pool. It wasn't a swimming pool, but a garden pool. In a public park it would have been called a lake. The hill continued beyond, and thus above the house. A lot of earth had been dredged to form that pool. On the far side the rise, having been cut into, presented itself as a cliff surface. Down this draped trailing plants. But this was October. The world might have been searched for suitable plants to provide a backdrop of colour in the summer, but the colour had now gone, leaving a drab drape of green. Golden carp lazily drifted amongst water lilies. A frog sat on one of the leaves. It was orange, with lumps on. Probably imported. Did frogs have to go into quarantine?

This was the whole concept of the house, the southerly sun-trap. In spite of the time of the year, it was warm. And secluded. There was nobody, in any direction, who could overlook you. The impression was of self-inflicted claustrophobia. No cold breezes ventured. You were safe.

He gestured, and I took a canvas lounging chair beside an oak table. There was a jug of drinkable liquid squatting in a bowl of ice. The autumn sun slanted along the terrace. Aubrey Wise had seated himself facing me, and the Australian was sitting on the flagged edge of the pool, his feet only an inch from the water. I realised that he, too, was wearing a light suit, something in pale blue with narrow lapels, and knife-creased narrow slacks. Perhaps the formality indicated a degree of mourning. Her body was not in the house, so it was not necessary actually to wear black. Or to weep.

"Grant," said Wise dismissively, "this man claims he knew Philomena in Killingham. Isn't that so, Mr. . . ."

"Paul Manson."

"And I am Aubrey Wise. This is Grant Felton."

"Howdee," he said over his shoulder, not looking round.

"It's been more than two years since we left Killingham," Wise commented. "Lemon juice?" His casual manner was forced.

"Thank you, I'd like that."

He carefully poured me a tumblerful. I took it up and tasted it. There was more in it than lemon. Rum, I thought. White rum.

"I find it strange," he went on, "that two of you from Killingham should suddenly appear, a strange person claiming to have been a boyfriend, and now you. I know she had a large number of dubious acquaintances, but I don't recall anyone called Paul Manson." He was being smoothly insulting.

"No." I tried to match his casual voice. "I didn't mean that long ago. I've known her in Killingham for the past few weeks, until a week ago. That's when she came to Sumbury. Returned to it, perhaps."

He took off his glasses, stared at them, and put them on again. Grant Felton slowly uncurled himself and got to his feet. He stood over me.

"You trying to be clever, feller?"

"Leave it, Grant," said Wise quietly and wearily, but there was command in his voice. "I'm sure it's only a mistake."

"How many more of these drifters we gonna have, then?" Felton drawled in disgust. "Homing in from Killingham, wherever that God-forsaken dump is."

"It's two hundred miles north," I offered amicably.

"So it is from our ranch house to the boundary fence," he told me in contempt.

I tried to imagine a fence around a spot two hundred miles away. Pi times four hundred, give or take. Did they have a fence-run of twelve hundred miles?

"But I reckon you still get drifters?" I asked with interest.

He had the craggy good looks of a man who's lived long in the sun. It wasn't so much sunburn, I thought, as what was left after the sun had pared it down. He was rangy inside that suit, though with bulky shoulders. I could imagine him on a horse, his feet barely missing the ground, or upending sheep to be shorn with the ease I was using to tilt my glass.

"Let's keep to the point," said Wise irritably. "You say you've known her in the past weeks in Killingham. That is quite impossible. She has been here."

I put down my empty glass and stared at it. "The young woman you identified as your daughter was not the Philomena Wise I knew in Killingham."

When I looked up into his face there was a touch of colour on his cheeks, just clear of the fuzz. The hair partly covered his lips, but I could see they were compressed.

"I didn't identify her 'as' my daughter, she *was* my daughter."

"Let me hoof him outa here," growled Felton. No patience, there.

"Be silent," Wise told him, acid in his voice. The younger man's head jerked as though he'd been slapped. "Explain yourself, Manson."

I looked from face to face. Felton knuckled his mouth with his fist. He was aching to knuckle somebody's and mine was forbidden. I noticed that the top joint of his left thumb was missing. Sheep shearing had its dangers, no doubt. All the same I made a mental note of it, realising that his stump would make a useful weapon in a roughhouse. It therefore seemed a good idea to smile from one face to the other, though I'm not much good at ingratiation.

"I've known a woman," I explained, "in Killingham, for the past month or so. She's called Philomena Wise. She told me she was coming to Sumbury to clear up some business. That would make it two women with that name at the same time in a small place like Sumbury." I lifted an eyebrow at Wise. "But you say you know nothing of this?" I put a small emphasis on the word "say" in response to his earlier insult.

Business consultancy probably required a calm and analytical mind, not like, say, a public relations man, who was expected to be able to lie cheerfully and with open candour. Wise couldn't do it. He fluffed it. He need only have made the statement, "I know nothing," and I'd have been up against a brick wall.

Looking past my left ear, he said, "If I knew anything . . ." And was at once involved with his glass.

"I thought she might've come here," I said blandly.

"She did not."

"Are you sure? If you knew her under a different name—"

"Y' see," cut in Felton. "He's admitting she's a fake."

I grinned at him. "One of them must've been, sport."

Not being able to hit a sitting man, he turned away with disgust.

"Surely I'd know my own daughter," said Wise sharply, flapping a hand to restrain Felton. His eyes tried to hold mine in challenge.

"But you haven't asked me to describe the other one," I pointed out quietly. "Perhaps you'd know her too."

"I think that's enough." He rose to his feet. I noticed he had to support himself on the chair arms. "My daughter has been killed.

We were to have had a party. Her mother is deeply distressed, and I don't want anything more to upset her. You understand? You will leave now, please."

I stood. There seemed to be no further I could take it. "Well, yes, I'll go. One thing, though, that's puzzling me . . ."

"Hell, go'n puzzle somewhere else," said Felton, crackling with aggression. Perhaps, living amongst sheep, he had to remain forceful in order to show them who was boss.

"This party," I said. "No guests? I mean, nobody seems to have been using the road."

Wise held out his arm in an ushering gesture. I was leaving, so he could afford to be slightly more affable. "Family and close friends. It was to be an engagement party as well as her birthday."

I moved just ahead of his hovering hand. "But she went out. Nobody wondered why, or wanted to stop her?"

"That's enough," he snapped, his temper going. "I will not be pestered in my own home. The police—"

"They know I'm here."

"Then they'll know where to come and fetch you."

"You just let her walk off into the evening." I persisted.

Wise tightened his lips and marched off purposefully towards the terrace windows, I reckoned on his way to a phone.

"All right," I said quickly, not wanting to embarrass Lucy, "I'm on my way. I'm sorry to have troubled you."

We walked back through the room. One of the two women said, ". . . never get over it." Both men dogged my heels. They saw me to the front door.

"A nice day for the time of the year," I observed. The door slammed. I sauntered away down the drive.

I couldn't claim I'd discovered anything, only that there was something to be discovered. Aubrey Wise had known, and understood, what I was talking about, and tension had crackled whenever Grant Felton had moved a muscle. Perhaps I hadn't uncovered anything useful, but I had certainly stirred the surface of some very murky water.

I stood beside one of the gateposts, trying to decide my next move. In neither direction was there any beckoning inspiration. In view of the fact that I was already on the way, I decided to have a look at Port Sumbury, and had turned in that direction, had covered a hundred yards or so, when I heard the rasp of an abruptly accelerated engine behind me. It was the sound made by a car that has been coasted quietly down a steep drive, then suddenly been kicked into life on reaching level road. My instinct recalled incidents where pedestrians had been run down and left to die. I remembered the attitude of the brittle and horny-palmed Australian, and turned quickly, poised to leap in either direction.

But the vehicle was driving away from me rapidly, towards Sumbury. It was as though it had been waiting for me to get clear, waiting to see the direction I took. I hadn't seen it at the house, so it must've been parked round the side. I would certainly have recognised it. There was no mistaking the little red Fiat two-seater. It had a distinctive inset rear window, with a black grill just behind it. This one was the same metallic red—on the brown side of red—as was my Phil's.

It was just as inconceivable that there could be two such cars at Sumbury, as that there should be two Philomenas.

Heavens, I thought, she might well have been one of the two women seated on that settee. She could have been staying there as a guest.

I had to restrain the instinct to run back to the house, shouting my head off. But it would certainly have got me nothing but a stump of thumb in my eye. I began to walk back to Sumbury. I had to reassure myself that if it had been Phil she might not have recognised me, walking away from her in my freshly pressed jacket and slacks. I was not wholly convinced.

Apart from Phil, there were now two people I wanted to see. One was the ex-boyfriend of Philomena, Arthur Torrance. The other was Dougie French. Torrance, I thought, could wait. In any event, he was beyond my reach at the moment. But Frenchie had been watching me and following me. He demanded more immediate attention, as he presented a positive threat.

Back at The George, I found it was opening time. George was on duty behind the bar, and the usual crowd had materialised, so he was busy. I kept to my usual paltry half pint, and quietly waited until I could get a word with him.

"George," I said, when he seemed to have a second, "where does the riff-raff go when they get tired of here?"

"Start something and I'll show you."

"I'm serious. You're too classy for what I've got in mind."

He considered me with high-class concern. "Don't look for trouble, you've got enough already."

"All I want to do is meet it face to face before it gets a chance to creep up on me."

He went away and served a couple of customers, then slid back to me. "If Ada can manage on her own, I'll come along with you," he said quietly. "Watch your back, sort of." There was a wistful note in his voice.

"Thanks. But I know what to look out for."

"You'd get a lift in my car," he offered, sliding a gin and tonic towards a demanding and strident woman. "It's a fair walk."

"What is?"

"The Stormy Petrel. It's along a lane, at the other end of Port Sumbury."

"I see what you mean."

"It's where the rough stuff goes. They dunk 'em in the harbour."

I'd wasted a lot of time since I'd been out of Gartree, where round and round the yard barely opens your lungs. I hadn't done much to work myself back into condition, and I'd been on my feet most of the day. The offer was tempting, but I didn't want to involve George. This was me and Frenchie. Just a chat about old times and fellow villains inside, like two old soldiers talking about Dunkirk. Except that they'd been on the same side, and in Gartree nobody's on anybody's side but his own. Frenchie and I had survived. I had developed a thick prison skin, and I still hadn't sloughed it off; I didn't want George to see it if it showed itself in Frenchie's company.

"Thanks, George," I said. "But this is just me and an old friend. Reckon I'll have to walk."

"I'll get you a sandwich if the crush eases off a bit. Half an hour, and it usually does. And I've got a bike I can lend you. No bicycle clips, though. And no lock and chain, either, so watch the buggers don't pinch it."

"You know, George," I said, "I might just get to like it round here."

"Hah!" he said, not smiling. "Look at that idiot, banging his glass on the counter."

He went away. I waited for my sandwich. There was no hurry. Let Frenchie, if he was there at the Stormy Petrel, get a few down him, then perhaps his wits would be blurred when I tackled him. It would be too much to hope that his reflexes would, too.

It was Ada who eventually brought me my sandwich. I was listening to the talk around me. There was the predictable demand for an early arrest of the bastard who'd strangled the Wise girl. It was an arrest they wanted, not necessarily the correct one. Any old arrest would do.

There was still light in the sky when I set off on George's bike. I was back to jeans and scruffy anorak; I didn't want blood on my only jacket.

The saddle was hard and brittle with age and too low, only the front brake worked, and the chain needed oil. There were no lights, so it might be tricky getting back.

Port Sumbury was not what I had expected from its grand

name. The basin was very small, the harbour mouth all piled rocks and wooden stavings. There was a lot of mud. The tide was nearly out, leaving a skim of water on a stony and slimy base, on which yachts were perched like ducks waiting for enough water to take off. To the west, the sky was now a deep, purply-red, and lights were on in some of the yacht cabins. Beyond the tiny township I could see a hill rising, a misty grey with its back-lit sky. Alongside the harbour basin there was a car-park, set between the road and the sea, with a ticket hut crouching against a low wall, but now the parking was free because the holiday season had finished. So it was full of cars. I wondered where all the drivers had gone. Later, I found most of them in the Stormy Petrel.

I hid the bike between the hut and the wall behind it, where there was a yard of space. There was a fair-sized hotel backed against the hill and facing the car-park, and beyond the point where the road ceased to claim that distinction, a rutted lane. Along there I discovered two small souvenir shops and a row of cottages, and at the far end, when it looked as though I was about to walk straight into the sea, was the Stormy Petrel.

Now it was clear why all the cars had been left back at the car-park; you couldn't have got a car along there. They probably had to deliver the beer by boat, and had been doing that for a couple of centuries, though at that time some of it would've been smuggled brandy and perhaps the odd French aristo fleeing the Revolution, and not getting any further until he'd been stripped of anything valuable.

From the pub frontage, a bare five yards wide, narrow and worn steps ran down a low cliff to the water—to the rocks now that the tide was out. There was a foot-high wall guarding it. The noise from the bar nearly pressed me over the edge.

I walked across to the door and went inside. The beams were original, and I was ducking at once. The smoke was more recent, but not fresh. What with that and the beams I nearly missed the three steps down to the black oak floor. The jolly jack tars had brought it in with them.

I hustled my way to the bar, not wishing to be conspicuous by remaining passive, and shouted for beer. While it wasn't coming I hooked my elbows on the hallowed old oak surface and looked round casually. Here were the modern mariners, as proud of themselves and their seafaring as Columbus; and here was a different group, this year's crop of layabouts, centring on the romantic atmosphere of daring deeds and violence. Eight pints inside you and you were Black Harry, in from the storm with his brig loaded down with hooch and the bodies of customs men. Anything less than eight and you were just another thug.

A pint tankard was slid beside my elbow. I took the top inch off, to save spilling any down a customer—a circumstance ripe for violence—and began to ease myself, shoulder first and tankard high, through the crush, weaving like a cyclist in a traffic jam and searching for Frenchie's weasel face through the fugg. I located him in a far corner, looking set for the night.

As he seemed to be surrounded by acolytes, not a happy face on any of them, I didn't go over to join him. It would have been impossible, anyway, to hold any sort of conversation, and what we had to say to each other was best kept to ourselves.

I stood still long enough for him to recognise me. There was no change in his expression, no surprise. I jerked my head, put down my beer at someone's elbow—it was terrible stuff, anyway—and turned to commence fighting my way to the door.

When I got outside the silence slapped me. Out there the sea murmured, and a wet breeze cooled my cheek. It was now fully dark, but enough light got through the dirty pub windows to show me how far I dared to move, and illuminated a finger post with a sign, *Gentlemen,* which pointed out over the sea.

As I watched, two loaded customers stumbled out of a side door I hadn't noticed, releasing a flood of sound. They headed for the sign, one each side of it. With interest, I watched them, one tall and thin, the other tubby and awkward. They stared out over the low wall and at the black, placid sea.

Then I was aware that Frenchie was at my elbow. He always did manage to move quietly. Evidently he was in a reasonable mood, otherwise I'd have been a hospital case by then.

"Well, Frenchie," I said. "How long you bin out?"

"Month."

"Keeping outa trouble?"

"You bet."

Frenchie had protruding teeth, the upper set jutting beyond the lower. He didn't seem to be able to speak without spitting. If he was half my weight I'd have been surprised, but his size had nothing to do with the menace he presented. His nobbly little body looked undisciplined, but he could move like a snake striking. His narrow and always slightly watering eyes gave the appearance of myopia, but he could detect an aggressive move at a hundred yards. I had to be smooth and relaxed with him. Nothing must be said to disturb his equanimity.

"You've bin following me, Frenchie. You wanna tell me why?"

"What you doin' in Sumbury, Manson?" he demanded, his teeth clashing.

"Lookin' for a friend. Tha's all."

"Yah!" He patted his lips. With his left hand, I noticed. It was his right you had to watch. Contempt dribbled from the corners of his mouth. "Y're a bloody liar, Manson."

"Carl sent y', didn't he?" I asked evenly. "Remember Carl? A lifer. Don' look so blank. Carl Packer, in fer life. I bet he sentcher." I reckoned he'd feel more at home with the lazy prison vernacular. "But he didn't send y' to hunt me out," I assumed.

His patience went. You get a split second of warning, and I was poised for whatever he might attempt. But I'd made a mistake. The bladder-emptiers had been his heavies, and quietly they'd moved in behind me. I felt hands clamp on my biceps, and it was too late.

FIVE

Frenchie was a knife man. Even inside Gartree he'd always had something about him with a point to it. Outside, he was wearing his working clothes, always a loose jacket with once-white roll-neck sweater. He had a thin pocket, leather lined, inside the left half of his jacket, housing a knife, and another up his left sleeve. Long and short, depending on the exigencies of the moment. But he was most deadly with the long, slim blade that lay vertically between his shoulder blades and down his back, in another leather holster. It explained his shoulders-back amble. Once the knife was out in the light his movements became more supple. I saw it glitter. He'd become too supple for my liking.

This thing was his throwing knife. He could reach back and draw it and throw it, all in one movement. It spun in the air, the speed of rotation varying in accordance with the distance involved. However far away you were, whether running towards or away from him, you could bet that point would be there to contact its target.

But at that time nobody was running. I was held fast. The thing was as close to piercing my flesh as I fancied.

The tall one was to the right of me. I'd had time for a couple of quick glances before the presence of the knife kept my head still. This one was young, flabby, with a beer-gut just beginning to mature. On my other side was the shorter, fatter one. He'd perhaps been a middleweight wrestler a few years back, but his belly was now tumbling over itself to get out of his belt. His grip was viciously tight, but I guessed his reactions would be slow.

The point of the knife was a fraction beneath my left nostril. The blade was slim enough to slide right up without drawing blood, and then a couple of inches further, by which time I wouldn't be worrying about blood any more.

Frenchie said, "You wanna go on livin'? Nod once for yes." Then he cackled maniacally, though the point of the knife didn't move a millimetre.

I abandoned the vernacular. "You've got nothing against me, Frenchie." My voice was tight.

"Musclin' in, that's what."

He must have been referring to the business that'd brought him there. I shook my head. Started to, then remembered. Words not actions. "I'm here trying to locate a certain young woman. Not your affair at all." I was finding it difficult to keep my eyes on him instead of crossing them down the length of my nose.

"Saw y' talkin' to him in Gartree. You're lyin', Manson."

"You saw me talking to whom?" I asked meticulously.

"Packer. You said it y'self. Carl Packer."

Packer had been our only link in Gartree. It was now confirmed that Packer, having approached me unsuccessfully about Philomena Wise, had later approached Frenchie.

"So we talked," I said soothingly. "Frenchie, think about it. If I'd taken the job on, she wouldn't have lasted as long as she did. I've been out longer than you."

"It wasn' me. Take that back, y' bastard!" Anger vibrated the knife point.

It was difficult to talk sense to Frenchie. The psychologists probably had a word for him. "Take what back? Did I say you'd killed her? Never, Frenchie. She was strangled. That's not your line at all. You couldn't have done that." Psychotic, that's the word.

The more plainly I tried to put it the more he failed to understand. He still seemed to think I was accusing him, insulting him, even.

"I was here, wun't I! If I'd done it, I wouldn't have bin here!" he howled.

I couldn't concentrate because his fury now had the knife point bobbing about. But I managed to follow his distraught logic. If he

had killed Philomena he would have done it only if he'd already
had proof laid on that he was somewhere else. But he'd been here,
in the district, and he was still here. I wondered again why he'd
not left, and rapidly.

"I can see why you're annoyed," I assured him, trying to manage a conciliatory tone. "You came all the way here to do the job,
and somebody beat you to it. So . . . no fee for you from Packer.
But it wasn't me, Frenchie. I really was somewhere else."

"Lay off that!" he shouted.

"I'm only trying to put you right."

"Keep y'r slimy tongue to yerself!"

"No. Listen. She's dead. Carl Packer sent you. Right? And they've
got nobody for it, and it's a complete mystery. So what's to stop
you going to Carl—or Carl's moneyman—and claiming your fee?
She's dead. You were on the job. So you can collect. Easiest money
you ever did see."

"You bloody stoopid or somethin'?" He seemed genuinely baffled.

"I want to help you," I told him. "You've spent good money on
this. These two characters here—top talent—they must've cost a
packet."

"Well . . . yes," he said reluctantly, though not with enough
conviction to affect the position of the knife point.

"And with all that money," I pointed out, "you'd be able to get
away to Brazil or Mexico or somewhere like that. Exotic, Frenchie.
Sun and sand and warm, soft flesh."

"What the hell!"

Only by being jocular about it could I see any chance of seeing
the next day in. I had to take a risk. Somehow, his unstable anger
had to be turned in another direction from me.

"You'd need to get away, of course, because the police might
arrest somebody in the end, then Packer would have to invest in
another hit-man, to track *you* down, Frenchie, for cheating him.
And get his money back. If he had to open you up to find it."

His teeth meshed together, and he hissed past them. No sense of
humour, that was his failing. I was a second or two from feeling
that blade, and now I had to get it said fast.

"Unless it's you they arrest, Frenchie."

Life had never been friendly to Frenchie. Not with that face. As
a child, kind ladies had offered him lollipops, and when he'd
smiled they had snatched them away. Life was snatching things
away again. He now raised a howl of animal despair, then he
whirled about and expressed himself in his only possible way; he

threw the knife. It stuck quivering in the thick oak door of the Stormy Petrel.

But I was far from safe. There were two more knives to go. Not throwers, though. One slicer and one stabber. I had perhaps two seconds in which to do something positive, and Gartree training had taught me that you had to act fast, or you went under.

I tramped down the shin of the one on my right. I wasn't wearing boots, but the heel was hard. I finished the tramp on his instep. This was more telling. I felt his grip relax and before he got the howl out I had my arm free. Fatty, the other side, didn't release my arm, but I used it as a fulcrum, swinging round with my right fist into his beer gut. Ten years before he would've laughed, and the fist would have bounced. Now there was only flab between me and the stomach inside. He grunted and bent over. My left knee met his nose, and then I was free.

Frenchie was turning back to me. I saw his right hand flashing inside his jacket. I had to stop that knife from appearing. The movement of his arm projected his right elbow, so I kicked it. The knife was probably already out of its sheath, because he made a wheeing sound through his teeth as his arm jerked back. It was clear that the knife had done something unpleasant inside the jacket. His mouth opened and his eyes glazed, and I hit him in the mouth with all I'd got.

Even as my fist was on its way I realised it was a mistake. I was going to break my knuckles on those teeth. I tensed for the pain, and to my surprise the fist went straight through, mashing his lips. The teeth were false. Why would anyone have false teeth shaped so revoltingly? I didn't pause to ponder the question. He was choking and retching, bent over, and the two toughies still had to prove their worth. I ran.

Two sets of feet pattered after me. I could outrun them easily, I reckoned. Having coughed up his denture, Frenchie managed to shout a choked command. It sounded like, "Tramp him!"

So I ran into the dark and rutted lane, out into the light streaming from the windows of the hotel, then into the darkness opposite the car-park. I was outpacing them, but I couldn't beat their car. They would surely have one. There would be little cover along the road.

I dived into the darkness behind the shed, and fell painfully on the bike. Then I lay still.

At this point the reaction set in. I was trembling, and sweat was drying chill on my skin. Nobody had ever deprived Frenchie of the use of two knives, except when they were both sticking in him. He wouldn't be able to forgive that, and my luck wouldn't protect me for ever.

I heard a car engine start, gears bang in, the scream of revving tyres. It stopped at the car-park entrance. A door opened. Frenchie's muffled voice gave urgent choked commands, and full headlights swept the road as they headed for Sumbury.

When the pain became unacceptable, I eased myself off the bike. The main problem had been a pedal. I stood, motionless behind the shed, and tried to get my mind working. The shakes were still with me, and I could've slaughtered a double brandy.

With the fact confirmed that Carl Packer had employed Frenchie to kill Philomena Wise, I still hadn't progressed far. I didn't know why, and I still didn't know which Philomena. But the job had brought Frenchie to Sumbury. It was therefore a strange coincidence that she had died just at the time he was searching out his target. Yet Frenchie hadn't killed her.

Coincidences were pounding in from all directions. Phil had come to Sumbury, where there was already another Philomena Wise. Phil had said she had something to clear up, and the other one had died. Had this been what she had to clear up?

And there was the question of the scarf, Philomena having been strangled by the very same scarf that Arthur Torrance had been bringing to her as a present.

I wondered whether all these coincidences would ever present a logical pattern. So far, there was no pattern at all, and I still hadn't managed to contact Phil.

All this thinking in cool and salty air had left me calm again, and reasonably in control of my nerves. I needed to decide what to do in the immediate future.

I couldn't see how I would be able to use the bike to get back to The George. It wasn't so much the lack of lights, as the sky was clear and there was enough light for me to see the road surface. But I knew Frenchie wouldn't give up easily. He would soon realise that I had to be hiding back at Port Sumbury. They would return, and if I was on the road their headlights could sweep round a bend on me abruptly, and I would have no chance of diving for cover off a bike.

In circumstances like this, the thing to do is the unexpected. Go where you would least likely go. I therefore slipped quietly and circumspectly back to the Stormy Petrel. When I got there, it seemed that nobody had gone in or come out, unless they'd used the side door to patronise the whistling post. I knew this as soon as I approached the main door. Frenchie's knife, as I'd hoped, was still sticking in it. Nobody could've gone through that door without having it brush his nose.

I levered it out. This entailed a certain amount of effort, as it was embedded a good inch into the ancient and matured oak. But at last I had it in my hand, and could examine it. The maximum width of the blade was less than half an inch, both edges were razor sharp, and the point was like a needle. Its handle was two thin slats of hardwood.

I now had a weapon, though not one I would care to use. More importantly, I had deprived Frenchie of his number one, an encouraging thought when I had to consider he would inevitably come looking for me, even if I managed to get through the night.

Slowly, carefully keeping to the heavier shadows, I began to move back towards the car-park. What I didn't know was now more important than what I did. One thing was that there had been time for the car to return, and I didn't know whether they were waiting for me. Another was that I didn't even know that Frenchie had gone in the car. He could be lurking, with mud smeared on the blade of his number two to avoid reflections. I had now completely abandoned any thought of using the bike, so it would have to be on foot. I would have to hug the verges, prepared to dive for cover during every treacherous yard of the two miles.

But first I had to be certain about the car-park. Frenchie didn't know I'd come on a bike. He could be waiting for a shadow, Paul Manson size, to creep up to one of the vehicles. The first poor sloshed bugger . . . no, I didn't dare to allow myself to think of that. First, I had to reconnoitre the car-park—if I could only reach it safely.

I was running out of the better sort of shadows. Ahead and on my right was the hotel, my side of the road. The lobby light was dim, but I dared not cross it. One upstairs light was on, casting a pallid gleam across towards the car-park. Crouching low, moving slowly with my knees protesting, I slid across to the other side of the road. The overpowering impulse was to run, but this was one impulse I had to ignore. It's movement that's most easily spotted.

Gaining the poor cover of the four-foot surrounding wall of the car-park, I crouched for a full two minutes to recover my poise, breathing quietly through my nose. The throwing knife was now clammy in my right fist. I listened. Somewhere there was movement, but I couldn't place it. A cat yowled in miserable sexual endeavour. I edged towards the entrance. Just inside was the shed, and I felt I dared to straighten to my full height in its shadow. I could hear each tiny wave on the rocky beach, but nothing else. A shadow moved to my left.

Had he seen me? Was he circling round? The hair stood proud on my neck. Sweat dripped from the end of my nose. I could almost hear it, and didn't dare raise a hand to dash it away. I couldn't stay there; it was too dangerous. Slowly, my eyes not moving from where I'd seen the shadow moving, I slipped into the shade of the nearest car. There, feeling safer, I edged round, moved between two more, slid across the backs, round the next, always skirting towards the same point. And pausing to survey the complete prospect. Nothing. A star was reflected from the roofs of the better polished cars. It began to annoy me, following me round, pointing at me.

Then I saw the shadow again, over by the shed I'd recently left. I had him. The advantage was mine . . . but to do what? The best method of defence? Why not! I attacked, having not the slightest idea of what I would do if I reached him and confronted him. But not being too foolhardy, I chose the safest route, along the narrow lane between the noses of the parked cars and the side wall. I stumbled, jumped, aware that I must now have revealed myself, if only by sound. And then I fell sprawling beneath the wall.

For some moments I was dazed. My right hand, still frantically clutching the throwing knife, had been rasped painfully against the stone wall. I crouched, and edged my way round, bringing my knees up. What I'd tripped over had not been hard and metallic, it had been soft and yielding. With my left hand I explored, the breath hissing between my teeth. A jacket—I moved my hands—a lapel—higher—and a nose, which was resting on the tarmac surface. There it was, the identification: a roll-neck sweater, feeling greasy to the touch. I tried to shuffle sideways, but my foot touched something that clattered on the tarmac. I did not dare reach for it, but I knew what it was. This was probably his number two. I had found Frenchie.

Now that there was no longer any need to remain silent, I nevertheless stifled a whimper. My snatched-away hand was poised. I had to *know*. I reached forward again. There was only the palest glimmer of light reaching me, but the roll neck of the sweater was paler than the rest. I rested my fingers above it, on the neck, questing for the jugular. And found it. Nothing. Frenchie was dead.

It took several seconds for the implication to flood over me, which it eventually did like a dam-burst. I sprang to my feet. I'd killed him, killed again. Oh Christ! I nearly shouted out: I've killed a man, another one. No . . . not a man, an animal. Not even that —a creature, a beast. All the same, I had done it.

My right arm swept back, the throwing knife in it. Get rid of the weapon! Then I quelled the impulse. It wasn't the murder weapon.

It did not bear a spot of his blood. The true weapon lay there, beside his limp right hand. Get rid of that? But why? It would achieve nothing. Think, I urged myself, gulping for air. Don't panic. It'd been self-defence. It could be called an accident. And the two toughies—hell, they'd be gone into the hills and far away.

Then the nausea overcame me, and I leaned over the wall, retching drily, the bitter gall in my throat. It didn't matter what I did, that was the point. What mattered was that I'd killed again. Dear Lord, again. Self-justification hadn't got anything to do with it at all.

But here my Gartree training came to my help. To hell with my conscience. They'd have laughed at me—even the warders.

I found myself out on the roadway, swaying, wondering which way was which. Then, I began to plod towards Sumbury, the throwing knife still firmly clutched in my right hand. Dimly, I realised, I needed to keep that. It was a weapon unsullied by blood. That was important. I didn't know how, and decided to work that out later.

I had to bear in mind that the two heavies were still out there somewhere with the car. If they didn't know Frenchie was dead, they would be heading back. This made the journey more difficult because I couldn't keep to the smooth black trail of the tarmac. Every sign of a headlight, behind or before, had me diving for cover, and the moon had risen dangerously.

The road junction arrived, then I passed the phone box. Now there was more traffic, too much to justify panic reactions. Head down, I stumbled on, keeping my right shoulder well in any shadows available. When The George appeared, I skirted round to the rear. There was still the oppressive thought that I could be under observation. I gained the dark comfort of George's back yard. For five minutes I stood amongst the beer crates and the empty metal barrels, still, waiting. Nothing moved. The window to my left was softly lit and heavily curtained. I knocked on the rear door.

Ada opened up to me. She might well have been immune to uncertainties, because she merely smiled thinly, and nodded back along the corridor.

"They're in the snug."

I walked stiffly ahead of her, hearing the bolts slamming home behind her. I pushed open the snug door and stood for a moment in the doorway, feet apart to assist the balance, the knife hanging down my thigh. George and Lucy were sitting at the table, playing crib.

"So there you are," said George, hardly glancing at me and moving a matchstick along the board. "We expected you earlier."

"I've lost your bike," I told him, getting rid of one of my worries. "I had to leave it at Port Sumbury."

"I'm surprised to hear you got it that far." He raised his eyes, and they narrowed.

Lucy had turned, her trained eyes taking in every detail of my tattered appearance. There were no doubt fresh rents in my jeans, and I didn't dare imagine what she could read in my face. Her expression did not change when her eyes roamed down my arm and reached the knife, only when they lifted again to my face. "Paul?" she whispered.

"I reckon you'd better take charge of this," I told her, advancing to the table. My voice sounded thin and insecure. "It's making me nervous."

I put the knife down on the table under her eyes.

There was a moment of silence as they stared at it, then George slapped the cards together and put them away with the crib board.

"Tea, I think," said Ada, and out she went.

Lucy was nodding to herself. She touched the point of the blade with her finger. "Did you leave anything else behind, apart from the bike?" She was speaking primly, trying to make light of it, but my brain thumped inside my skull.

I dropped down on to a chair. Exhaustion flooded over me, and I rubbed my face vigorously. I'd felt the blood draining from it and my head was swimming.

"It belongs—belonged—to a man called Douglas French. You'll have him on record, because he was in Gartree with me. He'll be registered as a knife expert."

"We should've put you in custody," she commented, her voice flat. "Are you telling me you took this one from him?"

"Not exactly. He threw it. That's what it's for—throwing. But he didn't throw it at me. I hit him in the mouth, and probably I broke his upper denture. I don't know. When he tried to get one of his other knives out I kicked him on the elbow. I think I hurt him, because I managed to get away." There it was, without a stain of untruth.

Then Ada brought in the tea, and a thick slab of cheese and pickle sandwich for me. She joined us, and in between gulps of tea and swallows of sandwich, recovering second by second, I related all that had happened, not omitting the relevant fact that Frenchie had seen me talking to Carl Packer, and that I had to assume Packer had approached Frenchie on the same subject, which was the projected death of Philomena Wise. I made no mention of my subsequent discovery in the car-park.

At the end, Lucy nodded, her big eyes deep and thoughtful. "So

. . . if we can contact him, we take him in?" she asked. "And we charge him with what?"

"Not the killing of Philomena. Strangling isn't in his line at all."

"Then we'd better have another charge if we're going to take him into custody."

I couldn't tell her that it wasn't going to come to that. "He assaulted me."

"There's not a mark on you."

"That bloody knife was an inch up my nose."

"It's not bloody, that's the point. And it sounds to me as though he was the one who was assaulted. Look at your knuckles!"

I thumped the table, not all the tension having drained away. "Oh, fine! Great! Just what I wanted, the law right behind me. I'm overwhelmed." Which was a prime example of sick insincerity.

She stared at me with her face set and severe. Firstly, she was a policewoman. Only as a minor and secondary consideration was she at all willing to offer assistance to me. I recalled that I'd confided in her far too freely in the past. I had been naïve, sensing in her an empathy I'd been only too eager to welcome. I had been lulled by it. But I was now very much on my own, it seemed.

"I've got to remind you," she said in her official voice, "that you came here quite voluntarily. Nobody's really certain about you, Paul Manson. Now you tell me you've been involved in a fracas with an ex-convict acquaintance. What d'you expect me to make of that?"

She actually used that word: fracas. To me it had been a fight.

"Make what you like of it," I said shortly.

"I'll tell you what Inspector Greaves is going to make of it. He'll say it's a carry-over from some disagreement in Gartree. He'll assume you met by chance here, and it's all boiled over. We don't want your private squabbles in our town, thank you very much. We've got enough to handle as it is."

I looked round at the faces, George nodding as though he quite agreed, as he'd have to if he wanted to keep the police on his side, Ada mastering her natural cheerfulness and wearing the baffled look of a person who hates tension. And there was tension in that room. I had brought it in with me, like a deadly disease.

I took a deep breath. "You couldn't have been listening," I said, keeping my voice low and even. "He as good as admitted he was here on a job for Carl Packer. Packer had sent him to kill Philomena Wise. Frenchie was here to do that, and she's dead."

Lucy lowered her eyes. When she looked up—how else could I explain what I saw in her eyes? It was fear.

"And you?" she asked quietly. "What does it tell us about you?"

"Is there anything you didn't already know?"

She backed away from the challenge. "This Frenchie, as you call him . . . you've already said it was not his line, strangling. You said he always uses a knife."

"He's killed with it. Why d'you suppose he was inside Gartree?"

"So he wouldn't have strangled her?"

I shrugged, not willing to go over and over it, and wearied now to the bones.

"All right! But now we hear you were in contact yourself with this unsavoury character Carl Packer, inside Gartree. Are we to be told the gist of that—or make the obvious assumption?"

"Assume what you like." It came out sharp and curt.

"You see!" she cried in exasperation, her eyes blazing now. "But you . . . you tell us you took a knife from this Frenchie—"

"I levered it from the front door of—"

"All the same, you managed to avoid it, and inflicted your own damage. With your bare hands, damn it. What *are* you, Paul Manson? No—don't tell me. Why don't you get back to where you came from and leave us in peace!"

What was I? She'd hit on the exact point, and I wasn't yet certain. This diversion, in which I'd become involved, was in no way part of a scholarly research leading to my Ph.D. I was still too involved with the high-pressure tension in Gartree, too much the predator, poised for violence. I had no reply, but fortunately George saved me from the embarrassment of silence. His hand slapped down on the table. "That's enough, Lucy. He's a guest in my house."

"A paying guest," I reminded him, trying to regain my composure.

He glanced at me. "You haven't paid anything yet, so you're my guest. I'm not having Lucy throwing her authority around in here."

"Oh . . . damn you, George," she said.

I lifted my head. I didn't want to intrude between these two. Her authority carried the weight of the law, and I didn't want either of them in trouble.

"Easy on. There's no trouble here. Greaves said he wanted me to hang around—"

"Not to get into fights with killers!" Lucy snapped. "George, can you find me something to wrap this wretched thing in?" She gestured in distaste at the knife, still lying on the table.

Ada, uncertain and uneasy in the presence of discord, said, "I'll get it," and hurried out of the room. There was a short period of silence. I realised something was slipping away from me, but couldn't put a name to it. Yet it seemed I still had George's support.

Into the air I remarked, "I suppose I'd better give you prior notice. I'll be out of town tomorrow. That'll give you all a bit of peace." This was pure bravado, tossing it in to watch the effect.

"I don't know—" Lucy began.

I went straight on. "I want to clear up something in Killingham, but I'll be back. Tell Greaves. He'll have plenty on his mind, I reckon, but if he doesn't like it he can chuck me in a cell."

Then she was able to avoid my eyes by taking a bar napkin from Ada and carefully wrapping it round the knife. "We've got enough to justify taking you in for questioning, so don't be flippant with me."

I knew that. I'd been waiting for it to happen, holding my breath. But Greaves was playing his own game, and I guessed he wasn't going to show his hand at this stage. I got to my feet.

"I'll walk you back to the station—or wherever," I suggested.

"D'you think I can't look after myself!" she flared.

I shrugged. "There's some nasty types around."

"Aren't there!"

She was about to leave, but turned back at the door. The couple of seconds had given her time to retrieve her solemn expression.

"Tell me," she said coolly, as though it was purely a matter of abstract interest. "A little point. Don't you ever feel any regrets?"

"For what?"

"For killing your father," she jerked out.

I could feel the stillness in the room as a tangible thing. It was a challenge, an offer. I was too tired to make the most of it.

"Well now, I suppose I do," I admitted. "Mainly that I didn't give myself time to think. I lost control . . ."

"How often," she asked quietly, "does that happen?" She looked down at the bundle in her hands.

I couldn't meet her eyes. Before I looked up the door slammed and I heard her tramping along the corridor, heard the bolts shoot back and the outer door to the yard slam. There was a clatter, and I heard her curse.

I turned, rubbing my face with my palms. "I'm sorry, I'm keeping you people up. It's getting late."

SIX

In the morning I put on my slacks and jacket and caught the first bus out of town, at seven-thirty, the one George had advised. I needed to be away before they found Frenchie's body, because it was quite certain I wouldn't be able to move a finger after they had. I was tense, my eyes switching from the direction of the police station to the inland hill, from where the single-decker bus eventually came trundling, only five minutes late.

There were five of us waiting, two women, two men, and me. The women were clearly heading for a shopping spree. Of the two men, one was smartly dressed and carrying a folded *Times,* the other a sloppy youth with a morose expression. I sat where I could watch them. The smart one left the bus in the middle of nowhere. I considered the youth, speculating on the plausibility of his being a detective constable. You never can tell, these days.

The first part of the journey was tiring in its monotony, and in the regularity with which the bus kept stopping for no apparent reason and then hanging about. We seemed to cover the county in exhaustive detail, not missing any opportunity to dive down some inconvenient side lane, where the hedges brushed both sides at the same time and each corner offered new hazards.

I was relieved when the road we were on became more open and less obstructed, and we found ourselves between lines of houses and encountered more traffic. We were approaching my objective.

There were foot patrol officers in that town. I asked one of them where I might hire a car, and he directed me. The morose youth seemed to be following me. I took the direction indicated, and there he was again, outside the car-hire firm, watching as I made the necessary financial arrangements. My driving licence was still valid, my credit card worked its magic, and I drove out of the forecourt in a Ford Fiesta, pleasantly surprised that after four years I was still moving the controls in the recommended directions.

He was waiting as I paused at the exit, and put up his hand in a

halt signal. The nerve of it! Rather than lose me, he was prepared
to beg a lift. I wondered if he'd be discouraged if I drove over his
foot, but I saw he was wearing soft loafers so I stopped and wound
down the window.

"Thought you'd give me a lift," he said.

"Perhaps. If you ask nicely."

"Please."

"Where're you heading?" I asked, to catch him out.

"Same as you. Killingham, I reckon." And he grinned.

"Get in then." I reached over for the door lock. At least he would
be company, and we were still nearly two hundred miles from
Killingham.

He ran round and slid in smoothly. A fast mover. Early twenties,
I decided, and looking even younger. He had one of those naïve
baby faces that can be very deceptive, looking unworn, pink, and
shiny, with beneath it something resembling a brash hardness. He
had a snub nose and black, curly hair. When he smiled, he'd be a
devil with the women. His whole face glowed with the knowledge
of this.

"Been following you," he said as I got going. He didn't expect me
to resent it.

I couldn't spare any sideways glances. In strange towns you
have to be alert, searching for signs ahead, trying to sort information from too much data.

"I know," I told him. "Saw you."

That didn't worry him, either. "You're Paul Manson."

I'd detected a touch of challenge in this. It compensated, no
doubt, for his lack of bulk. "And you?"

"I'm Arthur Torrance. You can call me Art. Everybody does."

I had to think about my attitude to him, but also had to decide
whether I wanted Ring Road North or Ring Road East, this being
difficult because I was told to get into the correct lane. There was
no time to spare for Philomena's ex-boyfriend, he of the silk scarf.

"There's a map on that shelf in front of you," I told him. "Make
yourself useful and tell me where to go."

"Sure thing. Can't afford to run a car meself."

"Rough."

"I'm not supposed to leave Sumbury."

"Nor me."

"Think they'll have a road-block?" he asked with keen anticipation.

"I'm not that important to them, but you might be."

"Garn. They got nothin' on me."

By this time I was going round and round a huge island, looking for the correct turn-off. "Suppose you look at that map. I hope you know where we are."

"Sure do. Did a job here once."

There was silence as he searched the map. I continued to circulate. He hadn't said he'd had a job, but he'd "done" a job. There had been mention of Philomena's dubious friends. He was certainly dubious, but seemed quite contented with it.

He looked up from the map, gave the traffic signs a quick glance, and said, "Two more, and we turn off. Not that one, the next. That's it. How long since you drove a car?"

"Four years, you could say."

"Thought so. Want me to take over?"

I guessed what that would mean: unadulterated terror until we reached Killingham. "No thank you. It's all coming back."

"Yes. Well, watch that old dear on the crossing."

"I see her." He was talking as though I was senile.

Five minutes later we were out on the open road, and I put up the speed a little, fighting a tendency to wander on to the wrong side of the road. The last vehicle I'd driven had been in America. You could have fitted this Fiesta in the back of that big Cherokee.

"How did you know my name?" I asked.

"It gets around. I've got contacts."

"Good ones, too, to know where I was going."

He had a ready answer to that. "Oh, sure. An' if you wanta know, I picked it up in the police station."

I might have guessed. "From what I heard, Art, you can't be their favourite person. You buy a young lady a present and it's found knotted round her neck."

"Don't *you* start. I've had a skinful. All night they've bin at me, and I'm fed up to here."

"They had you in for interrogation, I heard."

"Couldn't hold me. I know my rights. They'd got nothing. I was outa there late last night."

I glanced sideways to catch a pout, a gesture of immature self-pity. "And how did you come to hear about me?"

"They was out there in the corridor, with the door open. Talkin' quiet, but I've got big ears. Just that Paul Manson was going to Killingham, and I knew it'd be by bus, 'cause the trains . . . Anyway, I reckoned you'd be after a car."

"And you just fancied the trip?"

"My folk're in Killingham."

"There'll be a warrant out for you if you don't go back."

"Goin' back, ain't I! Just tell me where and I'll pick you up."

"Well . . . thanks," I said. "Much obliged."

"It's all right."

We drove another thirty miles in reasonable silence, then I saw a Little Chef ahead and pulled in.

"Coffee?" I asked.

"Why not! It's on me, though."

I agreed, without reluctance. We sat in a corner, cradling our coffees. I could now face him squarely and watch that open and mobile face chasing through all the emotions, and was able to understand why the police couldn't get anywhere with him, all that bland innocence beaming at them, and with that eagerness of his to co-operate. Throw a question at him and a willing answer came bouncing back.

"You've told it over and over to the police," I said, making it a statement.

"Fifty times."

"Care to make it fifty-one?"

"Why not! Anything for a mate." He looked round. "Here, I ordered egg and chips. It's taking a hell of a time." He half rose to his feet. "Miss!"

He was the sort who gets the best attention at restaurants. From waitresses, anyway. Egg and chips appeared like magic. He waded in, elbows flying, talking as he ate and waving his eating irons.

"You never met Philomena, did you?"

I'd seen her once. "I didn't know her," I said.

"Had no breakfast," he explained. "Now . . . there was some little raver for y'. Into anythin' for a bit of a giggle. Lor', but we had some great times. One big laugh after the other. She was my girl. Everybody knew that, or I hadda teach 'em." He waved his knife under my nose. For one brief second I was facing a tough little layabout. Then it was gone, and he was grinning over all the good times they'd had together, which always seemed to start with nicking a car before they went on to carve up the town. Great fun, bring the kiddies. It hadn't been like that in my day. I was getting the impression I'd missed out on an important element in my development.

"From time to time we did a warehouse or somethin'," he went on with undiminished enthusiasm. "When there's a load o' spirits just come in, that's the time. You know."

I didn't, but I nodded agreement. "You mean . . . you and Philomena?" I had visions of Bonnie and Clyde. He was completely and happily amoral. The them and us jungle, it was, "them" being the ones who'd got it and "us" the ones who wanted it.

"You ain't listenin'. Me an' a few of the fellers. But Phillie"—so that was what he'd called her—"used to stick her nose in. Wanted to keep cavey for us. Things like that."

He'd chomped his last chip and we got up and left. He was silent as I got the car moving again so I had to prompt him.

"This was at night, you say?"

He knew what I was thinking. His mind bobbled about like a globe of quicksilver. "She used to sneak outa the house. They didn't know. We didn't want her, but you could reckon she'd be there, parked in her little Mini with the lights off. Stupid little bitch," he said fondly. "We coulda made it great if we'd put it together."

So she'd had her own car, but they'd had to steal one for a night on the town. But of course, stupid old-fashioned me, it wasn't so much of a giggle unless you nicked a car.

"She sounds a real ball of fire," I said admiringly.

"She sure was. It's left at the next roundabout." He seemed to be able to read a map and talk at the same time. "But that one job, it all went haywire. The cops got a tip-off or somethin', 'cause up they popped and took us all in. Me, I was the getaway driver. No good, they cut me off, and they raked in Phillie at the same time."

"That must have raised a stink," I observed.

"Have you seen him? That Aubrey. There's a poncey name for y'. But he'd got pull, 'cause she was out the next morning, and no charge. Wish I'd got friends like that." But he said it with pride, and with no sign of rancour.

"He wouldn't consider you a friend," I suggested.

"You are so right," he said in a prim Aubrey voice. "Me, I got a year inside."

"Not Gartree?"

"Nah. That's for the nobs. Winson Green f' me. No class to it. And while I was inside the family up-and-offed. Couldn't stand the scandal or somethin', or keeping her well away from me."

"That'd be it." I took a bend on the wrong side of the road and had to pull myself together. "And when you came out?"

"D'you always drive like that? When I came out, I hadda trace her—didn't I! And there she was, livin' at Sumbury, so I went down and saw her."

"Heh! Hold on a sec'. When was this? They've been there two years, and it didn't take you a year—"

"It was back in January. Took a month, is all. But she'd changed."

"They do."

"All snooty and la-di-da. Couldn't get anywhere with her. So I went back to Killingham, and dropped her a line now and then. Got nothin' back, though."

"Perhaps she couldn't read your writing. Did you get as far as joining your letters up?"

"You're cute, you know that! So anyway . . . d'you want to hear this or not?"

"Go on, I'm interested." I felt I was going to hear it anyway. He was in desperate need of a friend, and who better to sympathise with him than a fellow suspect? His flip tongue was all camouflage, and beneath it there was insecurity. I was beginning to wonder whether I'd met the best liar in the country. It was a great loss to politics.

"Then watch the road," he said tersely. "I was going to say—I heard she was as good as engaged to some Aussie clown."

"You heard it in a pub, I understand."

"And why not? Gotta keep in touch, ain't you! So I reckoned I'd better go an' see her, give her one last chance. Who'd want an Aussie when they could shack up with me?"

He seemed genuinely puzzled by this. He did not lack self-esteem. The fact that this particular Aussie had loads of money and a huge ranch did not in any way qualify him to challenge Art's charm. The fact that her family would prefer her to be even further away from Art, and would thus apply persuasion, did not disturb him.

"It does sound unbelievable," I agreed.

"Yeah. So I hadda go along and sort it out. I hitched down to Sumbury and got her on the phone, and in the end she said she'd meet me."

"At the bus shelter, the town end of the road to Port Sumbury," I said, just to make it clear that I knew the background, and he'd be wasting his time loading me with too many lies.

"Right. It was her birthday, see, and I reckoned she'd be expectin' a pressie. Nearly cleaned me out, that did. A silk scarf . . . got it at a cute little shop in town. They wrapped it up, nice as you like. She'd said she'd be there at seven. No later. Said there was a party she'd gotta get back to, and she'd need time to change. Why're they always changin'? Suggest anythin' and it's, oh, I'll just have to nip upstairs an' change into something. Can't understand women."

"It's not necessary to understand them, just learn to make the right moves. Carry on. She didn't turn up, so you—"

"If y' know it all, why trouble!" He'd gone all prickly.

"I was waiting for a bit of common sense to crop up. What I heard sounded so damned stupid!"

"What was stupid about it?" he demanded, offended.

Deliberately, I provoked him. "If you wanted to strangle her, why did you use the scarf? It was a dead giveaway."

He puffed his lips in contempt. "I didn't use it. You ain't heard it right. Admit it. I stood waiting there like a prune, for nearly half a flamin' hour. Quarter past seven, and she still hadn't come . . ." His voice faded away dismally.

"She'd stood you up. Anybody else would've realised that, but not you, I suppose. Always come running do they, Art?"

"If you don't wanta hear . . ."

"What I heard was that you ran back towards the town to the nearest phone box."

"Sure I did. I'd come a long way. Nobody was gonna stand me up and not hear from me." Then he sounded uncertain. "And I'd gotta know, hadn't I!"

"Of course you had. You went to the phone—"

"Her mother . . . you ever met that ice-pick of a bitch? Who is that? Speak up young man. Who? Took me ages to stick a word in she could understand. Then she said Phillie had gone out ages before. Well, I ask you! What'm I gonna think then? Ran back to the bus shelter. No Phillie. Boy, was I worried! Somethin' musta happened to her—"

"Hold on. You're forgetting something."

We were only three miles from Killingham, and I was reducing speed gradually. I didn't want to miss the end of this. "The present," I prompted.

No response. I glanced sideways. He was rubbing a hand over his face, not meeting my eyes. Art Torrance was embarrassed. He, who was God's gift to womankind, and who was well aware of it, was temporarily silenced by the memory of an emotion for which he felt shame—concern for somebody else.

"Well?" I demanded.

"I panicked, didn't I! Belted outa that phone booth and back to the bus shelter, and left the scarf behind. Didn't give it another thought. Stood there. Gave it a few seconds—"

"For a quiet smoke?"

"Walkin' up an' down, and I don't smoke. Then I ran for the house. And after that it was coppers and takin' me in and askin' me this an' that. Till last night."

"But they believed you?"

He recovered his self-confidence. "Well . . . got 'em baffled, ain't it! I'd left the scarf in the phone booth an' they say she was dead before then—"

"And there it was, knotted round her neck when they found her."

I pulled into a lay-by and stopped the engine. He was staring straight ahead, chin up, lower lip quivering. Art Torrance was close to tears. I decided to give him time, and spoke to the windscreen.

"But of course, they'd think you wouldn't strangle her with your own present and leave the wrapping behind, then come up with such a stupid story." I said it quietly, waiting for a reaction, prodding at his pride. "You're a bright lad. Always had your wits about you. Nobody as bright as you would make up such a load of rubbish. So you'd be recognised as too clever to have done it yourself, and then come out with that story."

I was being sarcastic. The police had certainly not based any of their reasoning on Art's brainpower. They had been constrained only by the awareness that they had to link a charge with logical continuity, and they hadn't got it. But if my remarks pleased Art, they might also lure him into indiscreet confidences.

He turned to me. His eyes were still moist, but he was grinning that triumphant smile of his. "Well . . . that's it!" he claimed. "You've got it in a nutshell."

I matched his grin, changed it to a scowl, and shook my head. "But the snag is, Art, that the police'll see through that. In the end. Then what d'you think they'll come round to? Go on, give it a guess."

I watched him steadily as we called each other's bluffs. He was street-wise and had always lived on his wits. He wasn't big enough to have survived otherwise. And survival had boosted him into a smug complacency. On his own turf he might be considered a genius, but he was getting too old for the street-boy act and he had nothing solid to replace it.

"Can't you guess?" I taunted him, when he still hesitated.

I watched for his eyes to flicker, and at last they did. "I ain't makin' any guesses," he muttered.

"So I'll tell you. Art, you bought that scarf and you had it gift-wrapped. There'd have been no intention of killing Phillie at that time, so that fits. You went to the bus shelter at seven, as arranged. But you didn't wait there. No, don't interrupt. You were ten minutes early, because you were eager and anxious, and for the same reason you couldn't wait there. She meant a lot to you. So you walked to meet her half-way, and you did meet her, where that patch of woodland is, beside the road."

He gave a too-expressive shrug. "Of course, you're talkin' crap."

"Perhaps not. You met her, I'd say, and she told you she was going to marry the Aussie, Grant Felton. She was going where you wouldn't be able to reach her again. It wasn't what you wanted to hear—"

"Don't wanna hear it now."

"You can get out of the car and walk into town, if you want to."

He made a move towards the door latch, then hesitated. The police were going to shove this under his nose, so he'd better have time to sniff round it a little. He turned back.

"Get on with it then." His voice was tight.

"It wasn't what you wanted to hear, but all the same you gave her the present. And I reckon she opened it up, looked at it, and said who'd want this, 'cause she'd got hundreds of them. So you made sure she kept it by tying it round her neck."

"No!"

"It *was* tied, I suppose?"

"For Chrissake, drop it!"

I was forcing him into facing it. "A single knot or a double?"

"Lay off!" he shouted.

"Double, was it?" I tilted my head. "You'd know, because the police would've told you. In full detail, I bet."

He thumped a clenched fist on his knee. "It was double-knotted. That make y' happy, does it?"

"Not particularly. I suppose a single knot would've slipped. Being silk. At the front, was it? The knot, I mean. Was she attacked from the front, Art?"

"Yes, yes, yes!" he choked.

"The knot at her throat?" I persisted. I had him shaken, and was wondering how far I could push him. But I had to have the facts, and needed my own assessment of his guilt or innocence.

Apparently I'd pushed him beyond a personal psychological barrier. His jaw was set and his eyes were dark and angry. "It was under her jaw to the right. You can bet they gave it me, item by item, the stinkin' rotten bastards."

"Right, so that'd make it difficult to untie. But you can see what those same rotten bastards are going to get to. They'll say you stood there, over her, and realised you'd buggered it up. It was your scarf, and you found you couldn't untie it, so you couldn't take it away with you. You'd realise it then, standing over Phillie's body."

"Don't keep sayin' that!"

"I'm pretending to be a police officer, throwing it at you. Devil's advocate, they call it."

"I needed to know that." He was, bouncing back, recovering fast.

"But whereas you can get out of this car and walk away, they'll have you where you can't go anywhere. And that's what they'll say, that you stood over her and realised you'd dropped yourself right in it. You deliberately left the wrapping, with your name on it. You dragged her into cover. Not far—you wanted her to be found pretty soon, because of the timing. You ran back to the phone box to make your call. It was around seven-twenty by then. Then you ran all the way to the house to get things rolling, and waited around while you polished your story about leaving the package in the phone booth. Because *that* would really stop 'em in their tracks. As it has done." I grinned at him. "There, how's that for a bit of logic?"

I had embarked on this theory with no confidence that I could carry it through, but in an attempt to undermine his self-esteem. But I hadn't, apparently, dented it. He was staring at me with contempt, waiting, it seemed, for an apology. When I did nothing, he jutted his lip and turned away.

"Why don't y' gerron with yer driving?" he said in disgust, his vernacular thicker than ever.

But he was silent and thoughtful for the rest of the way into town.

I dropped him in the square. For a moment I thought he was going to forget his intention to return to Sumbury. But no.

"Give me a ring when you're ready to go back," he said, holding the door open. He found a stump of pencil in his pocket, an old cash-till receipt in another, and wrote something on it. "Here. The phone number of Sam's Caff. They'll know where I am. Don't forget."

He was back on form. I promised not to forget him, and drove on. Sam's Caff. They would know. Not his home. I couldn't decide whether to be amused by his flip brashness or feel sorry for him. He was an insignificant predator in a world of slavering lions.

SEVEN

My approach to Phil's place had to be made cautiously. Frenchie's body must surely have been found hours before, and the police net would be out. Time was closing in on me, though they couldn't have known the location of Phil's flat unless they'd managed to trace her. The odds were well in my favour, but all the same I cruised past a couple of times before I risked the drive entrance and parked outside the front door. I still had her keys.

Again the house was quiet, but today the furniture polish smell was overlaid with a cigar tang. Three other families lived there, but you wouldn't have guessed it. People could die and nobody'd know for weeks. Silently, I mounted the stairs to the flat.

I should have gone through the place when I had the chance. I'd certainly had the opportunity, but at that time I'd had reservations. Not now. It was clear that I hadn't known much about Phil, and I needed to know more. I got out the key ring she'd given me and let myself in. At once, before the door had shut behind me, I knew that somebody had been there.

When you spend five solid days shut up in a flat you get to know every item around you. Now, there were minimal changes, a stool a foot from where I remembered it, the door to the bathroom shut when I hadn't closed it. I stood very still. The silence was oppressive.

Quietly, I opened the door behind me, went out, and closed it again. I'd heard it said that you can open a cylinder lock with a piece of thin celluloid (loid it, they'd said in the nick) or even a credit card. But that works only with a loosely fitted door. You couldn't have slid a razor blade in the crack of this one. I examined the frame, and there were no marks of force having been used.

So Phil had been home. She had seen me at Aubrey Wise's place —had perhaps even heard me—waited until I was clear, then driven like hell for Killingham. Whatever I might have found before, it would not be there now, not if it had any meaning for me.

In the bathroom she'd left the scent of bath oil. That smell was the only thing personal, and there was nothing else.

In the kitchen I discovered she'd eaten one of the frozen dinners I had left in the fridge. I turned on the cooker and prepared to cook the other. She hadn't thought to water her plants so I did it for her.

I said she hadn't left anything, by which I meant accidentally. On the Formica surface of her tiny kitchen table there was a note for me.

> Paul,
>   I'm certain you'll come back here to see what you can find, so I've had to make sure there's nothing. I don't want you in Sumbury. Please stay here at the flat, and I'll phone you when I can. I can assure you, it is far from finished.
>   Phil

While I sat and ate I read it over again. She had written it on half of an A4 sheet of notepaper, folded and torn roughly. Idly, I turned it over.

Oh, Phil! So much energy expended on keeping me in ignorance, and you had to go and make such a mistake! The notepaper bore a printed heading and phone numbers, but it clearly had not been something sent to her. There was nothing else on that half but the heading, and nobody starts a letter halfway down the page. She had carefully torn the sheet in half, to keep the heading from my sight, and then left me the wrong half. Somewhere in her shoulder-bag she would now have a screwed-up ball of blank paper. It had, before being torn, been a sheet of her own printed notepaper.

The heading was: WISEMANN AGENCY, 3rd Floor, 37 Parkin Road, Killingham. The phone number was: Killingham 7397. Out of hours: Killingham 5964.

The number of the phone on the tall table beside Phil's front door was Killingham 5964.

Wisemann, I thought. The Wise part of it was obvious, but was the Mann part of it a partner? Or herself? She'd said she worked alone, so the latter was more likely. If the name Wise was not her own, and evidence was growing that it couldn't be, then perhaps Mann was. But that got me not one jot or tittle further. If she was known in Killingham as Wise, she would not also be known as Mann.

After I'd finished eating I looked round the flat, wondering if I'd be seeing it again, then left. The door closed on an episode in my life.

Killingham was not my home town, and though I'd spent some time scouting round it I was till uncertain of its precise geography. I'd never heard of Parkin Road. I took the car into town and left it in a multi-storey and bought a street map. On a bench in the shopping precinct, I studied it. Parkin Road was on the poorer side of the town centre, not far from where I was sitting at that moment. I decided I could walk to it.

At that end of town they were demolishing slums. Already there was a new bus terminal, and the street flanking it, which was marked as a narrow thoroughfare on my out-of-date map, was now part of the new ring road. Parkin Road had crossed this street, but was now cut by the ring road into two halves, Parkin Road East and Parkin Road West. I explored the eastern half first. No Number 37. Across a foot-bridge I went, and down into a row of dirty old terraces waiting anxiously for the bulldozer and nearly fit to beat it to it. A few of the houses, judging by the dusty lace curtains, still housed residents.

Tucked away amongst all this there was a tight, narrow door with the number 37 on it. The lock was new. There was a recently painted board: WISEMANN AGENCY. If you required a private enquiry agency, and you didn't intend to dig too deeply into your pocket, this was where you would come.

There was a second cylinder lock key on the ring Phil had given me, that and two small flat ones. I tried the key that wasn't for her flat, and it didn't fit. This was a set-back I hadn't expected.

I crossed the road. Traffic hummed along the ring road but nobody drove along Parkin Road West. I stood on the far pavement and looked across. Third floor. Counting the ground floor as number one, the third-floor window looked just as dirty as the others, way up there under the guttering. I wondered how it would be possible to get round to the back.

There was no access at all from the ring road end, so I tried in the other direction. There was a five-ways junction there and more traffic. An active garage used one whole corner, and on another was an easy-fit exhaust and tyre service. Running back along the rear of Parkin Road was an alleyway. I strolled along it.

The surface was cobbled, and on one side there was a rudimentary pavement of blue bricks, a yard wide. On the opposite side to this, the Parkin Road side, there was a six-foot wall, just too high for me to see over without jumping. From the pavement I could see the tops of the buildings, which were far enough back from the wall to indicate that the space had been gardens or rear yards when Parkin Road had first opened its welcoming arms to residents. How they must have rushed in delight through the pristine, cramped homes, exclaiming in awe at the water available simply by turning a tap, at the gas lamps, the outside toilet. Now all that glory was gone. A ring road, bearing modern-day facilities, had sliced Parkin Road in half with a shrug of disdain.

Doors were set at regular intervals in the wall, each with a small bricked arch over it. They bore numbers, but most had eroded. I found 25, then 33, and counted two more to 37. The paint had been green. I probed a finger through the hole, but there was no latch to lift. So I pushed, and it gave slowly against a bank of riotous nettles. I thrust my way in far enough to shut the door behind me, and considered the prospects.

The blind rears stared at me impassively. Most of the windows were boarded up. The garden space to Number 37 was choked with weeds—nettles, thistles, and a clutch of bramble. What looked as though it could have been a rambler rose clung to a side wall. A linepost leaned limply. Someone had once hung washing out there.

It was possible to detect where the path had been by the thinner growth. I thrust my way through it, past the end privy, the coalhouse, the kitchen, all on the right in a line. Here I faced what had been a window, and was now solidly planked over. To my right was the back door, next to the kitchen window, which still retained its glass. Nobody had used the door for years. It was solid, had the keyhole of an ancient and probably rusted deadlock, and was apparently sealed by old paint and the accumulation of filth.

I stared at the barrier facing me, and turned away defeated. There had been a phone number for this place, so Phil must have used it for something.

On the way back to my car I passed a post office, and checked in their phone directory. To my surprise Sam's Caff was listed exactly as it sounded. It was apparently a transport café, out on the Markham road, which had been the main route north before the motorway cut its throat.

I dug out my car and drove there. It was just as I'd expected, a broken-down one-storey building, fronted by a parking patch and the concrete bases from which petrol pumps had once sprouted. Now only two ramshackle cars and a clutch of fast motorcycles decorated the frontage. It was the haunt of bikers and out-of-workers, killing time with endless cups of tea and meaningless chatter.

I pushed open the door, assailed by the beat of a jukebox and the screams of female pillionists. Sam might once have been fat, but was now thin and lugubrious, with the fluff of a moustache high on his upper lip, like a little furry animal seeking refuge up his nose.

"Tea," I said.

"Do you a beefburger?" He was pitifully eager.

"Later maybe. Is Art in?"

He nodded towards a far corner.

I had not expected to find him alone, and he was not. There were half a dozen of them round the table, which was cluttered with empty cups and saucers. Sam was clinging to his standards and holding on to the saucers. All of them were dressed in Art's style, the loose cotton jackets, sweat shirts, and denim jeans. They were not bikers. Put them all together and you wouldn't find a finger honest enough to operate a clutch lever.

I took my tea over to the table. There was a scattering of empty crisp packets, a tray full of cigarette stubs, and a smell of cannabis. Nobody looked up.

"Room for one more?"

Art raised his head at my voice. "Already? Thought you'd phone. Move over there, Ken. Let the man in."

Ken moved with reluctance. He looked as though he accomplished nothing without a sullen consideration. I slid my tea on to the table surface, where fortunately it was at once lost, and sat down.

"It isn't finished yet," I told Art. "How're you at breaking and entering?"

There was an abrupt, brittle silence. I smiled around the set faces. Art said: "It's okay. This character's from Gartree." Art had, apparently, ready access to all the facts.

They relaxed. There was a softening of the expressions towards respect. I was still kept at a distance, but now it was because of my higher status. Sheer snobbery.

"What y' got in mind?" Art asked.

"The rear entrance of a house in Parkin Road West. Know it?" He nodded. "It's now offices, or pretending to be. I want to get in."

Art was all professionalism now. You'd have thought it was the Bank of England. But he had to show me what a big gun he was amongst all these little pistols of the criminal fraternity, how attentive he was to detail.

"What're we after?" he asked at the end. "A safe? Could need a couple of guys . . ." His eyes went round the table. There was a general show of interest.

"We're not going to take anything," I said. "Where shall we meet?"

We arranged the meeting at the open end of the alleyway behind Parkin Road West at nine. It would be good and dark by then. He said he would bring the necessary equipment.

I left, and went back to the flat to fill in time, and in case she phoned. She did not.

At nine I was waiting for Art. He slid to my side from the shadows, dressed for the part in somebody else's black donkey jacket. What he had brought along for the job was a torch and a crowbar. This was clearly going to be a delicate job.

I found the wall door without difficulty because I hadn't been able to close it completely. He plodded after me through the undergrowth, the town glow in the sky being sufficient at that stage. Along the whole row of buildings there was not one lighted window.

We reached the rear door. "Hold the torch," said Art. "Shield it with your hand. That's it."

Art was calm and practical. He thumped the claw end of his crowbar into the jamb of the door opposite the lock, forced it in further, then put his weight behind it. There was a crack, the door creaked open, and we stepped over a little heap of rotted wood on the ground.

I threw the torchlight around. We were in the kitchen, narrow, with all the equipment in a line beneath the window. There was an old black cooker and an earthenware sink with a wooden draining board, a small table beyond it. The table had an oilcloth top. On it was a brown pottery teapot, beside that a clean cup and saucer, and a stainless steel sugar bowl. There was milk in a bottle, but it seemed yellow, and when I tilted it the surface swayed rather than moved. I picked up the cup. It was Crown Derby. On the cooker there was a tin kettle.

The kitchen was still in use. Phil took milk and sugar in her tea, but she hadn't done so recently.

"Let's find the stairs," I said.

We climbed. The treads seemed secure, but the higher we went the more flimsy was the stair rail.

There was only one door from the landing on the third floor. A visiting card was thumbtacked to it: WISEMANN AGENCY. That was in case anybody ever came here, which I was beginning to doubt. The lock on the door was new. It was another cylinder lock. I tried the second key, and it worked. The door opened.

"You don't need me," said Art gloomily.

Oh, but I did. It was comforting to have him at my shoulder. For one moment I wondered about this, why I felt I could trust him, why I needed him. Then I gave my full attention to the room.

There was no denying that this was intended to be an office, though a very rudimentary one. There was a desk with a chair behind it and a phone on it. There was no visitor's chair, no desk lamp, no typewriter, no tape recorder, no pictures to break up the tattered expanses of the walls, no framed diploma signed by Philip Marlowe. There was a filing cabinet against the side wall. I saw it all in one sweep of the torch.

"Watch what you're doing with that!" whispered Art.

"No need to whisper. Let's see if the blind works."

He went over to the single narrow window, which overlooked the street. The blind was an old roller type. It pulled down raggedly, but the ratchet didn't work, so he tied the cord to the radiator beneath it. I put on the light.

"Go easy, can't y'!" he croaked, not so much the master crook now.

"Who'll trouble, around here?" I was short with him. Disappointment at the sparsity of information I was uncovering was reflecting in my voice. "Perhaps there's something in the cabinet." I had intended this as a thought, but it came out as words.

In the corner the light was dim. Hopefully, Art hefted his crowbar. "Hold it," I told him. "Let's try these keys first."

I was referring to the small flat ones, which were just the sort of thing for cabinets. The second one worked the trick. The four sliding drawers were all accessible.

There was nothing in any of them, except the little cotton bag in which the keys had been tied.

I pushed them shut and relocked them. Either she used this office as nothing more than an accommodation address (but in which case why did she need a phone?) or she actually conducted some of her work from this place. Perhaps the error in using the letter-headed half of the sheet for her note had not, in fact, been a mistake. She had cleared out her office and deliberately led me to it. But . . . to find nothing?

I felt a stir of anger, a tingle of unease.

"There's still the desk," I said, more in self-encouragement than anything else. But that would surely be cleared out too.

All the same, I went round to the other side and sat on the hard wooden chair, lifted the phone and discovered it was connected, and replaced it. There was a knee-hole, on each side of it a set of drawers. One set was unlocked. I went through them. Nothing but standard office equipment. There was a desk diary, the only entries in it being cryptic. Phone to confirm. Due date for receipt. Rates. Things like that as reminders.

I looked to the other set of drawers, which were locked. But my magic last key did the trick.

In the top drawer nothing. In the next one, half a bar of chocolate and a box of tissues. In the bottom one, two items.

One was a passport. I took it out, laid it on the desk surface, and opened it. There was a photograph, recognisable as Phil, though her hair had been longer and blond, and the usual endorsements, which could have been for holidays abroad or business trips. And there was her name. Dorothy June Mann.

There could be no doubt that this had been left for me to find. A passport is something a person would most certainly remove. It was a confidence. It was a seal of some complicity into which we had, presumably, entered. Uneasily, I wondered what that might be. I put it back where it'd come from.

The other item in the drawer was a different proposition altogether. I stared down at it for a few seconds before I reached down. It was a small automatic pistol.

Gingerly I lifted it out and put it on the desk where I could get a good look at it. Art said, "Cor blimey!" and took a pace forward.

I am relatively ignorant of weaponry, never having handled such a thing, though in Gartree you're exposed to a certain amount of discussion on the subject. I know there are pistols, sometimes called handguns, and that this covers two categories, the revolver and the automatic pistol, which in fact is only semi-automatic. This one, not having a cylinder to revolve, was therefore an automatic pistol, and probably of the calibre which I'd heard called a thirty-two. There was supposed to be a safety catch. This was the first thing I looked for. It was on the side, just above the handgrip. It was at the "on" position, so I therefore felt safe in handling the thing. There should have been a clip at the bottom of the handgrip. There was. I released it, and the magazine slid out into my other hand. It held a full load of cartridges. Seven. I found the slide and pulled it back. There wasn't one in the chamber.

Now I knew how things were.

All this useful information I had gathered from cocking an interested ear, and subsequently borrowing a book from the prison library. I slid the magazine back. Had Phil meant this for me? Surely not. But did the hint mean that I might well, in the future, be needing such a thing for self-protection? Was *that* what she was telling me? Or simply that I was into something that was beyond my ability—as would be using the blasted thing.

Yet all these hints could most easily have been committed to paper, to the other half of the sheet she'd so carefully left me.

I was so lost in these thoughts that it was Art's hiss that brought me back to reality. I looked up.

Standing in the doorway with his hands thrust in the pockets of a short topcoat, flaring it like wings, his feet apart and a sour expression on his thin face, was Detective Inspector Filey, whom I'd last seen in the Sumbury office of Inspector Greaves.

"Well, well," he said, teetering a fraction on his heels. "What've we got here, then!" His tone was of acid sarcasm, and there was a marked confidence in his casual control of the situation, remarkable in that the pistol in my hand happened to be pointing in his direction.

He glanced sideways at Art. "You!" he said. "Scat!"

And Art, after one quick and apologetic look at me, scatted. Filey was so complacent that he gave him not one more thought, though Art had slipped behind him with the crowbar still in his hand.

Filey was shaking his head in mock sorrow, the smile on his lips unpleasant. "Breaking and entering," he commented. "Technically, burglary. And in unlawful possession of a firearm! Oh, dear me, what troubles we do get into, don't we!"

I stared at him. He was holding out his hand. I placed in it the handgun, which hadn't done me any good at all.

EIGHT

It was a little mortifying to realise, too late to take avoiding action, that I'd advertised my intended trip to Killingham and then ventured into Filey's territory. He had been waiting for me, and it'd been unnecessary to have me watched from Sumbury. With reluctance I handed over the pistol. Filey checked it quickly, slid out the magazine, and distributed it into two different pockets. I remained seated. I felt this gave me an edge; I was interviewing him, not the other way round. This impression he soon dispelled.

"Explain your presence here," he demanded, moving around the room and prodding his long nose into shady corners.

I dangled the keys from my fingers. "I have the keys."

He shook his head, not impressed. "But all the same you had to break in at the rear. Not good, Manson. Not good. Try again."

He walked past me and fingered aside the edge of the blind, as though there might be a stunning vista out there. There was some-thing contemptuous in his attitude, implying he had no need to keep an eye on me in order to detect when I was lying. I felt that his general demeanour held a touch of theatricality.

"I'd got all the keys but one." I tried, stalling for time.

"Still not good enough. It's not your office, is it? Don't trouble to answer, I know it's not. So . . . why are you here?"

He went over to the filing cabinet and tried the drawers, which wouldn't open.

"There's nothing in there," I told him.

He turned, shaking his head. "Naughty. You peeked."

"Yes."

"And in the desk drawers? What were you looking for"

I tried to stare him out, but it didn't work. His eyes seemed dead, with no expression. Is there expression in eyes? I've always felt not. It's the surrounding landscape that reveals the character of the lake. His surrounds were smooth and placid.

"Whatever there was." I shrugged. It was the best I could do, and I was still shaken by his sudden appearance.

"Well now. Let's examine this a bit more deeply. You broke into an office in a building like this, scruffy and down-at-heel, hoping—just hoping—to find something? Is that correct?"

I didn't want to bring Phil—Dorothy June Mann—into it, but I couldn't think how to go on avoiding it. I was too long considering my options, though.

"Or I'll have to assume," he said evenly, "that you knew this was here"—he whisked out the pistol and showed it to me—"and came to get it."

I shook my head.

"Then you brought it with you. It's yours. This becomes very interesting. Don't you think it's interesting, Mr. Manson? Say something, so that I'll know you're still alive."

"It was a question of identity."

He cocked his head at me. "Which you have now solved, this question of yours, or you wouldn't be so cagey. And as there's nothing, you say, in the cabinet, it must be . . ."

He was very quick, brain and body. In a second he was round at my side of the desk, and was whipping open drawers. He did it like a burglar, for economy of movement, the bottom one first and moving upwards. It saves having to shut them, but the middle one was half open before his reactions took over. He slammed it shut and plunged down to the bottom one for the passport. I turned back to face the top of the desk. It was either that or his eyes, not

pleasant to stare into. Closer to, I could see they were inflamed
with strain.

He was making a mournful whistling sound through his teeth,
sad but complacent.

"Dorothy June Mann," he read out, strolling round to where he
could face me again. He seemed to be spending a ridiculously long
time staring at the photograph. Then, as though talking to himself,
he said, "So this is where she got to. Ex-Detective Sergeant Mann.
Dismissed from the force a couple of years ago." He tossed it on to
the desk. "So now you know."

I knew, and it meant nothing. I didn't comment.

"Dishonourable discharge," he amplified, smacking his lips on it.
"Now you're happy. Go on, say you're happy."

I cleared my throat. "Dishonourable? It's news to me."

"You're not happy? Oh, dear! Ask me why."

"Why was she discharged?" I stared at my clenched fist on the
desk surface, and deliberately, with force, unclenched it. No anger,
I told myself. It blunts the mind.

"For striking a senior officer."

"Any chance that was you?" I asked hopefully.

"I was deaf for three days, and she dislodged a tooth."

"Then it should've been an honourable discharge. Perhaps a
medal or something."

"A comedian!" he cried. "We have a comedian in our midst." But
the line of his mouth was hard, and his tone implemented it. "Any
more of that, my friend, and you'll lose more than a tooth."

I sighed, sensing that most of his attitude was forced. I probed,
risking it. "You should've brought a back-up." I was wondering
why he hadn't. Did he want this interview to be unofficial? His
ready release of Art indicated something like that.

He seemed to realise what I was thinking, and put both hands
on the desk in order to lean forward, his face much too close for
my liking. He smelt of a rather piercing aftershave. "I want you
alone, Manson. Anybody with me and I'd have to take you in.
Now . . . wouldn't that be a treat for all of us! Wasting time on a
paltry break-in and a possession of firearms! That's not for me. Not
for you, either. No. I've got better things lined up for you. Much
more tasty. Have a guess. Drugs? No. Pimping? No. I'll be taking
you in for murder, Paul Manson. Back to Gartree for you. Ain't it a
pity we haven't got the death sentence any more? It'd save all this
trouble, in prison, out of prison, back in. But this time. Mr. Manson sir, it'll be for good and you won't see daylight again."

At the end of this, he was spitting the words in my face. He was
making it personal. He was enjoying the stalking, the hunt, the

eventual kill, and he was playing with me, I felt. His contempt riled me, which was probably what he intended. But he was pushing too hard, overacting like a rotten juvenile lead.

Gartree training came to my rescue. You traded in your anger for a measure of composure, thus giving yourself a minimal advantage. I managed to answer him calmly. "I'd have to commit a murder before you could achieve your ambition, Mr. Filey. You'd need a case to throw at me." And too late I realised that by now he must have heard about Frenchie's death.

He thrust himself back from the desk, plunged his hands again into the pockets of his coat, and grinned at me. This uncovered one unpleasant canine, the left one, the other presumably being the one that'd been dislodged. Taking his attitude as a clue, I sat back in the chair, almost resigned to his attack.

"Does it disturb you," he asked, "if we discuss Philomena Wise?"

It didn't disturb me, but it certainly surprised me. I couldn't help smiling; it was the relief. "There's nothing for you there."

"She was strangled. You're a strangler. It's on record."

"She was strangled with a silk scarf. I'm a bare-hands man, myself. Fingers Manson, they called me in Gartree."

He cocked his head sideways. "So you think it's funny!"

I sometimes found that by treating it flippantly I could possibly live with it. But that wasn't what he'd meant. "I'm tired of having it thrown at me, that's all. What else have you got?"

"No alibi for the Friday she died. Talk your way out of that."

"I was here in Killingham all the week."

"Witnesses? Go on, tell me you've got no witnesses. I can't wait."

"I was staying in a flat, and hardly went out all the week."

"What a pity. Would you like to whisper its location."

"I don't see why."

"But you must've gone out some time, and these things can be checked. If you could persuade me the effort's worth it," he suggested invitingly, dragging a lure. "One sighting, and you're in the clear."

"I'm in the clear now. Convince me I'm guilty. Go on. Give it a try." I was feeling more buoyant, relieved that he didn't seem to want to talk about Frenchie. I was trying him at his own game. His eyes sparked and his lips drew back.

"Motive," he snapped, trying to regain the initiative.

"That's just what I haven't got."

"Oh, you're a corker," he said with acid admiration. "Staring you in the face, it is, and you can't see it. Go on, be a devil, risk it. What motive do you see?"

And there he had me. Everybody seemed to assume that

Frenchie's motive had to apply to myself. It must have shown in my face. He removed his hands from his pockets, flapped them in the air as though calling on somebody to be his witness, then came and perched himself on the edge of the desk and leaned towards me. This was all confidential now, though there was nobody within a quarter of a mile.

"You were in Gartree. You came out about two months ago. While inside you had the chance to speak to Carl Packer. Deny it? You can't. What he asked you to do for him, for cash, was kill Philomena Wise. Miss Wise is now dead. Right. I've finished. You have permission to speak."

I seized the chance. I'd been almost choking to interrupt him. But all the same, I managed to keep my voice level. "One thing. One small thing. Tell me . . . why did Carl Packer want Philomena dead?"

"You know that. You must. You'd have asked him that."

"Assume I didn't."

He shrugged. "You wouldn't need to know, I suppose. All right. It was because she shopped him. It was her evidence that put him inside."

That fitted neatly with what Art had told me. She'd been on the periphery of a crime. She had been arrested, and released the next morning. She had been in an ideal position to see what had happened. So they'd needed her as a witness.

"And whose case was it?" I asked. "Can I have three guesses?"

One corner of his lip lifted. "It was mine." There was no pretence in this; his pride was genuine.

"Good for you."

"But bad for you, Manson. It all begins to fit together."

"Conjecture," I said. Then I recalled what Lucy had told me. "You've got nothing that'd stand a chance in court."

"I'm willing to give it a fling."

"It's got one basic snag, though. It wasn't me who got the contract with Carl Packer, it was Frenchie. Dougie French. D'you know him?"

"I know him."

"All right. Pick him up, he's probably in the Stormy Petrel every evening. That's at Port Sumbury." No harm in a bit of background bluff, I thought.

"I know that."

"Take a squad of men and winkle him out. Stick one of his knives up his nose, and he'll tell you he got the contract."

"I might've done that," he mused, "but there's a bit of a snag.

Unfortunately, he's dead. What a pity, Mr. Manson. That's life for you, always kicking you in the face."

I felt it had done just that. He'd known all along, and had been leading me around with a ring through my nose.

"When?" I asked, still desperately trying. "Where? How?"

"You're throwing around a lot of questions. More than your quota." He lifted his sharp chin in challenge. "And you know all the answers before I say a word."

"When did he get himself killed?"

"I notice you're assuming it wasn't natural."

"People like Frenchie don't live long enough to die a natural death. Are you going to tell me? Why else did you follow me here?"

"Well now . . ." He went behind me to the window again, and once more peered past the edge of the blind. "Your mate's down there, thinking he's invisible. We don't want him bored . . ." He turned abruptly. "Frenchie died last night. In the car-park at Port Sumbury." I felt his hand on my shoulder and glanced sideways at it. His fingers were slim, his nails carefully manicured. On his little finger there was a signet ring, with a garnet. A snappy dresser was Inspector Filey. He bent his head close so that he could speak quietly, for greater emphasis. "The car-park, Manson, where you disappeared when he and his two heavies chased you there. They say they drove off in the car, looking for you, and Frenchie was left in the car-park. I suppose he reckoned you were hiding there. And of course you were. I wonder who spotted who first. Give me only one guess."

This didn't make any sense to me. Another of his traps? I was now looking directly forward, and when I spoke it was into the air. "I didn't hang around." My voice sounded empty to me. Whatever I said wasn't going to make an impression.

The pressure went from my shoulder. He moved sideways, and stood where he could intercept my words and consider my face when I said them.

"Remember the car-park?" he asked in a coldly reminiscent voice. "It's got a storm wall along the seaward side. Made of rocks from the shore. A lot of 'em loose. Lying there, just waiting to cause trouble. Can you see it?"

"I see it." And something else, lying beneath the wall.

"I'm sure you can. One of those rocks, heavy enough to need two hands to lift it, was used to bash in the top of Frenchie's head. It made quite a mess. Crushed a couple of vertebrae in the neck. Nasty."

I couldn't say anything. My mind was racing to accept the proposition, and elation was surging through me. "Certainly sounds it," I managed to whisper.

"You wouldn't have liked to see it. Oh—silly me—you *did* see it. You did it, Manson, with that chunk of rock. And where d'you think we found his body this morning?"

He stopped abruptly. The draught from the open door gently moved the single light bulb, and his shadow moved backwards and forwards across the wall. It was difficult to tell whether he was standing still, and the effort to do so was hypnotic. He shook his head, his long face gloomy. I said nothing, waiting, though I thought I knew the answer.

"You disappoint me, Manson," he went on after a few moments. "Anybody else would say they didn't know. Where we found the body, seeing you're so interested, was lying behind the car-park attendant's shed. It was on top of an old bicycle."

I breathed in deeply, ashamed that it made a shuddering sound.

"This bike belongs to George Rice," he said, his voice almost a purr, as though I might be tickling him behind the ear. "A good man. Knows where his duty lies. He says he lent it to you, so that you could get to Port Sumbury."

I hastened to confirm this. "I put it behind the shed for safety."

"And who," he asked, "returned late to The George, saying he'd lost the bike? Why . . . you did. Surprise, surprise. But of course, you hadn't lost it. You dumped the body, and then you couldn't get the bike out. Tricky. And who walked in, looking exhausted and without a mark on him, carrying Frenchie's knife in his hand?"

He waited. Damn him, I wasn't going to feed him, like a comedian's mate. I stared at him silently, until he shrugged and went on.

"It was you, my friend. His throwing knife, this was, and you'd managed to take it earlier from a man like Frenchie, and without suffering a scratch. So you'd be aware he was without his full armoury, and you could risk tackling him. In the dark. And you've got the utter gall to sit there and tell me you didn't kill him."

"I haven't said anything."

"Then say it, damn you."

"I didn't kill him." The impulse was to shout it out in glorious relief, but I managed to hold it to a flat statement.

"There we are then."

I sighed. They had obviously questioned Frenchie's two goons, who would've told them exactly what had happened. I could explain my possession of the knife, and even show them the groove where it had dug itself into the door. He knew that, and I knew that. So we were playing games, and I was getting a bit fed up with it, my relief from hearing the manner of Frenchie's death now leaving me weak and exhausted.

Nevertheless, I had sufficient energy left in my mind to realise that Filey must have been reasonably certain of my innocence throughout. So what was he after?

"Look, Mr. Filey," I said, "this could go on for ever. Why're you throwing this at me—and here—if you think you've got something on me? Why did you come on your own unless you intended to do nothing more than throw around a few words?" He didn't answer, so I pressed on, more confidently. "Why're you skating all round the case when it isn't yours, anyway? Sumbury's not your patch, it belongs to Inspector Greaves. So stop playing about. What're you getting at?"

He didn't even blink, but ploughed on vigorously. "You slay me, Manson. Here you are, up to your neck in the nasties, and all you can do is try to change the subject. Greaves knows what I'm doing. This is my manor, and you're in it right now."

"I'm going back tonight."

"To The George? You've left it a bit late for that, and I don't fancy he'll leave the door on the latch for you. George Rice knows the score."

"Which is?"

For the first time I heard him laugh, a shishing sound, stifled by his scorn. It was a little-used laugh. "The score is that both of you, Frenchie and you, were offered a contract to kill Philomena Wise. One of you succeeded, but it occurred to the other one that if a convenient death took place, then the survivor could collect. Packer wouldn't quibble. That was what the affair at Port Sumbury was all about. You and Frenchie were sorting it out, and it was you who came up lucky. All we've got to decide now is which of you killed Philomena Wise."

There was also the fact that the manner of her death did not fit Frenchie's personality, whereas it could be made to fit mine with only a small amount of distortion. I didn't see why I should offer him this idea, and wondered why he hadn't produced it already.

Looking him directly in the eyes I said, "I throw myself on your mercy, Inspector."

What he did next startled me. He threw back his head and laughed out loud. There was something empty about it, like a laugh in the Gartree exercise yard, but it was a true laugh. His eyes held no humour at all.

"You'll be the death of me, Manson. I've got no mercy for the likes of you. What you're throwing yourself on is my sense of humour. Laughing Harry Filey they call me round here. And I'm just going to sit back and laugh, while you dig yourself deeper and deeper in the mire. Because you know who she is now, Dorothy June Mann, and you can't wait to get to her and find out what's going on. And there I'll be, laughing my head off, because you're not going to like it when you know."

"Tastes differ."

"Now get out of here and get yourself lost."

He stood to one side and watched as I levered myself to my feet. There had been a tone of bitter defeat in his voice. Perhaps, to compensate, he expected me to scuttle past him, so I straightened my back and took my time. Why the devil was I aching all over when all I'd been doing was sitting? I looked at his set face, and felt a sudden stab of pity.

"After you," I said. "I've got to lock up." I picked up the passport and dropped it in the bottom drawer of the desk. Then I looked up. "Am I to have the pistol."

"It's evidence," he said flatly.

"Of what? That you took it from me, Inspector? But she might have a licence for it, in which case that'd be theft. I'd better put it back. Don't you think?"

With a grim twist of his lips he handed it over, in two separate parts. I locked them in the drawer, had a look round, went and untied the blind, followed him to the door, turned off the light, and made sure the door locked after us.

"We might as well use the front door," I said.

"Why not? I used it to get in."

I glanced at him in suspicion, but he was expressionless. We went down the front stairs. The street door had a few letters in the little cage. For Wisemann Agency, no doubt. We went out into the street and I slammed the door after us. I seemed to be initiating all the actions at the moment. The air, heavy with car fumes, smelt good to me.

"Tomorrow," he said, "I'll have somebody come round and secure the back door. Can't encourage burglars, can we!"

"That'd be terrible. They might nick her Crown Derby."

"Hmm! That's your mate over there, the fourth shadow on the left of the lamppost. We'll meet again, no doubt."

"In more congenial circumstances," I agreed. They could hardly be worse.

He turned on his heel and stalked away, a trim slim figure disappearing into the night. I found it impossible to visualise him going home. To a wife, to laughing children clinging to his legs? No. He no doubt disappeared in a puff of smoke, reappearing in unblemished glory the next morning.

But I was being cynical. I said to Art, "A minute." Then I left him in his shadow and moved quietly after Filey to the corner where he'd disappeared. He was walking towards a parked car, but now his shoulders were slumped, his legs moving with a weariness close to exhaustion. Yes, he'd possibly go home to a family, but he'd be too involved to notice them, absorbed and defeated. The car pulled past me and I stepped back into a doorway. A flick of light from a street lamp slid over his face, slack and old and grey.

Art slid to my side. "Cor strike! Reckoned he had you there." He hadn't even noticed the car.

For all his flip and worldly-wise confidence, Art was nevertheless shaken. And worried. He was worried because he was a known villain in that area, and he'd been committing a crime—and yet Filey had dismissed him with disdain. It could only mean that Filey was saving something more interesting for Art. Even when trouble was around, Art had to see himself as its centre point.

We began to walk to where I'd left the car. "Didn't it make you feel small," I asked, testing him out, "being dismissed with two words, so that he could devote his attention to the big wheel?"

"Why d'you have to talk all fancy?"

"I've just spent half an hour—an hour?—anyway, a long time fencing with our friend Filey. I'm having a job getting back to normal."

I could detect his shrug, but his answer was wary. "He knows me. I ain't anythin' to interest him."

"Exactly. Now, you've got a choice. You can go home to your folks, or you can let me put you up for the night."

"I'll stick with you," he decided, without hesitation. Perhaps he wasn't sure of a welcome from his folks, who probably didn't even know, or care, that he was in town.

"I'll phone The George, and you can call Mrs. Druggett."

"She ain't on the phone."

"All right. In the morning you can stick with me, or make your own way back to Sumbury."

"Depends where you're goin'."

"Gartree, I thought."

"Heh! That's great. Always wanted to see what it's like."

"Don't expect a guided tour. You go in—you don't come out again."

"Same thing for you, then."

"They'll welcome me. Old friends, me and the governor."

"You're kiddin'."

I was. I'd met him twice, once going in, once coming out. In fact, I wasn't at all sure I would be able to get to Carl Packer. But I had to try. He was the only one left to ask.

NINE

Art had recovered his bounce by the time we were twenty miles on the way towards Gartree. The previous evening, at Phil's flat, he had been subdued, showing no enthusiasm for Beethoven's Ninth. But on the next morning, he missed no chance to advise me on my driving, or to criticise my lack of attention to his enthusiasm for his various adventures with Philomena. There was no mention of anything remotely legal, but I noticed that none of his activities had involved violence. He seemed to avoid it fastidiously. I simply drove and said nothing.

"Why're you going to see Carl?" he asked at last, changing the mood, shading it.

"Something I need to know."

"You don't wanta believe anythin' *he* says."

"Of course not. I'll watch my step. I never believe anything I hear."

He caught my meaning, and grunted. There were a few moments of silence as he chose his words carefully. "He'll tell you anythin' to get out of it."

"Out of what?"

"Shooting that copper." He turned away and stared out of the side window.

Now the silence became oppressive. I hadn't heard of a shooting, certainly not one that'd involved a police officer. A darker shade of violence had crept in.

"Shot him—you mean as in murder?" I asked, managing to keep my voice casual, as expected from a Gartree graduate.

There was no need for him to study a map, because I'd worked out our route before we left. He had no excuse for avoiding the question. "Yeah, you could say that." His voice was slurred. The incident was tasteless and stale in his memory.

"This was on the warehouse job you told me about?"

"What else?"

"Then I take it you won't want to meet Packer again?"

"You wasn't thinkin' . . ."

"I could arrange it, perhaps, if you wanted to. You should've said something, when I told you who I wanted to see last night."

"I don't wanna meet him!" Panic gagged his sense of humour.

"You'll wait outside in the car. I don't need an introduction."

He pouted childishly. "Don't see why you wanta talk to him."

"It's necessary."

Then I explained as much as I thought he should know and could appreciate. But in fact, I was trying to justify it in my mind. "With Frenchie dead, I need to know—"

"Frenchie's dead?" he cut in.

"So you know him?"

"Never met him, face to face. Everybody knows about Frenchie. How'd it happen? When?"

"The night before last, apparently. His head was bashed in with a chunk of rock. Or so Filey said."

"Nasty. But Filey's a bloody liar, anyway."

Not about that, I didn't think. "I met Frenchie inside Gartree," I told Art. "We weren't exactly friends."

"Well . . . you wouldn't be. Not from what I heard." The effort to sound disinterested put an edge to his voice. "Nippy car, this," he observed casually. "Never thought you'd get past that wagon."

I glanced sideways. There was a slick of sweat on his forehead, which my driving didn't explain. "Anyway," I went on, "with Frenchie dead, I'll need to have a word or two with Carl Packer."

"Such as?"

"Frenchie told me he was in Sumbury on a contract for Packer. What could that mean but the killing of your Phillie? But it doesn't fit, does it! I just can't see Frenchie doing anything like strangling. Can you?"

I paused, giving him the chance to take it on, and he took it reluctantly. "I wouldn't know what a character like him'd do."

"And if he did—how did he get hold of your scarf to do it with?"

There was a short silence. Subdued, almost sullen, he eventually answered. "You're gettin' at me again, ain't you!"

"Not at all. I was dabbling in amateur psychology."

"Oh . . . that stuff!"

"I learned quite a bit in college."

"You went to college? Oxford an' that sorta thing? Gerraway."

"It was Cambridge, if you want to know, and I was talking about my other college. Gartree. I picked up more there than I ever did at the university. More important stuff, such as the basic means of survival. And I had the chance to meet all the best murderers."

"Great. Brilliant."

"Did you know, Art, there're two categories of murders—domestic and professional. The first lot's to do with anger and emotion, the second lot with cash. Cold and unemotional. You with me? The odd car blown up, the pub raked with gunfire, those're pro jobs. No hatred, no fury. Or the contract killing. But of course, you know all about this, Art."

"Why don't y' write a bloody book about it?"

I stopped to fill up the tank and to stretch my legs. Art stayed in the car. I wanted him to think about it and get worried, and I wanted time to think about it myself. He'd been there; there'd been a policeman killed. That came under category two, professional. I felt I was within sight of something resembling motivation. I wondered how to get information from Art without having to thump him a bit.

"What're you gettin' at?" he asked, as soon as I'd got the car moving again. He was too eager, too anxious.

"I was going to tell you that the real pros, the ones who make their living out of it, they never touch their victims. It's a fact. They keep their distance."

"You live an' learn. Fancy that."

"Think about it. No contact, that's what matters. A powerful rifle, say, and your man's gone at three hundred yards. No difficulty for a marksman. Or poison—you don't even have to watch the poor swine dying. Or a hit-and-run. No contact—it's the car that does it. And Frenchie's always been the haft of a knife away, more if he threw it. But this one, Phillie's death, there was contact there. Only the thickness of a scarf away. Physical contact, Art. Personal. Let's hear your thinking on that."

"You're gettin' at me again!" he shouted.

"Am I? If you say so." Yet I'd overelaborated on purpose.

"You are! It was my scarf, and personal, if that's the way you soddin'-well want it."

I tossed a grin at him, but he was glaring stonily ahead. "Touchy, aren't we? Guilty conscience, is it?"

"Just lay off that!"

"I'm only saying it's very strange. There was Frenchie, sent to Sumbury to contact a certain Philomena Wise. An obvious pro killing was lined up and an obvious non-pro killing was done. So we have to accept that somebody else, other than Frenchie, came along and killed her. Are you going to believe that? Now . . . isn't that a fine coincidence for you!"

"An' that's all you've been gettin' at?" he demanded, his relief tainted with anger, that I'd left him on the hook so long.

"It's a big 'all,' that's what I mean."

"And what d'you expect Packer to tell y'?" Suspicion still clung to him, like fog to a prowling tom cat.

"I don't know."

"It's a hell of a way to go for no reason." He settled himself down into his seat, prepared to remain silent.

We were by then only a few miles from Gartree. The sky was heavy ahead. It could be raining there, but you don't have to worry about the weather, inside. You never have to get wet, or dig your car out of a snowdrift. Unless you're a warder, of course. But Gartree wasn't a place you'd want to return to, and even at the thought I felt a growing uneasiness. When it came in sight, though, I found it difficult to raise any emotion at all. The point was, I realised, that I'd never seen it from the outside before. That was strange. Going in, I'd been in a van with darkened windows. Coming out, in my taxi, I'd not cared to look back. So I was approaching a strange sprawl of buildings, which could have housed anything. Something innocuous such as the splitting of an atom here and there, or the production of next year's deadly disease— rather than the horror it did contain.

I parked the car and sat still for a few moments. Then I turned to Art. "You will sit here," I told him, "and mind your own business. If I'm not out in an hour, send for the police."

Thus joking, I walked to the entrance and demanded to be admitted.

But my nerve had gone. I wanted to turn and run. I was now too close to it, only the thickness of a wall away. I was asked my business, and then passed on to an office. There was no sight of the inmates. Only warders. The one behind the desk recognised me.

"Well, if it isn't Manson. Can't fit you up with your old room, I'm afraid. It's taken."

This tone I had never before encountered in there. I was now a civilian; better than that, I was a civilian with whom he could share an in-joke.

"I don't intend staying," I said. "What I wanted was to see Carl Packer, Mr. Morris."

"Now now, you know the rules. You can't just turn up and disrupt the whole routine like this." There were such things as visiting days and passes.

"It's important."

"That's obvious. Anybody who wants to see Packer must have a damned good reason. Care to confide? A word in the little shell-like, perhaps."

I could tell he'd had a boring day. In fact, all his days would be boring. He'd mentioned routine. That was his life, his work. For a con, it was nothing. You might just as well be doing one thing as another. Or nothing.

"A friend of his has died," I confided, making my tone solemn. "It was just that I thought he'd care to hear it from me."

"Why you, if I may ask?"

"Because the police think I did it, and I wouldn't want Packer getting that idea. He'd turn against me."

Morris shook his head in understanding, tut-tutting. "And we wouldn't want that would we! Who's died?"

"Dougie French."

"No! Well, that *is* good news. Here . . . I'll put it out on the Tannoy. Everybody'll want to know, and give a little cheer."

I sighed. "So can I see Packer, Mr. Morris, please?"

He eyed me with speculation. "You're serious?"

"Would I come here voluntarily if it wasn't important?"

"That's true enough," he said with feeling, then he turned away to a phone and spoke in a mumble I couldn't decipher.

I stood and waited. Now I could feel the pulse of life beyond the far wall, the never-silent murmur that closer-to becomes a perpetual clamour. There was a tingle in the atmosphere that nearly had me panting for breath, which is the constant pressure of detention, the smell of humanity in the mass, the prickle to the skin of violence not far removed.

He came back. "You can see him, Manson. You'll be subject to a search, and you will not be left alone with him. Ten minutes. The best I could do."

"Thanks. That'll do me." Ten minutes was about all I'd be able to tolerate.

It was the chief warder, Pierce himself, who came for me. Did I rate that honour? Now, I found, I could look him in the eye, though without pleasure. He was a bleak man. He never gave an inch, even if a yard was due.

"Watch your step, Manson. I'll be there."

"Suits me." I found I couldn't bring myself to give him his expected "sir." He noted that, and his mouth was grim.

We went to one of the small interview rooms. There was a table and two chairs, and four corners to it. Pierce wedged his shoulders into one of them, I sat in the chair facing him, and we waited. There was silence, until the tramp of feet. Carl Packer entered, the door slammed behind him, and I felt a chill all up my spine as I heard the lock thrown over.

"Sit!" said Pierce, quite unnecessarily.

Packer ignored him and sat opposite to me. His back was to Pierce. "Manson? You're out now. What's this, then?"

"Come to see you, to give you some news. Frenchie's dead."

I watched the thoughts moving round behind his eyes. Apart from the eyes, which were too light and too fishlike for comfort, there was nothing to indicate that Packer was a violent and devious crook. The rest of his face, cherubic and innocent, gave the impression of a lawyer, a barrister who would sway the jury with specious words in your defence. His eyes would terrify them.

"What a pity," he said calmly, when he'd absorbed it.

"Got his skull bashed in."

He shook his head sadly. "A great loss. Where was this?"

"A place called Sumbury."

"Never heard of it."

"It's in Devon."

"He must've been there on holiday."

I reminded myself that we were overheard, and that Packer would not dare to admit anything incriminating. We had to play it the way he wanted it.

"That wasn't what he told me," I said.

"Really?"

"I got the impression he was doing an errand for you, Packer."

"For me? I wouldn't send him to a place I've never heard of."

"Of course you wouldn't." But I'd seen interest stirring behind his eyes. "He'd gone there because that was where she'd got to."

"You've lost me there, son." He was, indeed, old enough to be my father.

"A Miss Wise. I got the impression you'd asked him to trace her. Something you owed her, he said."

"I seem to remember now. It's coming back."

"Though money wasn't mentioned."

"Wasn't it?" His eyes held mine. "Oh well, Frenchie always was close. Twenty thou, it was. He was going to offer her that."

If we were talking double meanings, he'd lost me. But he was giving me almost imperceptible little nods as his eyes remained on mine. He was transmitting, but I wasn't receiving.

"What'd she done to earn that?" I asked.

"It wasn't so much what she'd done, as what I wanted her to do."

"Five minutes," said Pierce briskly. "Hurry it up."

We ignored him. I said, "That'd be quite a favour, twenty thousand quid's worth."

"There's no price too high for the truth, son," said Packer blandly.

"That depends on what truth."

"Of the job. The job that got me in here. All I want is a new trial, or a pardon."

All he wanted! I heard Pierce's shoulders move against the wall. He'd heard it too, unendingly. To every villain, it is a basic principle that a verdict of guilty meant simply that the evidence had not been correctly manipulated. Whether or not you'd done it was irrelevant.

Oh, God! I thought, it's all been a waste of time. "How could you hope for a new trial, Packer?" I was still trying.

"The little bitch was lying at the first one."

"Easy to say. She'd have been on oath."

"She was lying." His voice had not changed. He was still speaking in a quiet, easy tone. But on the table surface his fingers traced the word: YES.

That he used this as a secret device, where Pierce could not see it, carried more weight than his words. I felt a stir of interest, but kept it from my voice.

"For that money, you expected her to go to the police and change her story?" We might have been chatting at a pub, the casual way I managed to say that. But my heart was beating faster.

"Yes." This time it was aloud. But I knew that he meant much more. If she'd been telling the truth, Packer would have been annoyed. But if she'd been lying, then Packer would've been livid with fury, and from then on she'd have been in constant threat. Not simply had the offer been twenty thousand pounds in cash, but it had also been a promise of the freedom from fear.

"In what way could she change it?" I asked, feeling my way and wondering how far I dared to go. But of course Pierce was no longer listening. He'd never heard of a trial that hadn't been riddled with lies. Packer could say anything now, and it would seem to be no more than the perpetual gripe, a buzzing in the background.

"She said it was me that had the gun," he told me, assuming I knew what he was talking about.

"But it wasn't?"

"No. And perhaps she'd tell them who."

"You mean you don't know?" I asked, testing him out.

"I don't know."

"But there *was* a gun?"

"They found a handgun. Nobody carried weapons on my jobs, Manson. I'm not a damned fool."

"Somebody did that time. Fingerprints?"

"We all wore gloves. Standard procedure."

"And masks?"

"Ski masks, yes."

"But all the same she identified you?"

"Why d'you think I'm here, damn you?" He lifted his chin. He'd had a poor shave that day. "And why're you here, Manson? Want to take over from Frenchie? Two thou in it for you, to make my offer to her, and do a bit of persuading."

"Didn't Frenchie let you know?" I asked in assumed surprise.

"Let me know what?" There was, at last, an edge to his voice.

"Philomena Wise is dead, too, Packer. She's not going to be able to give you any help at all."

He stared at me. "She couldn't be," he whispered.

"Time's up," said Pierce. "Say your goodbyes."

"Wait!" said Packer. "Manson, isn't there anything—"

"On your feet, man. You heard me."

Now plainly distraught, but willing to give Pierce no edge, Packer scrambled to his feet and went to the door. Pierce tapped and said something. The door opened.

"March."

Packer threw me one desperate glance, then he was gone.

I walked after them out of the open door, taking my own time. I was a free man. Nobody followed me back the way I'd come, nobody barked at me. I was free to come and go, yet strangely I felt a reluctance. Inside, I had at least lived with a solidarity, a backing against authority, and a barrier between me and the pressures of society. But now, outside, I was very much on my own.

Though not alone. I had forgotten that Art was waiting in the car.

"Get what you wanted?" he asked with eagerness, and before I had my seat-belt fastened.

"More," I told him. "Much more."

I drove away. Once again, not a backward glance did I give to the gaunt sprawl of masonry, and for two miles there was silence between us. I was allowing myself time to consider the visit, and it did no harm to allow Art to simmer for a while. There were clearly one or two things I wanted to hear from Art, and he wasn't going to be eager to reveal them.

At last he broke the silence. "You can take the motorway, direct to Devon."

"I just want to call in at Killingham again for a few minutes."

"Dashin' around everywhere, ain't we!" he grumbled.

"There was no contract out for your Phillie, Art. Carl Packer told me he sent Frenchie along, but to do no more than talk to her."

"Talk? Frenchie? The only words he ever knew were 'slit' and 'throat.' Talk! Gerraway.' He'd certainly known Frenchie.

He was so confident in his interpretation of the facts that I answered him with irritation. "He said it in such a way that I believed him."

He dismissed that with disgust. "Yah!"

I settled into a steady fifty along the open road. There was little traffic, and I needed only part of my mind to miss what there was.

"He said he sent Frenchie to make her an offer—"

"He sent him to Sumbury?" he cut in. "How'd Frenchie know she was there?" His wits were right in there, turning over at full revs. He'd been quick on that, and Packer had said something similar. I hadn't given that point very much thought.

"No, he couldn't have known that," I agreed.

"There y'are then."

"The same objection applies if you assume he went to kill her. All he'd know was . . ." I'd started this angrily, but it tapered off in sick despair. ". . . Killingham," I whispered.

"Go on, then," said Art after a moment or two.

But I couldn't say anything. I'd just realised how Frenchie had managed to trace the Wises.

"Cat got your tongue?" he demanded brightly. He was jaunty again. I'd been by-passed from my previous subject.

I couldn't speak. It had all begun in Killingham. The warehouse job had been there, and that was where the Wise family had lived. Immediately after the trial they had gone to live in Sumbury. But all Packer could have known was the town of Killingham. There I had gone when I'd got out, and there I'd met his Philomena Wise, as I'd thought, and become more deeply involved than I'd bargained for.

But Frenchie, too, must have started in Killingham, a month after I did, and he too must have traced the same woman—my Phil. Perhaps he'd had a better description of the real one, or even a photograph, but he had certainly not made my mistake. He had watched and waited until Phil, who was really Dorothy June Mann, had gone to Sumbury. And she had led him there.

It was I who'd initiated the trip to Sumbury, forced it on her, I who had activated the circumstances leading to the death of Philomena Wise.

"It was me!" I shouted in abrupt self-disgust, and I skidded the car to a halt because I could no longer see the road.

Tyres screamed behind me, and car horns blared. A trailer wagon and a build-up of cars, which had been waiting to pull past me, came to a similar abrupt halt. As they moved past me, comments on my parentage and driving ability were made. I could not raise my head to respond.

Art opened his door and got out. I heard him shouting obscene abuse on my behalf. Then he got back inside.

"Want me to drive?" He was always ready to help, almost too eager.

"No."

"You ain't safe on the road."

I started the stalled engine and drifted along until we came to a lay-by, where I parked and got out and walked around for a while.

It was ridiculous, I told myself, to take the blame. This I assured myself over and over, until I realised my anger at myself was based on my acceptance of failure. My naïve enthusiasm had led me into believing I was more important in the scheme of life than I really was. I'd wanted to be a knight, not a pawn, someone who was looking for a way to salve an uneasy conscience. But even this had proved to be invalid. I'd done nothing towards saving a life, because there had been no threat to Philomena. It was to have been nothing more dangerous than an offer of twenty thousand pounds. What a right balls-up I'd made of it!

I got back in the car and sat staring straight ahead. Art again offered to drive. Again I refused. It would've been a concession to weakness, the thin end of a great fat wedge that was facing me. So far I'd been inadequate, and the pitfalls ahead were greater than those behind. All I wanted to do was go somewhere, anywhere, as long as it was away from it all. But I'd been the one who'd pitched myself into it, and there was now no way to withdraw.

Fleetingly, I remembered the grizzly I'd met in Montana. I'd been told what to do if this happened: face him. On no account turn and run, because he'd be faster and I'd stand no chance. That was easy enough to say, but when he was facing me fifty yards away, I stood, mouth dry, legs weak, and stared at him, praying he wouldn't smell the sweat of fear that poured down me. And then, after an eternity, he'd grunted, turned about, and ambled away. Then my knees had given way and I'd fallen to the ground with my hands over my face, sobbing.

This time I knew I had to advance. Swamped by a sick emptiness, my will dormant, I started the engine and pulled out of the lay-by.

TEN

With a diplomacy I'd not expected, Art remained silent for fifteen minutes. When I had recovered sufficiently to glance at him, he was eyeing me with anxious concern. In the end, when I was certain of being able to control my voice, I broke the silence.

"Packer spoke about the warehouse job."

"Oh yes?"

"He said he didn't shoot the policeman."

There was a hesitation, then he summoned up his usual aplomb. "Well, he would, wouldn't he." His shrug was a nervous reaction.

"They always do," I agreed. "You never find any guilty parties in prisons. But Carl told me your girl lied at his trial. Yes, I know . . . he would say that too. But I had a good reason for believing he was telling the truth."

"Phillie lie? That'd be perjury."

"Shall we try to rephrase it? We'll say that she could have given an inexact testimony."

He seemed pleased at the juggling with words.

"But if we assume that," I went on, warming to the problem, "then we have to ask ourselves how she could've made any identification at all, exact or otherwise."

"Don't get you."

"Packer said you were all wearing ski masks."

"Tha's right." He was distant, hesitant.

"Well then, you'd all look the same, scurrying around in the shadows."

"Not to her. She knew us all."

"Even so . . . were you wearing one? A ski mask, I mean."

"Sure was." He flashed a look at me. "They don't half make y' hot." This was a touch of colour, to add veracity to his statement.

"But I'm sure you told me you were the getaway driver. Don't tell me you were sitting in a car in the street and waiting, with a mask on! Anybody walking past, they'd see you. You could hardly claim you were heading for the ski slopes."

He went sullen on me, muttering his answer. "It wasn't like that."

"How was it then?" I went after him. "I'm only trying to make some sort of sense out of it."

"The street down the side. Parked down there—"

"Not good enough, Art," I said, borrowing from Filey's technique.

"Dark along there."

"I expect it was. And where was your Phillie waiting in her car?"

He took a long while answering. I knew it wasn't that his brain was going slow. What he was doing was planning his tactics. He was on the defensive, but I didn't feel any elation.

"On the opposite corner," he conceded.

"Not wearing a mask?"

"You crazy or somethin'!" he said savagely. "Of course not."

"So you sat there—"

"No!" The rejection was explosive.

"You didn't sit in the getaway car?"

"I was picked as driver at the last minute. The regular guy was in hospital. Turned a car over. So I was kinda doublin' on the job—helping inside—loadin', you know. There was only five of us on that job."

"Loading? Oh, I forgot. This was a warehouse. What was it, whisky?"

"Yes. Glenmorangie. Posh stuff, that is."

"You weren't expected to drive that load, surely."

"Only the car, when the wagon got moving. Him one way, us the other."

It was flowing along more steadily now. "Ah, so you'd got an experienced wagon driver?"

"Sure. He was the regular with that trailer-wagon. Off on sick leave. If the buggers hadn't unloaded it, we could've driven it straight out."

I found myself smiling. "This was certainly a well-planned job. So there you were, inside and loading like mad things, and up popped the law. Everybody running this way and that. Something like that, was it?"

"You've got it." He sounded proud of my ability but distrustful of my intentions. "For what good it'll do y'."

"But you . . . you ran for the car. But didn't wait for the others, it seems."

"Lay off, will ya."

"You told me the police cut you off in the car," I went on easily, not pushing it. "That sounds to me as though you were alone."

"They went in all directions," he said, his voice thin. "The cops were all round us. I was tryin' to lead the cop's car away from Phillie, but they picked her up on the way back."

It had a convincing ring to it. "All right. So you drove off, still wearing your mask and your gloves."

"No gloves."

"Packer said: gloves and no weapons. His two rules."

"Well, yeah. But I'd dumped the gloves. Can't drive in gloves. I like to feel the wheel. You know."

I knew, because I did too. "So tell me how the policeman got shot."

It burst from him as though he wanted to get rid of it. "Come runnin' in the side door, didn't he. A great bull elephant of fuzz, wavin' something long and heavy, an' roaring at the top of his voice . . ." His graphic ability seemed to run out.

"And one of you characters shot him?"

"Yeah."

"Who shouldn't have been carrying a gun?"

"Shouldn't have," he agreed in a fading voice.

I took an island carefully and silently, working on his nerves. "But it was Packer's own rule—have you thought of this, Art?—if it was his own rule, it's unlikely he'd have been carrying a gun himself."

He brooded over that, then muttered, "He made 'em, he could break 'em."

"I don't believe that. It was unlikely. Don't you accept that?"

"I suppose."

I nodded. "So it was you who ran out of that door, and it was you who got in the car alone. And drove away. The fired pistol . . . where was it found?"

He said nothing. P, the sign read, indicating another lay-by. I headed for it.

"Where, Art?"

"On the pavement," he mumbled.

I pulled in, and rammed on the hand brake. I shot the seat-belt clear so that I could turn and face him. It was so obvious—yet the police hadn't prised it from him.

"And that was what Phillie saw, you dropping the gun and you diving into the car. And don't tell me it was too dark, because there'd be some light from somewhere. And it was Packer she identified, when she knew it was you."

He had the door open in one movement, was outside, and running. I banged open my door and bellowed after him, "It was you shot that copper, you lying bastard!"

Then I sat back and watched his retreat, feeling drained of emotion. There was nowhere he could go. At first it was a blind sprint, which eased down to a trot, then to a walk. I allowed him to get two hundred yards away, then I drifted after him and hugged his heels. He was making little bursts of speed, then falling back to a walk, and with not one glance behind him. Art had used up all the places he could hide. Including inside his head.

Eventually he stopped, and stood panting and limp as I drew the car alongside. He got in, but wouldn't look at me. I drove on, steadily and without haste, realising it hadn't been all that difficult to drag it from him. Did the young fool trust me? When I picked it up again I didn't need to watch his expression in order to judge his reactions.

"The gun," I asked. "Where did you get it?"

There was silence.

"The gun, Art."

"Under the car seat," he mumbled. He cleared his throat, then it came through with more confidence. "Wasn't my car. Our getaway character'd nicked it. The gun must've been his. When I took the gloves off and put 'em down by the seat, there it was. Revolver. Not big. So I stuck it in my pocket."

"Thought you'd need it?"

"No," he said. "No!" More violently.

"Then what?"

"The car could've got picked up, with a gun in it . . . it just wasn't on."

"Right." There was a kind of validity to this. "But why use the thing?"

I could just detect his silent shake of the head on the edge of my vision. I glanced sideways, and he was staring ahead, face white and stubborn, patches of red on his cheeks. This was his sticking point.

"Remember what I said, Art? About domestic and impersonal killing? You must do. I'm going to tell you something, and I don't usually talk about it. Mine was personal. It didn't make me anti-social, and didn't turn me into somebody looking on the rest of the world as a trash bin to be looted. You get what I mean? Killing a copper—that gets you top marks for loutish brutality. Don't assume because I've been in Gartree that I'm not going to the police and tell them about you. Oh yes, I'm still a social animal. Don't let the Gartree image fool you, laddie. So you can tell me how it all was, and you can try to convince me that I shouldn't go to Filey and shop you."

No sound.

"Art!" I snapped.

"All right!" he shouted, leaning forward to slap the dashboard. "You should've seen him. Like a mad thing—runnin' straight at me. I hadda stop him, didn't I!" he appealed miserably.

It was not good enough. "I don't think so."

"You would've. Go on, say you wouldn't, you an' your bleedin' social conscience. Go on, say it, you rotten liar."

"I might have stopped him. But not like that. Not with a gun . . ."

"For Chrissake! What else'd I got? A bloody mountain, he was. A bear, chargin' at me."

I kept my voice steady. "Sure. A grizzly, say." Then I had to look away from his distorted face. I'd let the car wander across the road again. Association of idea with place, that was. "But not shoot him, for heaven's sake."

He leaned close and bellowed into my ear. "Ya wanta know! He scared the shit outa me, that's what. I didn't know what I was doin' . . ." He caught his voice on a choked, indrawn breath. "I didn't even aim the soddin' thing," he whispered in bitter admission.

I allowed it to rest at that, giving the emotion time to clear away. After a while I said quietly, gently, "And Phillie? Was she parked where she could see all this, across the corner?" I took his lack of response as agreement. "You must've known she recognised you. Damn it all, she saw you dive into the car."

"I suppose," he muttered.

"You *knew*. Admit it."

"Well . . . yeah . . . I knew." The fight had gone out of him.

"But nothing was said between you?"

"Nar!" I caught the jerk as his head came round. "Didn't get much of a chance. I was inside, and her people kept her at home."

I sighed. Even now it was like squeezing juice from a prune. "But at least it gave you some idea of what she thought about you —that she'd do that for you. I'm talking about this perjury of hers."

"All right!"

It was a measure of his distress that he could raise no breath of pride in the fact. Perhaps he was already aware that he'd come to the end of his leash, and soon it was going to be hauled in. Art Torrance was in a trap. I wondered whether he understood the full implications. He seemed blissfully unaware of them.

I knew him to be an unprincipled petty thief, in for anything

without thought for the consequences or consideration for the victims. He would claim he only robbed the rich, but that was because, Robin Hood fashion, it wasn't worth robbing the poor. But
now he'd shot a man. In terror, perhaps. Nevertheless, he'd taken a
life. Were we so much different?

"What're we going to do with you, Art!" I said at last. It was a
plea.

"Can't we talk about somethin' else?"

I laughed at his naïveté. Did he think it would sneak away if
unmentioned? "You're unique, Art, d'you know that? Do we chat
about football all the way to Sumbury? Or girls . . . or you?"

"Heh! I can't go back—"

"Don't be a fool. Of course you've got to go back. Me too. You
know how it is, you'd be considered as having made a break for it,
guilt sticking out all over you. There'd be a nationwide search . . .
have you seen this man? Your mug on the telly."

"So what else is there?" he jerked out. "You take me there and
you hand me in? Is that the idea?"

"Hand you in! Oh, they'd be pleased about that. From me it'd
sound great. All I've done is worked out that you killed the copper,
and it wasn't Carl Packer. With a bit of help from you and from
him. And I couldn't expect either of you to repeat it to the police.
They'd laugh in my face. Anyway . . ." Facetiousness crept in.
". . . I bet they'd rather have Packer inside than you. Who's going
to trouble with small-fry when they've got a top-rate villain already?"

I looked sideways. He was pugging again, like a sulky child.
Perhaps he thought the murder of a policeman should've raised
him several notches in my estimation. I resented that. He couldn't
claim his had been in the family, as could I.

"Don't sit there feeling sorry for yourself," I said sharply, angry
with him. "You're a lying, crawling, creeping crook. You'd sell a
black stick to a blind man. You disgust me. I've a good mind to
dump you—"

"Then why don't you!" he demanded. It was in no way a request
for me to do so.

"Because I want to keep my eyes on you. You're like a walking
time bomb, and I want to know when to jump clear. Don't you *see*
how you're fixed, you cretin! And I do mean fixed."

"Who the hell d'you think you are, the beak or somethin'?"

"You're in a trap, Art. Two traps. Just think about it. Think how
this leaves you with the killing of Philomena, for a start."

"I told y' what happened. I didn't do it."

"Now listen. Frenchie went to Sumbury to see her and make her an offer. Money was the offer, but more than that there was the freedom from fear of Packer's reprisals. All she had to do was tell the truth about the warehouse job. Is that too difficult for you, Art? Is it sinking in?"

He gave a deep, weary sigh. "I'm with you."

"Good. We don't know whether or not Frenchie got round to making the offer, but assume for now that he did. She'd need time to think about it. If she agreed, it'd mean she wouldn't have to go on looking over her shoulder, and on top of that there'd be twenty thou as spending money. But where would that leave you?"

"She wouldn't. Not Phillie."

"I'm saying she'd shop you, Art. Like that!" It's difficult to snap your fingers when they're round a steering wheel, but he got the point.

"It's a bleedin' lie. She wouldn't."

"You said yourself she wasn't encouraging on the phone. She'd gone off you, Art. Or is that impossible for you to imagine?"

He sneered, but he said, "If you want Killingham, you've just missed the turn-off."

"I'll take the next. Keep to the point. She wouldn't be able to convince the police it wasn't Packer without telling them who it *really* was."

"Well all right!" he shouted. "All bloody right."

"But it could've been best in the end if she had," I told him placidly.

"Now what the hell're you goin' on about?" he demanded, his voice breaking.

"I want you to appreciate all the facets of this. And don't you pout at me, Art. You've got to face it. Right . . . assume, then, that she hadn't died, and she'd dropped you in it. What would've happened would be that you'd enter Gartree at the same time as Carl Packer moved out. Now you must admit that could be the best arrangement. It's the only place you'd be safe from his revenge. Reasonably safe, anyway."

"You're tryin' to put the wind up me," he complained, already scared.

"Too right, sport, as our Aussie friend would say. I'm trying to get you to understand that this isn't something you can laugh away. You see, that's the *best* thing that could happen to you. But what would've happened if she'd got Carl Packer off in the end—a pardon, say—and managed to do it without even mentioning you? Packer would come out and there you'd be, waiting, and owing him two or more years of his life. Art, he'd age you twenty years in a day, unless he decided to stretch it out. And make no mistake, he'd be after you, my friend."

He wriggled in his seat. "Talk of somethin' else."

"Don't be stupid. I'm going through the options. What if Parker has to do his full time . . . think how many years you'd owe him then. You could start running right now, and you couldn't get far enough. Nowhere in the world. Just a thought, Art."

"I ain't listenin' to any more of this."

"No? Is it all right if I change the subject? Right. Then I'll mention Philomena's death. But I assume you'd rather I didn't."

"Don't be a prat!" he shouted. "Say it, and get it done with."

"All right. Just suppose, Art, that you did what I suggested earlier, which was go to meet her along the Port Sumbury road. And you met her by the woodland. But now we know a bit more. Now it's not just the old brush-off she's going to give you—it's something very special. She's going to tell you that she's intending to come clean with the police."

"I didn't meet her," he snapped.

"But look what a lovely motive she'd have given you if you had. She'd come to tell you that the police were going to pick you up for murder, and she was sorry, Art, but twenty thou isn't to be sneezed at—"

"It's a lie! It's a bloody lie!" he screamed, thumping the padding on the dash over and over.

"Maybe. Maybe not. But I hope you see, now, what you're into. Whichever way you look, you're caught—and the trap's got nasty big teeth."

"You rotten bugger."

"The flat's just along here."

I had no intention of handing him in, because I had no evidence worth a toss. I also felt I'd scraped no more than the surface of the truth, and at the moment I had information to which the police had no access. In the probably short time I had left to me, I was determined to use it.

"You're a masochist, that's what you are," he yelped.

"Big words, Art. Like the situation, too big for you. It's sadist you mean."

I stopped the car out in the street instead of pulling on to the small patch of gravel in front of Phil's block of flats. She was still Phil to me. I stopped out there because her two-seater Fiat was already occupying the patch. The sun was going down, and casting heavy shadows beneath the chestnuts that lined the street. I didn't think the Fiesta would be noticed.

I got out and slammed the door. There was the sound of Art's door opening, then his head popped up, and he was staring at me over the car.

"What're you goin' to do?"

"If it's any of your business, I'm going to see the woman who owns the office we broke into, and the flat we slept in. I'm going to ask her some questions, and hopefully—"

He cut in impatiently. "I was thinking about me."

"You usually are. If you want to know, I'm not much interested in you any more. This is your home town, and you can disappear into it if you like. You'll have to assume there'll be a net out for you any time, but that's your affair."

"You're just sayin' that."

"Of course I'm saying it. D'you think I'm going to chip it out in rock? I'm intending to go back to Sumbury afterwards. If they take me in for interrogation, and ask me about you, then you can count on the fact that I'll tell 'em everything I know, including my ideas on it, because I don't care one blind bit what happens to you, Art. Do you get what I mean? I'm going to look after my own skin. You look after yours. Right?" It was an attitude he would understand and appreciate.

He stared mutely at me, then he nodded reluctantly.

I turned on my heel and walked to the front door, not looking back to see what he did about it.

The hall still smelt of furniture polish, but somebody had changed the make. A touch of violets. It was quiet. The only light was from the door behind me and a similar stained-glass panel above me in the wall, where the landing curved. When I cleared my throat the walls whispered back. I mounted the stairs, aware that I didn't know what to say, how to face her. I would have to take it as it came.

I didn't use the bell-push. After all, I was a part-resident, and I had the keys to prove it. The latch turned with the key. I opened the door and walked in.

She was standing by the window, but I didn't think she'd been admiring the lake. Her face was flushed with anger and her hair disarrayed. At the small sound of the key she'd turned, but from the emptiness in her eyes I could tell she hadn't brought her mind to it. Beside her was the Aussie, Grant Felton. He was turning slowly. They had been arguing fiercely.

"Why didn't you ring?" she asked tightly. She shook her head to settle her hair.

Trying to smile past them, I held up her keys. "I've still got these. Do I call you Phil? Or is it Dorothy? I mean, I'm starting from scratch again."

"You've been to the office." It wasn't a question, so she'd been there herself.

"Yes." I felt I could not move from that spot. The tone in her voice held me at a distance. I placed the keys down on the table beside her phone. "You're Dorothy June Mann. You are not Philomena Wise. She's dead."

Dorothy—hell, it sounded strange, even in my mind—moved at last. Noticing that Felton had turned to face me, and that he was tense as a towing rope, she made a small gesture to silence him, then moved a couple of tentative paces towards me. It seemed that her purpose was to hide her expression from him, but I couldn't detect any expression worth the trouble.

"So she's dead, and I failed," she said in an empty voice. "And you know it all now. So why are you here, Paul?"

"To return your keys. Perhaps to leave you a little note."

"Saying what?"

"I hadn't decided. Probably to say we ought to meet . . ."

"Which we've now done."

". . . and discuss how things stand."

Felton stirred. Remaining static for too long apparently did not fit his nature. He was impatient and aggressive. The room crackled with it. Whatever he had against me wasn't going away.

"Let me bounce him outa here," he said impatiently.

She whirled on him. "Keep out of this!" she snapped.

He stared at her with his eyebrows high, his jaw jutting, and his eyes glazed in surprise. "Now see here—"

"Be silent, or get out!" she told him briskly. "I mean it, Grant."

He didn't like it. Women did not give orders to Grant Felton. His shoulders firmed, then he shrugged. He turned his back again, and the view from the window captured him, dark as it was.

To me, her voice was more persuasive. "The way things stand, nothing's clear at all, and you know it, Paul."

"Seems clear enough to me. The police could charge me with the murder of Philomena, and they could make a good case against me for the death of Frenchie." I paused. Felton's head had jerked round at this. His lips had drawn back and his eyes were startled. "When the situation's like that," I went on, "I can assure you, Phil . . . oh hell, do I call you Dorothy or Dot?"

"I'm Dot to my friends," she offered shortly.

"Thank you. Still a friend then, Dot? I was saying . . . there're things I need to know, such as how you come into it, and what you've been doing. This is self-defence I'm talking about. I need facts in case I have to use them. You understand?"

"I can't help you—"

"I've got to know where I stand, damn it. Why don't we sit down and talk it over?"

"What's the point? You'll have to leave—"

"You went away," I interrupted. I tried to smile. "You were going to sort things out, you said, and depending on what happened you were going to give me an answer. Can you give me that answer now?"

I was half hoping she would take up the challenge, if only to clarify my own thinking. My feelings regarding her were in a turmoil. Nothing had changed, and yet it was all different. Dot was a different woman from Phil. What had been a tentative affection had become brittle and chipped away. I could see it in her set face. She was brisk and forceful, her way clear to her when mine was not.

"It isn't settled," she said, lifting her chin. "I'm not sure. Not with . . ." Her shoulder moved in Felton's direction.

"Not with him here? I'll get rid of him."

Her voice crackled. "Don't start anything in here. Either of you."

I found myself staring into Felton's bleak and threatening eyes. I grinned at him. "You hear, Felton? Relax. Nobody's going to hurt you."

She said with exasperation, "For God's sake—you two—stop it!"

We faced each other like two black clouds, waiting for the lightning to spark across. Then I shrugged.

"I suppose he knows about you, anyway," I said.

"How could he not know? You're a fool, Paul Manson."

I sighed. "Very well. You are Dorothy June Mann, ex-detective sergeant. Ejected for striking a senior officer. No reasons available to date, but I'm not surprised to hear it."

She grimaced. "You've met him?" Her voice was softer. I'd aligned myself with her.

But I was uncertain about him, too. "Filey? Yes."

"I hated him. Thought I hated him, anyway. But he's a complex man. All he ever wanted was perfection. He saw himself as a white knight on a charger, fighting all the wrongdoers and destroying them." She paused, smiling to herself. "He was even infecting me with it at one stage. Perhaps I encouraged him . . . I don't know. Hell—it was all a mess."

I glanced away from her, not sure I liked being equated with Filey, even though she couldn't know in what way. "And all this led to you becoming Philomena Wise? That's what I can't understand."

She walked across the room and began to fiddle with her record albums. Then she came back and stood in front of me with resolution. I could now see how she'd managed to dislodge Filey's tooth. At that moment I feared for mine, considering her firm and poised stance.

"Listen," she told me, "and don't interrupt. It began with that warehouse raid and the death of P. C. Adamson. You know about that?"

"I didn't know his name, but I've heard that one of your people was shot."

She nodded. She now had a base from which she could work. "Ted Adamson, a great lumbering fool of a man, with guts enough for twenty. He went in, and he was shot. We collected all of 'em, and dear sweet Philomena. Stupid girl, she thought it was all a game of cops and robbers, like on the telly. But when there're no cameras people really get hurt. We didn't want her, so we gave her back to poppa. He was appalled. He hadn't known she hung around with people like that. We let her go, but we knew what she must've seen, and that she'd know who'd shot Ted Adamson, so we wanted her as a crown witness. Filey gave me the job of persuading her. He'd got enough intelligence to realise he frightened her, and she wouldn't trust him. She was terrified by that time, anyway. She hadn't imagined what violence could be like, face to face. I spent hours with her, days, trying to persuade her. But she was scared. As I'd have been. Or you, Paul. You've got to admit it."

"Knowing what these people are like, yes, I'd have been scared."

I felt she was rushing her explanation, anxious to get it out and done with, and see the back of me. But this was her apology to me, and she was ashamed to have to make it. So I didn't waste her time, but let her get on with it.

She nodded. "Right. In the end I got through to her. I promised her police protection—anything she wanted—to persuade her she'd be safe, but I must've given her the wrong impression. We could protect her until the trial, but you can't protect anybody for ever. All right . . ." She looked past me, and her shoulders gave a small shuddering movement. "You can say I *let* her believe she'd always be safe. But I wanted her at the trial, and I wanted her evidence. Ted Adamson, well, he was something of a personal friend. Something special. I . . . oh hell . . . I got her to agree. Just to go and answer questions in court. I knew nothing about what she would say. I can see her there, her face absolutely stark white, there in the box, and when the prosecuting counsel asked her if she could indicate the person she'd seen fire the gun, she pointed at Carl Packer, and she used his name."

Her lips seemed dry. She moistened them. Felton was eyeing her with his head on one side. This was new to him, as it was to me.

But perhaps he made something different out of it. I said not a word, afraid I might shatter a very frail and delicate truth.

"Of course, we got his outburst and his threats." She moved a hand in front of her face. "He said he'd get her, and she fainted. But afterwards, Filey was delighted, you can bet. He'd wanted to put Packer away for years. I met him in the corridor outside, bouncing with smug satisfaction. But . . . even I knew . . . Packer with a gun? Never. Then I understood, or thought so. Filey had got at Philomena. Some time or other. He'd persuaded her to say it was Packer. Five of 'em, and she could've pointed at any one of them. But she picked out Packer. Of course, I realised later, he'd promised Philomena to do what he could for Art, if she'd say what he wanted. The tricky bastard—and he couldn't do anything, not for Art, nor for Philomena afterwards."

She stopped abruptly, leaving me with my mind racing, searching for implications. It didn't look as though she was intending to pursue it, so I prompted her.

"But you hit him! I don't understand . . . nothing you've said—"

She turned a shoulder to me and spoke over it. "Can't you work *anything* out for yourself! Packer had made his threats—and I knew he'd keep 'em. But . . . did Filey care a toss for that? Not him. And it'd been me who'd persuaded her, so the responsibility was mine. And the bastard laughed! So I hit him. Isn't that enough for you, for God's sake? It got me thrown out of the force."

Then she left me in order to wander round the room, apparently searching for cigarettes. It was finished. I was dismissed. I was supposed to creep away, the naughty boy glad to get out of the headmaster's study.

I wasn't going to be dismissed so easily. She had changed. Was she so caught up in that past case that she couldn't, even now, release her involvement? Or did she mistrust me now, my motives and my intentions?

I walked after her and seized her arm. "But you've told me nothing!" I shouted, anger suddenly bubbling to the surface.

ELEVEN

She turned on me furiously, bending over a table and glaring back with her hair falling forward like a screen. What I could see of her eyes implored me to let it drop, but I didn't know when there'd be another chance.

"It's all you're going to get, Paul. Now will you please leave." She sounded exhausted.

Felton assumed he'd been given the go-ahead. He advanced on me, grinning. It was lopsided. I backed off a yard. No trouble, if I could help it.

"The police," he decided, "we'll have the police. What d'you people dial . . ."

I reached back and lifted the handset and offered it to him. "It's nine, nine, nine."

Dorothy moved quickly to come between us. She snatched the phone from my hand and slammed it back in its cradle. "All right, Grant." She seemed short of breath. "I'll settle this. What d'you want to know?" she asked me, her cheeks flushed and her eyes moist.

"What the hell d'you think I want to know?" My voice was still too loud, my control hanging on a very slender thread. "The meaning of your stupid impersonation, to start with."

She lifted one hand and let it fall to her side. Felton threw himself into her Queen Anne chair, disgusted and sulking.

"I knew I'd have to change my name if I wanted to go on working in the town I knew," she said, picking her words carefully. "I thought that Filey would throw trouble at me if I tried anything under my real name. All I could think to do, because it's the only thing I know, was to try to make it as a private investigator. But it's a slow game getting it established, and I hadn't got any savings. I needed a steady income to tide me over. So I changed my name."

I didn't understand her. "But why to—"

She cut me short with a flip of her hand. "I arranged it with her father. I knew Carl Packer's threats weren't empty, and that he'd

pay somebody if necessary. Aubrey Wise was intending to leave
the district, and he didn't want people chasing him from one place
to another. So I agreed to use the name of Philomena Wise. I got a
monthly retainer. All right—so I haven't got far as a private eye.
Just try concentrating on a job when you've got to keep one eye
open to cover your back!"

So it had turned out to be more than she could handle. "You
certainly put yourself in a spot," I agreed cautiously.

"I know how to handle myself. I just had to be prepared."

"So?" I prompted carefully, realising that if her nerve had gone,
an offer to go to America could have appeared a godsend. It wasn't
a warming thought. I waited for her answer. "And?" I asked,
when I seemed about to get nothing.

"I laid it on. The Wisemann Agency was a lure. Anyone looking
for Philomena Wise would find it, and from it trace me . . . her. I
was waiting for somebody. An approach. Anything."

Fleetingly I wondered whether the choice of name for her
agency might have been prompted by a personal fear, that Packer
might wish to punish her, too. She'd concentrated both targets in
one persona.

She wasn't going on with it. Felton muttered something. It
sounded like, "Bloody stupid idea."

"And?" I said again, my voice a little tighter. I hadn't begun to
scrape the surface of it.

She didn't want to continue. We were coming to something approaching truth, and it pained her to express it. When she spoke
again there was bitterness in her voice.

"And you turned up, Paul, damn you, with that blasted smile of
yours . . ." She bit her lip, shaking her head again. "I didn't know
what Packer's man would look like, but I'd been expecting an
approach—been expecting it for two blasted years. And it was you.
I had a . . . a check made on you. I've still got friends at the
station. And you'd come from Gartree. What did you imagine I
was going to think! I didn't know . . ." Looking me in the eyes,
she whispered, "Even now . . ."

"Tell him, tell him," Felton cut in.

I stared at him. Tell me what? That I was a bloody jailbird, and
that meant I must have killed Philomena? Was *that* what was
haunting him? I nearly walked over to shut his mouth.

"And they told you I was a strangler?" I asked her. "All you had
to do was watch my hands."

She flinched. "It wasn't like that."

"No? Did you get some sort of perverted kick from leading on a
strangler, to see how far I'd go?"

"No!" she shouted, her head jerking forward.

Felton was on his feet. "Let him try it on me. So help me—"

"Sit!" I snapped, not even glancing at him, seeing only his movement on the edge of my vision.

Dorothy was drawing in deep breaths with her lower lip between her teeth, her eyes blinded by tears. "What in God's name could you expect from me, Paul? Once I knew—thought I knew—who had come from Packer . . . what could I do? Wait to be attacked? And you . . . there was no sign of intention. I was completely confused. And then you spoke about taking me abroad. How could that fit in with Packer's schemes? You wouldn't need to take me all the way to Nevada in order to kill me." Her voice was breaking, but she managed to get out, "I was all mixed up . . ."

Her distress made me uneasy. I'd put her in an impossible position. Both of us. There was nothing left to say.

"I'll go."

"Wait!" She fought for her composure. "Why d'you think I went to Sumbury? I wanted time to think, and I wanted to discuss the situation with Aubrey. Oh, heavens, Paul, can't you understand?"

I nodded, anxious to get away now. "I can see you'd want a consultation. The trouble is . . . oh, Phil—Dot—can't you see what you're telling me?"

There had been only one way in which she could've made certain of her future. "What could you find there, what action could you take?"

"For me to withdraw from my arrangement with Aubrey Wise," she said, dismissing it with a curt gesture. "The trouble was," she said, "that whoever Packer sent wasn't fooled. They knew I wasn't Philomena. So I was followed to Sumbury, and I led him there."

"I see what you mean. 'They knew' and 'led him.' But you mean me. That you led *me* to her, is that it, Dot? Dot! It's like talking to a stranger."

That was the block I couldn't get past. I was talking to a stranger, who no longer possessed the response and warmth I'd found in my Phil. Because this had been false? She was now demonstrating a hardness and determination that belonged to somebody called Dorothy Mann. Underneath, she was still a police officer. Right and wrong, that was all there was for her, with no shades of compassion in between.

"That wasn't what I meant," she protested. "But I certainly led somebody."

"Not me. I didn't kill her."

"I don't know who killed her." Her voice was cold, the distant bitter cold of a wind that's come a long way.

"But you were there when she died," I said, trying to keep my voice even and persuasive. "She was dead, so your job for Aubrey Wise was finished. Let's say that you'd failed."

"I tried, damn you, I tried!"

I gave a sigh. "I'm sure you did. But you went there, you've said, to sort things out. And you'd have found Philomena was going away with Australia's great white hope. That's even further than Nevada. So you would soon be free of it, and you knew I was waiting back here. Remember what you said: you'd let me know, yes or no. But you didn't. In fact, you've been keeping out of my way."

"I'm getting out of here," Felton said with disgust, but he didn't do anything about it until he realised that neither of us intended to dissuade him. With a grumbling sound in his throat, he weaved his way round us. The door opened behind me, then it slammed. I didn't look round. Her eyes were on mine, and she didn't spare him a glance.

"And what the hell's *he* doing here?" I demanded.

"That's no business of yours."

"No? Isn't it?"

For a moment her eyes left me. There had been a flicker of self-disgust in the line of her lips. "It was yes or no. As you say."

"And it's no?"

She shook her head violently, rejecting something I couldn't understand. Then she turned away with a gesture of despair. "Take it for no, then, if you want to."

"Your business with Wise is finished," I reminded her, gently persuasive, giving it every chance.

She turned back to me, pouting, trying for a smile. "Do you really believe that?"

"No," I agreed, "it's not finished. We're both dead in the middle. Perhaps we could hurry it up." I was offering her an alliance, but her eyes rejected it. I took a deep breath. "Can you tell me . . . something I don't know about . . ."

Her shoulders sagged and she sighed. "If it's something you think you ought to know."

"It was just . . . last Friday evening. I understand there was to have been a party."

She seemed to lose interest. She shrugged. "It was her birthday."

"I know. She went out before seven. She had to be back in order to change into her finery. But—didn't anybody object or go after her, something like that? It'd seem strange—her party coming up —and it was getting dark. The sun would've gone down, anyway."

"I went after her—yes."

"*You* did? Why was that?"

"She'd had her hair done, and set."

That stopped me. "I don't understand."

"The mist was coming off the sea—you could see it in the tops of the trees. It would've ruined her hair. But she . . . she wasn't thinking about that."

"About Art. Yes, I know. What time did she leave?"

"Oh, around ten to seven, give or take. Paul, please, this isn't really your concern."

"Accept that it is. You knew she was going to meet Art?"

"He'd phoned. Yes, I knew."

"So you ran after her to make her change her mind."

She twisted her lips in a cynical smile. Then it softened. "Nothing would have done that. She had to see him. At the party she was going to become formally engaged to Grant Felton. Of course she had to see Art. No—I ran after her with a headsquare."

"Not a fawn one . . ."

She laughed. "As though that hasn't been asked, Paul! You don't think much of the police—I've told Greaves all this. I ran after her down the drive. It would've looked fine, wouldn't it, dressing up for her party with her hair all dangling round her ears . . ." She stopped. There had been a catch in her voice.

I realised, then, that Greaves had known more than he'd admitted. No wonder he'd given me a loose rein.

"So, you took off after her with your scarf."

"Not mine. Grant's." Then she laughed openly at the expression on my face. "Not *his,* you idiot. His present. A nylon headsquare."

"Are you telling me he bought her a measly nylon head-square—"

"No! *Will* you listen. He's got one of these peculiar senses of humour. He piles things on. Expect a dozen roses, and he sends one bunch every hour. You know the idea—the diamond ring hidden in a box of cheap chocolates. He was going to give her the headsquare, then watch her expression, and after a few seconds tell her it was for holding her hair in place when she drove the brand-new BMW convertible he'd got hidden in one of the garages."

I grinned at her. "But that was for the party," I said.

"He's too eager. Like a child. He couldn't wait. He gave her the headsquare too early. He couldn't have realised he was giving her too much time, and she'd see through him. Anyway, there it was, lying on one of the tables on the hall—"

"I know where you mean."

"And I just picked it up and ran after her with it, calling after her."

She said this with her head on one side, waiting for my obvious reaction. My response was out before I could stop it.

"So she was wearing—"

"You're much too impulsive, Paul. No, she didn't take it. I caught up with her by the gate. I gave it to her. She just said, 'Oh, it's Grant's present,' and walked off with it in her hand. And I saw her hold it up and drop it on the grass verge, less than a dozen yards from the gate."

That, I could understand. Grant had sprung his joke too early. She had not been amused, not knowing the second part of the surprise. So she was miffed.

"Grant wouldn't like that."

"He was sulking."

"You mean . . . he knew where she was going? To see Art."

"It wasn't that. He'd seen the way she'd accepted the headsquare when he gave it to her. All pleasure and smiling thanks. Gracious. I was proud of her. He'd expected a pout of disappointment, at least."

"Ah, yes." Good for her. "It rather dented his joke, didn't it! Perhaps it would've done him good to see her drop it in the road. But I suppose he didn't."

She threw herself into the chair Grant had been using, reaching for her cigarettes on a side table. "Why're we discussing this, Paul?"

"I'm groping for the truth."

"The truth is that she died. Keep out of it, that's my advice. It's a police matter."

I tried to smile at her, realising I was losing her confidence. "And the nylon headsquare? What happened to it?"

"I went and picked it up, of course. The grass was already damp."

"And where was Felton, not to have seen it dropped?"

"He'd shut himself in one of the garages with his precious car, polishing and polishing. I wouldn't be surprised if he was hiding her engagement ring somewhere inside it. Like a big, soft kid."

Not the Grant Felton I knew. Big, yes. Soft, no. "You know that?"

She gestured impatiently. "He was still at it when Art got to the house, and I went to tell Grant she was missing. I had a job holding him."

"How come?"

"Paul, I'm ex-police. I knew the ropes. She couldn't be far away, and he wasn't going to do any good crashing around . . ." She gestured again, scattering ash.

"You restrained him?"

"I locked him in with the car."

I laughed. Poor Grant. Restrained by a woman!

"Will you please leave now, Paul. I don't understand you . . . these questions. You know she was strangled with Art Torrance's scarf—"

I shook my head. "Not with the scarf. When she died, Art still had the scarf in his possession. In fact, he hadn't even got to the phone box, where he left it."

"I'm glad he's got such an alibi, though it's a measly poor thing."

I grinned at her, trying to lighten the mood. "Of course, he might not have been telling the truth. Here . . . I've just had a nasty thought. You don't happen to have owned a fawn silk scarf, by any chance?"

It's my rotten sense of humour. The suggestion was too absurd to be considered seriously. But it jerked her to her feet.

"I did not!" she snapped, her protest too violent.

"It was a joke," I said gently.

"Was it? You'd better leave, I think. We've talked ourselves to a dead end," Her voice was weary with the strain.

"Yes. Right. I'll go." I turned, hesitated. "Oh . . . something else."

"Not more of your damned questions!"

"A simple one. You were in Philomena's confidence." It wasn't a question, but she couldn't prevent the tiny nod. "So she'd have told you things, private things, even her secrets. Did she tell you whether Dougie French had contacted her?" Now her eyes were blank. "Dougie French," I repeated. "The man Carl Packer sent."

Her lips were bloodless. "Then it wasn't—"

"No, it wasn't me. He sent Frenchie."

"I don't . . . oh, God!"

"You've made your explanation," I said. "You're entitled to mine. Packer did approach me—I thought it was about a killing. So I refused his offer, but I came here, to find her—to warn her or protect her, or whatever. And found you. Then things got all confused, and in the end, partly to get you away from trouble and partly for myself, I asked you to come to the U.S.A. with me. That's all there is to it."

The blood had run from her cheeks, and when she spoke there was no tone to her voice. "Thank you. That's very clear." She lifted her chin. "Dougie French, you say." She knew his name, knew of him. "He was Packer's man?"

"Not to kill her. To make her an offer."

Her eyes slid away. "Offer? What offer?"

I sighed. She had known about the offer. "He sent Frenchie to offer her money, to persuade her to change the evidence she gave at Packer's trial. It wasn't Packer who shot your Ted Adamson, and he wanted her to say so. He hoped it'd get him a new trial, or a pardon. I'm not sure of the legal aspects. But Frenchie didn't intend to kill her. Packer was shocked when I told him she was dead. She was his only chance."

She was confused. A blush bloomed on her cheeks and her eyes hunted. "I don't . . . what? . . . don't understand. What're you saying?"

"I wanted to know whether or not he'd contacted her, and if she'd decided to retract her evidence. That's all. You obviously don't know. I'd better leave. It's a long drive to Sumbury."

I turned to the door. Her left hand clamped on my arm. "Wait!"

"I thought you wanted me to leave."

"You get me all mixed up, and then you walk out!"

"I didn't intend to confuse you. I just wanted to ask that one question. To tell you the truth, I'm glad you didn't know the answer."

"*Now* what d'you mean? Paul, I'll brain you if you don't explain yourself."

I ran my fingers through my hair. It was embarrassing. "Well . . . you see . . . if she was intending to go back on it all, you wouldn't have been pleased. You'd been turfed out of the police because of your loyalty to her, and you'd spent two years waiting for a killer to come to *you*. So . . . if you found out she'd been lying all the time, and she was going to broadcast the fact that she lied—"

"Damn you!" she said throatily.

"And—sort of—that would've given you a bloody good motive for killing her."

"Damn you!" she shouted, on top register.

I reached quickly for the door. "So I'm glad you didn't know," I managed to get out.

Then I was out in the hall with the door shut, and from behind me there was silence. I'd expected noisy fury—but there was nothing. I hurried from there into the darkness of the landing, imagining her distress and afraid I might weaken and return and take her in my arms and apologise, and . . . oh, I don't know. All those stupid retractions that hamper a man's journey through life. Because I knew it was over. I'd been talking to Dorothy June Mann, whom I didn't know. Both Philomenas had died together.

I slowed on the stairs, having to feel my way. I realised I'd known neither of them. The fault was mine. Or it was the fault of the prison system, where reality recedes and the outside world becomes vague and illusive. Women, for instance, become either the figures of excessive eroticism, or the heroines of ridiculous romanticism. My mind had taken the second course, otherwise I wouldn't have involved myself in a stupid idyll in which the gallant Sir Paul was intending to save the life of the innocent Philomena. This basic concept had clouded the whole issue, and I'd not come out of it very well—I was even now departing in disorder.

But nevertheless, the sense of loss was devastating. I couldn't handle it soberly; my memories clashed with cool logic inside my head. I had to have time.

Consequently, I rushed from the front door without thought. I hadn't seen any shadow on the landing that could've been Grant Felton. This, apparently, was because he'd been lurking outside, to one side of the porch. I had the warning of feet on gravel, a second in which to half turn and duck when I saw the shape of a left hand coming at me. I knew he'd be aiming that stump of his at my left eye.

He got me on the forehead. I could only hope it hurt him as much as it did me. For a second I was dazed, unsteady. A man such as Felton needs no more. He'd have had me on the ground, and heaven knows what would've happened then, but we were interrupted.

With a howl, a shape burst in from the shadows. Compared with the bulk of Felton it was small, but Art was all flying fists and feet and teeth, and though he distracted Felton for no more than a second or two, it was enough. By the time Felton threw him off I'd been able to make some sort of a recovery. When he returned his attention to me I had both feet firmly spread on the gravel and my right fist was poised. He ran into the punch, deep under his heart, and with a grunt he fell to his knees.

There was another howl from Art, and he would have finished him off in true alley style, but I grabbed his arm and hurried him away, and together we stumbled out of the drive to the car. I leaned against it, still dazed, my head throbbing.

"You'd better drive," I managed to say, and I fell into the passenger's seat. We slammed our doors and snapped down the locking catches. If he'd recovered in time, Felton could've torn off a door.

The first few heavy drops of rain hit the windscreen as we

started away. Art said nothing. The wipers began to lash. He screamed the tyres whenever an opportunity arose, just to prove how good he was. He'd have made a lousy getaway driver; they'd only have needed to follow his tyre screams.

When I was feeling a little more stable, I said, "We'll have to make good time if we're going to get there before our landlady and landlord lock up, but it'd be marvellous if we could do it more smoothly. With a good driver, it doesn't have to show, but he gets there just as quickly."

"Does that mean you don't like my driving?" He sounded offended.

"Let's say it'd be fine to watch, from outside. And talking about outside, that's where you're supposed to overtake."

Poor Art had been suffering many damaging blows to his ego recently. He grunted in response, but from there onwards we progressed rapidly but with comparative safety. This needed his concentration. He was silent. The rain now lashed down, and the headlights cut into the gleaming spikes. The slicked tarmac allowed him to demonstrate his four-wheel drifts round corners. He couldn't resist that, and seemed to get some enjoyment from it. It was more than I did.

After an extended period of silence I said, "Tell me again. All about the scarf and the timing."

"Aw hell!"

"No. Please. It matters."

So he told it again, and it did not vary one iota from the previous account.

"I suppose your watch wasn't faulty?"

"It's a quartz digital."

"Marvellous. I make it eight thirty-three. What d'you make it?"

He spared himself a dangerous glance at his wrist. "Eight-thirty. Get a good watch, mate."

"I suppose you only nick the best."

"Lay off me, will ya!"

"And you're sure you saw nobody along the Port Sumbury road?"

"Nobody. Why can't you believe me?"

"Because you've already told me one lie."

There was a pause as he thought back to which one I might mean. "Such as what?"

"You said you weren't wearing gloves when you fired the gun."

"That wasn't a flamin' lie."

"Then how d'you explain the fact that it was clean of fingerprints?"

"I don't have to, do I! Let me get on with the driving, damn it."

So I did. Problems tumbled around inside my head, jostling for precedence. And thrusting them aside, each time I had them sorted into some sort of sequence, was the throb of pain from the blow on my forehead. I twisted the rearview mirror—Art never glanced at it, anyway—and in the dim reflected light from the instruments I could see the bruise blossoming. I owed Grant Felton, and I'm meticulous with debts.

We ran out of the rain, and into it again. We stopped for a quick meal, dashing through the downpour into a café, where Art downed his chips like a dolphin his fish.

"I never thanked you," I recalled.

"Whaffor?"

I touched the bruise and winced. "This. Your intervention."

"It was a pleasure. You scratch my car and I'll scratch yours."

"I'll remember that."

We proceeded another ten miles before he asked, "What y' gonna do about me, then?"

"In return for the scratched car? I'm not going to do anything. Nothing I know will affect the investigation into Philomena's death. And as to the copper's—what could I tell the police that'd cause any reaction at all? Your Phillie's dead, and only she could've given evidence." I thought about that. "Except you, of course."

"Come off it."

"Which I doubt you will. No—what you've got to worry about is Carl Packer, and there I can't help you at all, Art."

"Don't put yourself out."

We drove on. Out in the open countryside, for the last twenty miles before we reached Sumbury, the road was more tricky. I didn't expect it to affect his speed, but I noticed he was slowing. In the end he drew in to the side of the deserted road and spoke miserably.

"I don't know what to do, and that's the truth." It was the first hint of defeat I'd had from him.

"You go back to Mrs. Druggett's, and you wait it out."

"Easy to say. I feel lousy."

"I don't feel too good myself."

"I'm scared," he admitted, so quietly and modestly that the rain almost drummed the words out of sight.

"The very fact that you've gone back voluntarily will be in your favour."

"It wasn't voluntary. You couldn't 'ave driven yourself. You've bin asleep half the way."

"Have I?"

"An' anyway, I feel safer with you."

Oh, Lordy me! He felt safer with me! How crazy could you get? "I'll drive the rest if you like."

"No. No, I'll do it."

He started again, and we rolled quietly and placidly into Sumbury. It was eleven o'clock, and it'd been a fast run.

"Straight to Mrs. Druggett's," I said, "and I'll take it on from there."

He didn't argue. A light in him had faded. Art was a very frightened young man.

The house was a small cottage along one of the dim side streets, with the grey bulk of a church lurking opposite. There was light in the front window and he hopped out smartly, attracted to it like a homesick moth. I got out and went round to take the wheel.

"See ya!" he said.

"Sure."

I had one foot inside when a shape moved to my shoulder. My nerves were so taut that I'd whirled and had my fist ready before I recognised her. Sergeant Lucy Rice was wearing a plastic hood over her head, the rest of her covered with a police slicker. It was made for a taller person, and reached right down to her ankles.

"We've got to talk," she said.

"I need to be in before George locks up," I answered inanely.

"He's waiting for you. And Inspector Greaves. They'll wait a little longer."

I looked at her, what I could see by the spill of light from a far street lamp.

"We'd better get inside the car," I decided.

TWELVE

She edged her way on to the passenger's seat. The slicker seemed to fill the car with angular, wet folds.

"How come you were waiting here?" I asked her.

"I saw you and Art getting on the bus, and guessed you would be going somewhere to hire a car. George said you'd been asking about that. So I reckoned you'd bring Art back with you."

Into three sentences she had condensed the complex pattern of her theorising, and on it based a long and dreary wait. Possibly more than one.

She was a direct and uncomplicated person. Her confidences gave the impression of being naïve, in that she offered them freely and didn't expect them to be betrayed. A romantic, too, it seemed. I looked at her with curiosity. She was also a police officer, but this could well be a trusting attitude she had perfected, and maybe it worked well with the locals who knew her. I didn't know her. Suddenly I wanted to.

"I'd thank you if I knew why," I said, meaning whether the trouble had been taken officially or personally.

She answered obliquely. "Greaves reckons he's got enough to be able to take you in."

"And you don't?"

"It's not for me to reckon anything. I'm only a sergeant."

"But you trust him?"

"Certainly. We've worked together for several years. I trust him. He's a straightforward country copper with no tricks."

"Does he trust you?"

"I like to think so."

"And yet—he wouldn't be pleased that you're talking to me now."

Her face was in shadow, so that I could judge only by her voice, which sounded tentative when she replied. "He'd trust me not to say anything that could ruin his case."

"The case against me, you mean? I suppose you're talking about the death of Philomena?"

"Why do you ask? Have you been mounting up a collection? All I know about is Philomena, and Douglas French." Her voice changed gear and became a crawl up a slippery slope. "Are there any more?"

I opened my door an inch to put on the interior light. Now I could see her more plainly. She'd thrown back the hood and shaken out her hair, as much as it would shake. Her expression was her usual one of solemnity, but I thought I could detect the control this involved. Her eyes danced, with the devil behind them.

"I've lost count," I said, shaking my head at this weakness.

She looked down at her hands, counting her fingers, then her eyes darted back at me. "There's nothing to be flippant about," she told me severely, though the devil was still there.

"Of course not. I sit corrected. And what makes Greaves think he's got enough on me?"

"Two things." She patted my knee. Twice. "One: Filey's been back to Killingham and he's phoned in." She waited for my nod, which I did. I waited for her to mention the Wisemann Agency. Which she didn't. "He's been making enquiries about your so-called alibi. He'd managed to trace the flat you stayed at, apparently. You were not seen by anybody during the whole of last week."

"That's exactly as I said it would be. Anything else?"

"Inspector Greaves, who's brighter than he likes people to think he is, had to guess where you would want to go yesterday that was so urgent. He worked out that you would probably go to Gartree to report to Carl Packer—assuming, of course, that you'd strangled Philomena as Packer's agent. So he phoned there. And you did visit Packer."

I could appreciate that she would be a good police officer. Her reports would be succinct and precise. She had left me in no doubt that I was in difficulties. Yet in the back of my mind was the fact that I'd already been mistaken in my assessment of one woman. I was not yet certain whether Lucy Rice was a police officer or a friend, and which one I was listening to. When in doubt, ask. So I did.

"Why've you told me this, Officer?" Making it formal.

"I didn't want you dashing in unprepared." She was challenging me to assume what I liked from that.

"That wasn't what I meant, and you know it. This . . . waiting here and warning me . . . surely it could get you into difficulties. You've got no reason to trust me. I could now turn around and drive away, and nobody would ever know I've been here."

"Except me."

"If I drove away and left you to explain to Greaves—"

"But you're not going to do that," she said with confidence. "Otherwise you wouldn't be concerned about me. And you've come back, anyway. No, you're not going running now, Paul."

"But how can you be so sure of that?"

"Something you said." Then, as I didn't ask, she told me. "About your father. If you'd had time to think, you said."

"So?"

"You've had time, and you're still here."

"Ah . . . yes."

"You're impulsive, Paul Manson. Act first, think later."

"Too true."

"I'm impulsive myself."

I allowed that to mature for a few seconds. "Trapped me, haven't you!"

"Only if my reckoning is correct."

The thrum of the rain on the roof, the interior light, the surrounding darkness, all these conspired to give an impression that we were the only two persons still existing.

I took a deep breath. "If you know I've seen Packer—"

"More important, I've seen your file. I know what you did. You wouldn't do it again, certainly not for money."

I stifled a laugh of delight; it would've come out shaky. "What a pity you're not in charge of this case, Lucy. You'll never make inspector, you know, if you let your personal feelings control your judgement."

"They're not my personal feelings," she told me severely. "They're the result of cold reason."

"Then I thank you for your crystal-clear mind, Lucy, and your lack of warmth. Now—forewarned and forearmed—I'll get along to The George."

I reached over and kissed her on the cheek. For a second she glanced at me with mischief in her eyes, then she was remote again. "Never kiss a police officer," she advised, nodding severely.

"Somehow I got the impression I wasn't talking to one. Lucy Rice, not Detective Sergeant Rice."

"Even off-duty, I'm still a policewoman."

"Then, ma'am, I apologise for the kiss. It wasn't one of my better efforts, anyway."

"Which are you apologising for, the fact or its performance?"

I reached back and shut the door again. It went dark inside the car, but I had no difficulty in locating her face, which was still wet and caught reflections on her cheeks wickedly. It still wasn't one of my better ones—you can't do much in a Fiesta. She drew away. My shirt was soaked from her slicker.

"I'll repeat," she whispered, "never kiss a police officer. It could get you into all sorts of trouble."

"I'm in that now."

"It could get worse," she warned. She opened her door. The light went on again. "Never kiss any other police officer. With either sex there'd be a ready charge."

"I'll remember that. Greaves wouldn't like it—you think?"

She slid out of the car and slammed the door. It cut off what she said, so that I only got, "Idi . . ."

I allowed her to get well clear, not wishing the headlights to slide over her. Then I drove to The George.

There was no alternative. My only chance of remaining free was to face Greaves and hope I could argue him into a certain amount of freedom. Besides, I could never face Lucy again if I turned and ran. If I did that, I might not even see her again. I had no choice.

I drove into the tiny cobbled yard beside the pub, allowing the lights to sweep across the windows, and even gave a short peep of the horn to indicate I was back. I tried the front door, and it was unlocked. I went in and slammed it behind me.

"We're in here." George shouted from the snug.

I went on through.

George, I could see, was keeping to traditional standards. He was feeding free beer to the police after hours, on the principle that it was illegal to sell it. The table bore empty and full tankards. Greaves looked pink and warm, but George knew how far he himself could go with his own beer, and was well in control.

"Had a good trip?" he asked.

"Profitable."

Greaves thrust back his chair and got to his feet. His features chased around until he found the face for officialdom. "Paul Manson," he said, "I am charging—"

"Heh, heh!" I interrupted. "Don't you take that as far as a warning. How does it go? Anything I say may be taken down, et cetera. Because then I wouldn't be able to say one word, which would include what I've found out."

"Found out?" said Greaves, slowly lowering himself into his seat.

I pulled over a chair and sat facing him. "You'll never guess where I've been," I said confidently. "George, is one of these for me?"

"No. But I could find you a pint. Bitter is it?"

"Please."

"Ada's gone to bed, but I could get you a sandwich."

"No, it's all right. Just the beer. And make it a half."

George had been very quick to pick up my lead. Bland confidence, that was what I had to feed Greaves, because one glance had told me that he was suffering from a struggle against outside influences. Not only had he to deal with a couple of murders, when his worst crimes had been no more than indecent exposure, but he had also become involved in a partnership with a much more forceful character than himself. Filey. He was being hustled and outmanoeuvred. On top of that there would be the thought that if he didn't clear it all up quickly his chief constable would ask the top county brass to take over.

Greaves, therefore, was in urgent need of an arrest, and at the moment I was this week's bargain offer. He clung desperately to my last interesting remark.

"And where *have* you been?" he asked grumpily, because he'd wanted to throw it at me.

"Go on. Guess."

His tankard banged on the table surface. "Where?"

"Gartree prison, to look up my old mates."

He stared at me above the rim of his tankard. His jowls wobbled, his nose twitched. "Such as who?" Then he plunged his lips for the rim, his mouth forming the correctly shaped spout before it reached it.

"Carl Packer."

"Well, now," said George at my shoulder, putting a brimming glass in front of me. "Fancy that. Who'd have thought it!"

"What did he have to say?" asked Greaves, his voice now far from slurring. There was a moustache of froth on his upper lip.

"You'll never guess—"

"A straight answer, Manson," he snapped, "or I take you in."

I caught George's eye. He shook his head gently, and his expression told me I'd already gone far enough.

"Carl Packer told me he *had* sent somebody to Philomena Wise," I said seriously. "Not me—he'd approached me before, but I'd backed off. No, it was Douglas French he hired. Frenchie. But the contract wasn't to kill her. Packer told me he didn't shoot that policeman. His name's Ted Adamson, by the way. He said that Miss Wise had lied at his trial."

"This is nonsense." Greaves spoke with complete conviction.

"Then why was he shocked when I told him she's dead? He was relying on her to get him his freedom. And he *was* shocked. The chief warder was there, and he can tell you. Phone the prison. His name's Pierce. He'll confirm that Packer was shocked."

George nodded solemnly and spoke to his beer. "It's a point."

"Never mind the points," Greaves grumbled. "What if he *was* shocked? Tell me that."

I knew then that I'd made a breakthrough. "It was Frenchie he sent, but it was only to offer her money for her to change her story and tell the truth. So why should he also send me along to kill her? It's contradictory. And it's no good falling back on Frenchie as a suspect because he couldn't have done it. Not like that. Not Frenchie."

"Another point," said George lugubriously, not looking at Greaves.

"So," I went on with growing confidence, "what we need to know is whether—"

"We?" barked Greaves. "We! When were you taken into the force, Manson?"

"I, then."

"Who cares what you need to know! It's what I need to know that matters." And his face set into an aggrieved expression of stern and craggy resolution.

"What *you* need to know," I went on, picking my way tenderly through the undergrowth so as not to trip over daisies, "is whether Frenchie did or did not make the offer to Philomena, and if she'd decided to accept it if he did do so."

Greaves waved his mug and spoke grandly, trying another tack in order to control the situation. "I feel no compunction to discover that."

"No," I agreed. Then I held my silence.

George stirred in his seat. He was embarrassed for Greaves, who had apparently drunk enough to muddle his thinking. Perhaps George blamed himself for that, though it would've been difficult to refuse a pint to somebody who wasn't paying. Cautiously, he assisted him.

"Manson is playing it cute, Inspector. He's got sources of information you can't reach. That's obvious." He looked at me from beneath lowered eyebrows. Suddenly his grey eyes were as expressive as Lucy's. "Isn't that so, Manson?"

"I find I've picked up quite a number of weird acquaintances," I admitted, thinking of Art. "And it does mean—subject to contradiction from you, Mr. Greaves—that the whole thing has come from that earlier case, when Packer was tried and convicted for a murder he says he didn't do."

"Tcha!" snapped Greaves. I was on his wavelength again. "They all say that."

"But if, in Packer's case, it was a true verdict, and he really did do it, why should he be upset when he heard of the death of the one person who knew the truth?"

Several pints separated the clarity of our respective thinking. But mine was blurred by the throb in my head from Felton's blow, and though Greaves was having to struggle with it we were on about level terms.

Abruptly placid, he thought about it, assisting the process by producing a scarred black pipe, which might have been a light cream colour before he introduced it to the black plug he now rubbed between his beefy palms. When he lit it I realised it was probably his principal interrogation weapon. One blast of that smoke in your face and you'd confess to anything. Even to smoking cigarettes.

"Interesting," he observed, sucking in six inches of flame from his lighter. "Interesting but iffy. If Packer didn't shoot the policeman. If Douglas French came here to make an offer to Miss Wise. If he made it. If she'd made a decision on it. Isn't it interesting that all these ifs disguise the fact that you're my prime suspect!"

He stabbed the pipe stem in my direction. "But you don't convince me, Manson. Oh no. Why the hell've you introduced this diversion? What the devil has the murder of a policeman in Killingham, two years ago, got to do with the strangling with a scarf of a young woman in Sumbury?"

Once again his ogre had raised its head. It was Filey who'd introduced the warehouse murder into the local investigation. Greaves resented that, but wherever he looked it leered at him.

I shrugged.

"Nothing!" he cried. "Strangling is a domestic crime. Who better to know that than you, Manson?"

It was a low blow. Greaves could inflict more discomfort with his voice than most coppers with a truncheon. Deliberately and carefully I answered him.

"But your case against me, Mr. Greaves, exists only on the assumption that I came here as a professional to commit a professional killing. In no way can you fit me in with a domestic killing involving Miss Wise."

George buried his mouth in his beer. I'd caught Greaves in mid-suck, and he coughed hackingly.

"Isn't that so?" I asked.

He rallied. "But you have a personal and perhaps emotional contact with Miss Philomena Wise." He managed that much before the cough got him again.

"Not the same one."

"They were both at Aubrey Wise's house that night," he said briskly.

"So you're arguing that I might have made a mistake in identity?"

"That's my argument."

"I made this mistake face to face?"

"It need not have been." There was no force to it. He was merely leading me on.

"The scarf was double-knotted," I said, displaying a knowledge I should not have possessed. "It would have been possible to have approached from behind, thrown the scarf over her head, and pulled it tight. And then held on until she was silent." I had to gulp there. It was not a pleasant thought. "But this was done from the front, and we know that because it would've been almost impossible to tie a double knot under her chin from behind. Agreed? Go on, agree to something."

He nodded, his eyes bright. "From the front."

"Then I could not have failed to recognise who I was killing. Oh, come on, Inspector, it would've been impossible. And double-knotted, as though there was a panic to get it done and be away from there."

He lifted his head. "I don't get that."

"Double-knotted to make sure it wouldn't work loose. Why? So that I'd be free to turn and run and leave her? Why would I need to run? I'd have had all the time in the world."

He cleared his throat, stared with disgust at his pipe, and looked back at me. "You make a point. I wonder, though, where you get all your information, if you weren't there, on the spot."

This was soggy ground. I didn't want to tell him too much about Art, and I wondered how much he knew about Lucy's activities. I trod carefully round the issue. "So if you've made up your mind . . ."

"Mind? What about?"

"I'd like to know where I'm going to sleep, because I need it, believe me. Here or at the station? If you could make up your mind . . ."

I heard the front door slam, then a voice. "Where are you? Ah, there you are, all matey and sloshed."

Filey strode into the snug. There was a briskness about him, preceding him like wind ahead of a thunderstorm. Not one of us uttered a word of welcome, but Filey was quite capable of ignoring such things. He wouldn't have acknowledged a direct snub if he'd tripped over it.

He walked over to the table, missing nothing. A finger jerked out, nearly prodding my forehead.

"He's been fighting again. Left any more bodies hanging around, Manson?"

I stared at him, not amiably. He grinned lopsidedly, the corner of his mouth twitching. Then he forgot me and turned to Greaves.

"You charged him yet?"

Greaves took his pipe out of his mouth to say, "No."

"Just as well. He's rubbish. It's no good wasting words on him."

He was on an emotional high. This was not the attacking, sneering approach he'd previously used on me, but a jaunty confidence designed to carry everything before him. Only the dark patches beneath his eyes betrayed his intense weariness. He was pushing himself to the limit.

Greaves lifted his eyebrows. He had no words to waste on Filey, either.

Filey allowed his hand to float above the empties on the table. "Any going spare?"

"Afraid not, Inspector," George said, also expressionless. "It's way after closing time."

"By heaven, so it is. Will you look at the time! We'd better get moving, Greaves."

But Greaves looked as immovable as he could, like a plaster cast of himself. He allowed himself a few dry words. "Where do you suggest?"

"I know who killed your Miss Wise. Let's go and pick him up. It's time to put an end to it."

"Pick who up?" Greaves poked at the dottle in his pipe with the sharp end of his reamer.

"Arthur Torrance."

"There's a difficulty in that. The scarf . . ." He blew through the stem.

"I can explain all that. Come on, let's rake him in."

"Thank you for the offer, but no."

"Please yourself. I'll arrest him for you."

Greaves spoke so quietly that he barely disturbed the air. His pipe held his attention. "Any arrests around here will be made by me, Mr. Filey. This isn't one of 'em."

Filey was stirred to bitter anger, moving round in small circles chasing his nerves. "You know I can make an arrest anywhere—"

Greaves stabbed downwards. The point of his pipe-prodder stuck quivering in the table surface. "Not here." Then he lifted his head, and I was surprised at the fury in his eyes. His calm voice had not hinted at it. "If you'll let me explain about the scarf—"

"To hell with the scarf." Filey gestured it away. "I can cover that. Are you coming or not?"

"I am not coming, and you are not going there."

Filey made a sound of disgust and turned away, his shoulders hunched. "It's about time one of us did something."

Greaves's voice cracked out. It stopped Filey in mid-pace. He'd heard only a gentle swish from the whip before, now he heard the snap. "Do what I say, or I'll have you out of this town, Filey. Quietly. Officially or otherwise. No fuss. A word to my squad, you know how it works. You won't be able to move a finger in any direction I'm not pointing. Do I make myself clear?"

Filey was half turned. His eyes were narrowed and his glare killed the head on my beer. He said nothing.

"Your patch is Killingham," Greaves went on. "Your murder was there. It's not here. Nothing for you here. It's a domestic matter. Do you understand?"

"My God, you're a great help!" Filey snapped. Then he was out of the door, slamming everything in his way to the open air.

"This damned pipe's not drawing," Greaves complained. "Is there any more beer, George?"

"No," said George. "Could find you a short, though." It was a time for celebration.

"Ah yes!" Greaves prodded again with his instrument.

I hardly dared to raise my voice, in case I attracted his anger, but I risked it. "Can I go to bed now?"

Still prodding, Greaves asked, "Who've you been fighting?"

"That was domestic, too."

"Don't play with me, Manson. Who?"

"Grant Felton."

"That figures. Now get off to bed with you. I've got some thinking to do."

I downed the flat inch of my beer and complied. The last I saw of him he was blowing something very nasty from the stem of his pipe, and beaming at it in triumph.

I was beginning to realise where I stood—dead in the middle. I knew both sides of the legal war, the criminal and the police. At this time I was neither, simply a civilian who was involved and in some ways informed. So I was both suspect and investigator, with no more than a moral obligation to discover the truth. Moral? Well, yes. It was I who had triggered it, who had been the cause of Dorothy Mann's coming here, which had brought about the death of Philomena. All right—so I couldn't be certain of that. But I couldn't leave before there was something in all this mess of which I could feel certain.

With this self-justification firmly in my mind, and exhausted from the last two days of effort, I turned my steps towards the bed, but I don't remember reaching it.

THIRTEEN

There is a vast difference between walking up to a house and driving up to it, especially if it's on a steep slope. With the car, I arrived with no shortness of breath or excess of perspiration.

I swept up to the frontage of Seagulls, parked, and got out as though I owned the place. This time I had not been observed, because no one appeared. It was a dull day, with the rain hanging around over the sea. The run of glass along the frontage looked black, offering an oppressive welcome. No one would be out at the pool.

I first walked to the corner of the building and peered along its side. There was an array of garages, set well back, like the rear of a housing estate. Two of them had their doors open. Two expensive vehicles were on display, and I knew at once that one of them was what had been intended as Philomena's birthday present.

Also on display was Grant Felton himself, hovering round the very neat black BMW 320i, with its top down. This was how it would've been presented to Philomena. If he'd also hidden her engagement ring somewhere inside it, I guessed he'd have recovered it by now.

He hadn't heard me, and was standing with his fists on his hips, three feet of cleaning rag dangling from the fingers of one of them, his head tilted. The zest would have gone from any aspect of cleaning or polishing, now that there was no point. Nevertheless, he couldn't stop. It occupied his mind, stopped it from wandering where he dared not venture. The car shone. There was no possibility of improving it, but he had a bucket of water against a side wall and the rag looked wet. Somebody had given him an old sheet to tear up.

"Nice car," I said, pleasantly enough. "This the one with the six-cylinder engine?" I wandered up towards it.

He whirled round, like a startled kangaroo, poised to fly at me, his fists now well clear of his sides.

"Get lost! Ya hear me! Bloody jailbird." His voice was contained, menace in every word, but quiet.

"What the hell's the matter with you?" I asked.

"Why ain't they got you inside?"

Was that it? He believed I'd killed Philomena! Yet who but Dorothy could have fed him that idea? In a sudden surge of anger I snapped out, "She'll have told you more than that. Give your brain a rest, cobber."

I didn't know what a cobber was. Perhaps it's an insult over there. He took a slow pace forward.

"I'll kill ya, you bastard!"

His fury was too bitter to be real. He was poised, with every muscle tingling for attack. I watched his right hand as it swung back idly, trailing the yard-long streamer of rag. It was only subliminally that I recognised the movement, then I knew. He was going to snap it at me. A glance at his eyes, with all their menace focussed on me, that was all I could spare, then I had to watch the end of the rag whipping towards my face, to try to duck, to bring up my left hand to protect my eyes. It cracked at me like a heavy bullwhip.

They'd done this sort of thing in the changing room at my prep school. A wet towel snapped at a naked buttock could raise weals. A wet cleaning rag could take out an eye. It got me across the back of my hand, hot pain rushing through it. He was shouting—an Aboriginal war cry, perhaps. I heard the rag whistling again, and frantically dived forward to get inside its arc.

My head took him in the chest. He went back into the boot of the car, and I heard the air whoosh out of him. For a second he couldn't bring himself upright, and I used the interval to plant my right fist on his nose.

And stepped back. Dazed, he raised the wet rag to his face, his eyes flinching above it. I could have finished him off right there and then, but the fight had gone out of him, and what was the point? He was a pitiful fake, I realised, a macho puppet, all show-off and nothing but strutting ego.

"Here," I said. "This'll stop it bleeding. A cold shock . . ."

I finished the sentence by throwing the bucket of water over him. It was a pity that the top of the car was down.

I walked away from him. His comments followed me. "Bleedin' pommy slob!" At full pitch.

The back of my left hand was red, and was swelling. The knuckles of my right hand were sore. I cursed him, found the bell-push, and waited. The house seemed dead and empty, but by the time

I'd decided to ring again the door swung open. It was Aubrey Wise himself.

"*Now* what do you want?" he demanded wearily.

I was getting used to studying people closely, so that now I realised his pose of masterful top executive was suffering under the strain. On his own subject, finance and management, he would no doubt be very telling, but anything else, such as a domestic crisis, left him helpless. Steadily, the tragedy of his daughter's death was undermining him. His eyes were moving round with no certainty as to purpose. Except perhaps for escape. There had been no authority in his voice.

"I'm sorry to disturb you again—"

"Haven't you brought us enough trouble?" It was a plea. No more, no more, he cried silently.

I didn't think I was wholly responsible, but I didn't say so. "It's your wife I really wanted to see."

"That would not be possible." But his phrasing indicated he could see no valid reason to refuse.

"I don't want to upset her . . ."

"I'll not have it."

"But perhaps she wouldn't mind." I was speaking very gently. "I wonder if you'd care to ask her for me."

I was like a tap dripping, jangling his nerves with persistence.

"She can't bear to hear one word about our daughter."

Our daughter? Not Philomena. Not my darling child. But . . . our daughter. So she was that to him, connected by a slim cord of filial devotion, the devotion being to the effort he'd expended in an attempt to sever it. Perhaps he hated his daughter, for the shame and distress she had brought. To him the shame would be personal, in the same way as it used to be thought that shame was deserved by the raped girl, when the shame was the rapist's to bear. I didn't think his wife would feel the same. She'd be a strange mother if she didn't want to speak about her daughter. On and on, unendingly.

"Could you ask her?" I asked gravely.

He made an annoyed little click with his tongue, and turned away. "You'd better come in." I prowled the corridor, staring sightlessly at the paintings. They stared back, uninspiring.

He returned. "She will see you." Like royalty. "But I intend to be present." Not conceding too much.

Did he think I was going to bully her? Or was I expected to try to trick her into indiscretions?

"Thank you. That's all I'm asking."

This time it was a small living room, and if it was darkened by half-drawn shades it was not from bereavement, but to protect the lady's eyes.

There wasn't much to look at, anyway, the furnishings matching the heavy velvet curtains, hideous ornaments and the dreary tock of a clock, marking off each second closer to the grave. A room to which you could bring your miseries. They lay thick underfoot, waiting to be picked up and fondled, and their harrowing memory revived.

She was seated in a winged easy chair, placidly, dressed in a plain grey blouse and a black skirt long enough to enable her to rest her clasped hands in her lap without displaying her legs. I had the impression that she had reached the chair just before I entered, dragged from her Jane Austen.

She inclined her head, and the light caught it. She had blond hair so pale you wouldn't notice that it had turned grey.

"If you will sit there," she said.

It was a light, musical voice, but with a reserve of strength behind it. I've heard the same in Wagner, just before Brünnhilde lets fly on a high note. So I was not impressed, merely braced for whatever was to come. The chair she had indicated was directly facing her, a Hepplewhite which he had intended to be looked at rather than sat on. My stay was to be limited.

I made a murmuring sound of compliance, and sat. I couldn't see what had happened to Aubrey, and licked the back of my left hand.

"And you are?" she asked.

"My name is Paul Manson. I'm a friend of Dorothy Mann. I knew her as Philomena Wise in Killingham."

"I've heard of you." There was no longer any need to dispute the fact that Dorothy Mann was known there.

"I wanted to talk to you about the real one. Your daughter."

"But you didn't know her?"

"No. We never met."

Now that my eyes were getting used to the gloom, I could see her more clearly. She had what must have been a pretty face, though with a nose too long for it, and now it had the smooth appearance of well-tended skin. Her eyes were dark. Even without the assistance of reflected light they blazed with an internal passion. Her mouth was firm, but there were stress lines around it. She compressed it often. With disapproval, no doubt.

Here was the strength of the marriage. She was the driving force behind Aubrey, and the force that had tried to drive her daughter, though perhaps she had succeeded only in driving her in the wrong direction.

She had hesitated a long while before deciding what to say next. "If you never met her," she said at last, "I can't understand your interest."

"I'd have liked very much to have met Philomena," I told her, and even to me it sounded empty of sincerity. "I'm now in a position of being deeply involved with her . . . with what happened to her."

"And why is that?" she asked politely, but with distant interest.

"Because the police are building up a case against me. In sheer self-defence I need to know more about her, who her friends were and who she'd approach for advice. That sort of thing."

To my surprise she gave a strange little snigger, as though I'd made a joke, a slightly blue one. But no, it seemed it was only an expression of bitter cynicism, judging by what she said next.

"You'd have difficulty in understanding Mena, young man. That's what we called her—Mena. And you're not young enough to relate . . . is that what they say these days? . . . relate to her. She was always a difficult child, obstructive and sulky, and even argumentative. She managed to give the impression that she demanded something from us we couldn't give, yet we were always generous in our help and advice."

She touched her lips with a handkerchief. It was real lace, and wafted a musky scent at me.

"Of course," she went on, as though he wasn't there, "her father was useless. With a boy he might have related—there it is again—related to him. With a girl it was difficult, though if she asked for it he gave her money. Whatever she wanted. And he was generous in his advice on how to invest it."

Again she hesitated. I caught on a half smile and suppressed it. For a second I'd suspected her of humour, even if it was something that had gone sour with age and disuse. But no, I decided, she had simply stated fact. There was no murmur of protest from Aubrey, who was now no more than a pattern on the wallpaper.

"And I," she said with distant pride, "did what I could for a young girl in the way of moral advice. Don't you think, young man, that personal morality is so very important in an age when society is in danger of crumbling from a lack of self-discipline? So I taught her morality. Tried to, but they have no use for that these days. In my day . . . but never mind that . . . but now they use sex as casually as they do a knife and fork. For pleasure!" she cried, her voice thin with disgust and long-repressed emotion.

I said nothing. It was clear why they had only one child. I murmured encouragingly.

"No," she decided, "I think I was quite correct in not trying to advise her on sexual matters. But on social morality I did what I could. She was a girl who could have cultivated the most refined friends. There were numerous opportunities for improving relationships. But she rejected all my offers to help. Ungrateful child. She went her own wild way, and associated with riff-raff from the streets. And of course . . . well, you know where she finished— in court." She nodded, tight-lipped.

"But as a witness," I tried in consolation.

She rejected it with a break in her voice. "She *knew* them!" Her voice faltered, and she went on close to a whisper. "How *could* she have done this to me! I tried. I argued, I discussed, I pointed out the ways in which she'd been led astray. But she rejected me. She went off with that crowd of . . . of back-street thugs."

I thought that in Philomena's position I too would perhaps have gone off. With anybody, for a little light relief. Dracula, if necessary.

"A great disappointment," I murmured, moving uneasily and cursing Hepplewhite.

She had pulled herself together, looking down at her fingers, which were tearing the handkerchief to pieces. Then she looked up. Her eyes were as dominating as ever. "If I've been of any assistance . . ."

"Thank you, yes. I take it, then, that she'd have hesitated to confide in you?" What a useless question! I was trying only to keep the conversation going, feeling my way.

"I'd have been very surprised."

"A man came to this district, to see her, to make her an offer—"

"As though I'd know about that." She cut me off shortly.

"If he managed to contact her, and did make the offer, it would've given your daughter one or two problems to worry about. She might have needed advice. Urgently."

She was shaking her head. "She'd have made her own decisions. She was very wilful."

"But Dorothy Mann has been staying with you," I suggested. "Would your daughter have confided in Miss Mann?"

"That is conceivable."

"Even have asked for her advice?"

"Possibly."

"Do you know if she did? Did you hear them discussing anything kind of secret?"

She lifted her head in surprise. It was as though I'd suggested she would lower herself to eavesdropping. "Certainly not." Then she unbent a little. "They were friends. Always whispering together."

"She's not here now?"

"Not at this moment. She's been staying with us until all this dreadful business is over. Now . . . if you have nothing more to say . . . I am feeling very tired."

I was glad to comply with her suggestion, and got to my feet. I was tired and stiff and frustrated. But I didn't say so.

"Thank you for seeing me, Mrs. Wise. I'm much obliged. I'll show myself out."

"Certainly not," she said, lifting her chin. "Aubrey. Show Mr. . . . er . . . er . . . out, please."

Aubrey separated himself from the shadows, appearing at my elbow with stately dignity. "This way," he said, as though I didn't know.

We went back through the house. We saw nobody. There was silence. Such a large and magnificent home, with so few people rattling around in it! How would they manage to extract their full quota of enjoyment from it unless they moved quickly from one room to the other, perhaps completing the circuit in a week? Shall we go to the Thursday room and have an exciting game of Scrabble? No, we're in the Friday room today. Yes of course—didn't you have a grand piano put in it last Saturday—I must see it.

"I'm afraid," he was saying as we reached the front door, "you'll have to make allowances for my wife. It's the shock. My wife is not herself."

Had I not, then, met the true Mrs. Wise? "I appreciate that. Will you let Miss Mann know that I called?"

"Yes, of course, though we don't expect her back until quite late." He closed the door behind me.

There was no sign of Grant Felton, with whom I might have engaged in casual conversation. I walked round the side, but the garage was closed. A pity. Philomena might have confided in Felton, and with a bit of persuasion he might have been prepared to tell me her intentions.

Which left me, I realised as I sat in the car, with a day to fill in, and with no way I could see of forwarding the investigation. If that was what I was doing. Yes, I decided, it was. How the professional investigators managed to keep themselves amused, in between discovering clues, I couldn't imagine. Watch them on the telly and they're at it all the time, not a moment free from action, violent or amorous.

All I had was one clue. It seemed that Philomena could have confided to Dorothy more than she'd admitted. But Dorothy would not be there until late. The day drooped ahead.

It now seemed imperative to discover whether Frenchie had actually contacted Philomena and made the offer, and what she'd intended to do about it if he had. Perhaps she herself hadn't been certain.

I drove to Port Sumbury, where all the action should have been, yachts moving in and out and sails being run up.

It was not like that. I pulled on to the parking patch. The season having finished, there was no attendant at the hut. George's bicycle was still between the shed and the wall. I left it there. I was the only car visitor so far that day, and I had the whole car-park to myself. It was confusing. Usually the choice is made for you, the one empty slot. With all the choice in the world, I did a couple of circuits, and finally parked nose in to the far wall, got out, and had a look around.

The place had died, as though everyone had fled from a deadly plague. Too late for any holiday-makers, and the locals were skulking in their cottages. You couldn't blame them. The clouds, racing in from the sea, were heavy and black. It was a day of gloom and despondency, when depression could easily become despair, and the sea could become inviting. I stared over the wall, and there the sea was, ten feet below me, and already tramping in to make it less. The bitter, cutting wind lashed in at my face, and the grey water was broken into white-caps far out, as the seabed shoaled. The tide was coming in fast. Spray was reaching up to me as the waves rushed in, excited to discover the stone barrier.

This was the wall by which Frenchie's body had been found, initially by me. It might even have been where my car was now parked, though I couldn't remember accurately. And here were the rocks, loosened from the wall by the persistent sea. But at that time it'd been dark, and many more cars had been here. It would have been easy to stalk him. No, not easy. Frenchie had possessed ears like satellite reflectors. It would, however, have been noisy with the sea. Or had it? Surely the tide had been out?

Putting my head down against the wind, I went to look at the yacht basin, which is more accurately descriptive than harbour. The vessels were stirring uneasily as the water surged in and lifted them. It would have been a fool who raised his sails that day. Nobody so much as lifted a head. I walked back, wondering whether to drive away, and wondering where to.

Art was sitting in the passenger's seat. I unlocked the driver's door and slid in, slamming it after me.

"I locked it," I said, not severely, because Art provided a break in the boredom.

"I know. Wastin' your time, weren't you!"

"You're in a grand mood, I can tell that. Why d'you have to inflict it on me?"

He took that to be rhetorical and didn't reply. He was down, right down. Port Sumbury on a grey, wet morning was no place to bring a fit of the miseries.

"What shall we do," I asked at last, "play 'I Spy' to raise a laugh?"

"Manson," he told me, "I'm about fed up to the eyeballs with your funnies."

I stared at him. His eyes were morosely ahead at the blown spume that speckled the windscreen. This wasn't the Art I knew. Where was the sparkle, the self-approval?

"What's got into you?"

"What you said—I bin thinkin' about it. A trap, you called it, and you ain't kiddin'. What'm I gonna do, Paul, for Chrissake?"

"Sit it out," I advised, "as I told you."

He pouted. "It's not Filey. He's haunting me, but he don't scare me—just gets on my nerves. It's Carl Packer . . . *he* scares me. Scares the pants right off me."

Now at last he turned and faced me. There were dark shadows under his eyes, which wouldn't settle. They flicked over my face, then away.

"Yes," I agreed encouragingly, "that's where your worry is. Packer. But he's safely tucked away at the moment, and I reckon he won't send somebody to get you. He'd have done that before now. No—he wants to keep you for himself. What's Filey been saying to you?"

He turned back to look sightlessly out over the sea. "Not sayin' anything. He's just there all the time, watching me."

I guessed that Art's imagination might be entering into the situation. If anybody was keeping an eye on him, as was very likely, it would be a lowly detective constable, not Filey.

"He had a go at me last night," I said. "Called me rubbish."

But Art wasn't going to be interested in my concerns. He hadn't changed that much. "Go for a cup o' coffee, an' there he is at one of the other tables. Go for a slash, an' there he is in the next stall. Pretends he don't know me. It gets y' down. I tell you, I'm thinkin' of making a run for it."

"I shouldn't do that. It's probably what he's hoping for."

"What else, then? What else?"

So perhaps it wasn't his imagination. Filey, after all, would have no authority to issue orders to the force in a strange district. He would have to do his own legwork, particularly after what Greaves had said to him. I wondered why Filey hadn't been re-called to Killingham. Was he taking a spot of leave in order to wage a personal vendetta?

"It's a war of nerves," I decided.

"Great. Just what I need, that is! That lump o' granite ain't got no nerves."

Yes he had, I thought, he lived on his nerves. That he also chewed into other people's was a corollary to his efforts.

"You could always put an end to it," I suggested casually. "Go to Greaves and tell him you killed Ted Adamson." No response. "You could do that."

He was nodding. "Oh yeah! Sure I could." Then he turned to face me abruptly. "Y' know, Paul, I thought it'd all go away, in time. Kind'f fade from me mind. But it don't. I can still see it, that big oaf . . ." He stopped, his eyes on mine. Then he looked down. "Can I ask y' somethin'?"

"Ask what you like." I was still off-hand about it, but Art was actually talking to me. For the first time. Before, it had been nothing but smart back-chat.

"About . . . inside. You know. Prison. D'you mind?"

I minded like hell. I smiled, because he'd thought I might. "Not at all." He'd been inside—he ought to know.

"Kind'f, bein' there and payin' for what you'd done, sort of. You know." He looked up again suddenly, his face drawn and his eyes bright. "Did it make it better?" But he hadn't been paying in full.

Barely breathing the words, in order not to disturb the mood, I said, "Make what better, Art?"

"What y' felt about it. What you remembered an' thought. I mean . . . did it help to get it outa your mind?"

Now, as at no other time, I had to be completely honest with him. "No, Art, it didn't. You just get more time to think about it. There was just one thing—they, the rest of the world, they reckoned I was paying a debt. Me . . ." I shrugged. "I came out still believing I owed something."

"A great help you are."

"But now I know I was wrong. I didn't owe anything to anybody. I was just fooling myself. All it was—I was starting again from scratch. Look at it like that."

"Yeah. Like that. Fine." He pouted, and stared again at the windscreen.

"Listen," I said, digging deeply for a cheerful voice. "There's that place over the way. Let's see if we can get some lunch. That'll liven you up."

He twisted round and eyed the hotel with contempt. "Looks too high an' mighty to me."

"They'll take our money. Come on, hop out. I'll lock your door, if you don't want to take the trouble."

"Yah!" he said, slamming it.

I urged him into the hotel. I didn't tell him I'd just caught a glimpse of Filey, who'd been entering a red phone box on the corner.

What had seemed to be a salt-scarred shell from the outside turned out to be a plush Victorian hotel inside, hushed but welcoming, though it was clear that dining guests were not expected, the reception desk being dark and deserted. It was a residential hotel, at this time of the year housing only those retired and too poor to go anywhere else, but not poor enough to have to live on the streets.

I pinged the bell on the desk, and it drew forth a man, nodding and smiling.

"May we have lunch?"

He was the *maître d'hôtel*, the waiter, and probably the cook as well. He said, "Certainly, sir. The dining room is through there. Sit where you like."

There were six elderly couples and two single old ladies already in occupation. We found a table. We ordered—choice of one. The food was plain but wholesome, not exactly filling, but they catered for depleted appetites. Art cheered up a little.

"I could hide out here."

"Sure you could. A white beard and bleached hair, and fend off advances from the two old dears over there."

He grinned. It was a welcome sight. We ate a leisurely meal, the waiter-cum-everything being as old as the residents, and left, feeling warmer if not full.

It had started to drizzle when we got outside. Then I realised it was flying sea-spray, and in fact the sea had begun to boom against the wall. The wind caught it and flung it at us. In the harbour, the yachts were moving uneasily at their moorings. We stepped out for the protection of the car.

In an anorak, and with an old peaked cap pulled low over his eyes, Detective Inspector Filey was leaning back against the boot.

"So there you are," he said.

FOURTEEN

Art stopped dead. I, not having his reactions or his incentive, was half a step later. All the same, I sensed him stiffen. In the corner of my eye I saw his chin go down and dig in. I knew he'd recognised the smile of satisfaction on Filey's face. This was the kill.

"Easy," I said softly. "It's all right, Art."

He grunted. I stepped back to stand at his shoulder, in case I had to grab his arm. Behind us I heard vehicles coming to an abrupt halt, and turned. Two police cars were now parked across the carpark entrance, blocking it. From one of them stepped Inspector Greaves and Lucy Rice, from the other came two large and impressive constables in uniform.

Art panicked, and before I could grab him he'd made a break for it. I made no move to go after him, as the constables were already running beyond the two side boundary walls, covering them, their heads going lower as they ran towards the sea. There were undisciplined rocks clattering there, I could tell. They stumbled, but they covered the territory as far as they could go, and Art had no way of escape. Filey didn't need to make a move; he scorned it. His expression was of amused contempt.

Art finished up with his back to the seaward wall. Beyond him the spray threw itself upwards unevenly. The waves were heavy against the wall. For one second he glanced over, and in that instant he was silhouetted against a backdrop of white water.

I shouted, "Art . . . no!"

He turned and looked at me, his eyes wild. Filey laughed.

Greaves and Lucy advanced steadily towards us, Greaves using the time to assess the situation. Lucy was wearing slacks and a loose jacket, a thin, inadequate outfit. She'd been dragged, unprepared, from the office, and already she was looking pinched with the cold. Greaves had thrown on an old donkey jacket, and was wearing trousers that were faded and blotched into decrepitude. The wind caught his sparse hair and threw it about.

I realised that Filey had forced a showdown in circumstances that made it difficult to back away and leave him to it. It was the culmination of Filey's morning of watching and tailing. Greaves had to see it through, but he didn't seem about to give assistance.

Ten yards away, they came to a halt. For several seconds nobody moved. Greaves then took his pipe from his pocket, and turned his back on us as he sheltered his flame-thrower inside the jacket's flap. He emerged. Smoke was whipped away behind him.

"What's this then?" he asked.

Filey had to raise his voice as the sea boomed behind him. He levered himself away from my car. "This not being my patch, I thought you'd better make the arrest, Inspector Greaves." This was gravely formal for Filey, but his tone left no doubt that he wasn't going to waste time on niceties. To give him his due, he didn't give up easily.

Greaves puffed placidly. "Who are we charging?" He glanced round as though there was a choice. I shook my head. Not me.

"Bright-boy here, Arthur Torrance," said Filey.

"I thought we'd cleared this away. The charge?"

"The murder by strangling of Philomena Wise." Filey tossed his head, as though throwing out a bluff.

"It's a lie!" Art shouted. "It's a bloody lie. You tell 'em, Paul." His shoulders were black with spray.

I shrugged. I'd warned him, after all. I caught Lucy's eye. She gave a little grimace, but the devil was back in her eyes. There was no indication in her attitude that she was in a supporting role to an officer who would probably be no match for the driving impetus of Filey.

"Have you made the charge?" asked Greaves, stalling for time. The previous evening's clash still stood between them.

"I left that for you. Come on, Greaves, it's damned cold standing here."

Greaves pointed the pipe stem at him. "When I'm satisfied I'll make a move. In the meantime"—he turned fractionally so that he faced Art—"you will be silent." There had appeared a snap in his voice. "Do you understand?"

Art shouted, "It ain't fair! He can say anythin', and I can't."

"You'll have your say. Now, Mr. Filey, let's hear this case of yours."

"Oh, we *are* gritty!" said Filey jauntily. "I can give you the details back at your office. Charge the young devil, and we can talk there."

Greaves thought about that. He made a great performance out of making up his mind. "I'll tell you what, Mr. Filey. When I hear a logical theory, then I'll make a charge. As things stand, I don't think we need to hurry things. Or make an unnecessary scene. Do you get my point?" He was being heavily patient.

For one second his eyes had slid over Art, who had the top edge of the wall digging into the small of his back. There was terror in Art's eyes. Greaves frowned. He didn't want a tragedy on his hands.

Filey missed the point. He said, "These big-town small-fry learn all the smart talk. You aren't used to it. Let me tell you—"

"Can we hear your case, please, Mr. Filey. Perhaps we should go and sit in the car? He's not going anywhere." Greaves was quite placid, but his voice grated.

"No!" shouted Art. He saw himself deserted. For some reason he trusted Greaves, but he believed Greaves would emerge from the car grim-faced and decided, without Art having been able to offer his side of it.

Filey realised this. It didn't suit him either. Perhaps he preferred something more theatrical. "I want him to hear this. Let him listen and know we've got him. Down to the finest detail. Let him squirm. Look at him, sweating already." He turned to confirm this. It was sea spray that streamed down Art's face, but Filey's words were having their effect. "If that's what you want, Greaves, then let him listen and take what action he likes."

Greaves's eyebrows had been rising steadily at this. Lucy stared with fascination at Filey, then lowered her eyes. Art was making backward flapping motions with his palms against the sea wall. I couldn't hear the sound of them.

"Your case!" demanded Greaves, his face set.

"You know most of it." Filey glanced at me, inviting me to share his contempt for Greaves. I stared through him. His eyes slid back to Greaves. "The young rat left Killingham to visit his old bit of tumble from the days when she lived there. She probably didn't want him any more. Got herself six feet of moneyed Aussie, hadn't she! Why would she give one thought to a work-shy lout from Killingham, with nothing to offer her?"

"Can we keep to the point?" asked Greaves flatly.

"Yeah!" cried Art. "Keep your opinions to yerself!" Art fighting back, that was, but he winced as he said it. This was the nudge technique, hoping for a hint of retreat.

Greaves prodded the pipe in his direction. "Be silent. I warn you. Go on, Mr. Filey, if you please."

Filey lifted his shoulders and jerked the peak of his cap. "I know him. As thick-skinned as a buffalo, so he wasn't going to be put off, and he headed in her direction to try his luck again. All it cost him was a cheap scarf. He got it gift-wrapped, phoned her, and made an appointment to meet her at seven at the bus stop. All right so far, Mr. Greaves?"

"I'm managing to hang on. Proceed."

"And he says he waited there until seven-fifteen. And he says he got worried. And he says he ran back towards town and phoned her house, and heard she'd left before seven. Or so he says—"

"That is confirmed," Greaves intruded. "Mrs. Wise is sure of the time of his call. We all accept that."

"We agree on something! Fine. So he claims he's so worried about her safety that he dashes out of that phone box and leaves his present behind. Have you ever heard . . . of *course* he didn't! It was already tied round the throat of Miss Philomena Wise, that's why."

I had difficulty in dragging my eyes from Filey's face, but I had to keep a wary eye on Art. He'd already heard all this from me, so he'd had time to examine it in his mind and admit to himself it had a certain validity. And Art was falling apart. Ahead of Filey in his exposition, he was also ahead in his reactions to it. Terror gripped Art. His eyes met mine in appeal, and with something of an accusation. I shook my head. It seemed to make him worse.

I had missed a few words, but it didn't seem to matter. Greaves was saying, ". . . but we know all this, Mr. Filey. What we don't know is why he went to the house if he'd killed her. Why he wouldn't simply disappear, taking his scarf with him. Can you explain that?"

"What you're doing," Filey told him with condescension, "is letting the scarf confuse you. What *is* this scarf, anyway? A magic scarf? Something the genie kept in his bottle to polish the inside of the glass? It was in two places at once, according to what this genius here told you. But in fact it was in only one. Round her neck. But he couldn't just run away and leave it, because he was caught in his own little trap. And," he said heavily, "he couldn't take it away with him."

"May we hear your theory?" asked Greaves politely.

Filey flicked the peak of his cap with his thumb, then he turned to face Art, walked towards him, and stood one pace away, holding out his right hand. "Let's have it, laddie."

Art stared at him, mesmerised. "What?"

"Your blade, your knife, wherever you've got it hidden."

Wild triumph lit Art's dulled eyes. Innocence of this charge he could assert with confidence. "Don't be stupid, I never carry one."

"Never?"

"Y' think I'm crazy!" Art cried.

Filey smiled. Then he turned back to face Greaves, calmly presenting his unprotected back. "There! He never carries a knife. Don't you see?"

"It's cold. Can we get on with it?"

Slowly and gently, so as not to catch Filey's eye, I began to edge sideways along the wall.

In marked contrast to his previous attitude, the sign of a born orator, Filey modulated his voice to a spurious solemnity. "He went to meet her. He'd assume she couldn't wait to see his smiling face again. He *did* meet her, at that patch of woodland, and he offered her his present. She unwrapped it while she told him she'd found somebody more appealing. Maybe she draped the scarf round her neck."

He half turned and threw his voice into the wind at Art. "And what then? It'd need only a cross-armed grab at the ends of the scarf, and a yank, and a double knot . . ."

With contempt he turned his back to Art again. Art's legs were failing him. Only his grip on the wall kept him upright.

"And there's your answer, Mr. Greaves."

Greaves looked puzzled. "Where?"

A hint of impatience sharpened Filey's voice. "The reason he did all the rest, running back to the phone to make that call, then to the house. You see, he couldn't untie the scarf, and he doesn't carry a knife." Without glancing round this time, he raised his voice to a shout. "Care to disprove *that*, Torrance?"

The offer of his back was for Art to prove that he carried one. Art clung to the wall.

"So he had to make up that stupid story," Filey explained to Greaves. "For God's sake, it all fits!"

Greaves didn't seem convinced. He was moodily tapping the pipe against his heel, and spoke down to it. "I'm not satisfied."

Filey lifted his chin. "All right, then, if you don't want to do it, I will. We'll argue about it later." He whirled to face Art. "Arthur Torrance, I'm arresting you for . . ." The words pressed against the wind.

"No!" Art croaked, forcing himself firmer into the wall. "You can't . . ."

Then he had turned and was hoisting himself up, the spray framing him as he slipped and fumbled frantically. I'd already started moving. I dived for his legs and caught them, but he was kicking and screaming hysterically. My left shoulder went painfully into the wall, and he toppled down on me, like a peeled clam from a wet wall. I hung on, then I felt him being hauled to his feet, and I pulled myself up his body until I reached an arm. Lucy had her fingers clasped on his other one. I spoke quickly into Art's ear. "Be quiet, you young fool. Say nothing."

He turned to face me, but without recognition. It was too late to reason with him. He mouthed something, but it came out all burbling with sea water. His eyes were wild, hunting for a way out.

Filey stood in front of him as we held him. There was no way Art could avoid the lashing of his tongue.

"Arthur Torrance, I am charging you with the murder of Philomena Wise. You do not have to say anything, but anything you do say will be taken down and may be used in evidence. Have you anything to say?"

And Filey's eyes were as wild as Art's.

I could see no sign of notebooks. Nothing was being taken down. Greaves had moved forward a few feet, but seemed unimpressed.

Art said nothing. He felt stiff and tense in my hands. He spat sea water at Filey. I think.

"There now," said Filey with satisfaction. Then, in his relaxation after the effort, he took it one move too far. "We'll put you away for life. Maybe in Gartree. You'll like that, Torrance. All your old friends'll be there. Such as Carl Packer."

It was the wrong thing to say to Art at that time. For a moment I thought we were going to lose him. In blind fury he nearly had us off our feet in his effort to get at Filey, who was smiling thinly and waiting for it. But we held on, until I felt a shudder run through Art, and something seemed to slip from him.

"All right!" he shouted, then he managed to go on more quietly. "Then you can take this down. If you can write. Are y' listenin', Filey? Put me away for Phillie, an' I don't care what else you do. I might just as well go down for the other. Two for the price of one. I killed your copper, Filey. Not Packer. Me. Get it? I'm admitting to the shooting of poor old Ted Adamson. Now charge me for *that.*"

There was a whole tangle of emotions involved in this outpouring. Say this for Art, he was a quick thinker. Part of it was the pleasure of throwing it in Filey's face. Anything to get back at him in some way—and indeed it would raise problems for Filey. And lurking in there were the trap jaws represented by Packer. Art was also not forgetting that he would probably get both sentences to run concurrently. Two for the price of one, as he'd said. All this I could see. But what really surprised me was his reference to poor old Ted Adamson. Art had carried it with him, his horror and revulsion for what he'd done.

Filey's reaction was even more unexpected. "What's the matter with you, you young fool?" he demanded, waving his arms in Art's face. "You cretinous oaf—what d'you think you're doing?"

Greaves put in, "He's admitting to killing your constable, Mr. Filey. That's *your* case. Your patch. So, for that one, you can make the charge. This one too," he added thoughtfully.

Filey dismissed this with an angry gesture. "I've got Packer put away for that. D'you think I want him out?"

"It's an admission. Act on it."

Filey stared at Art with exaggerated admiration. "Didn't I tell you he's cute. The young bugger's trying it on. One of his tricks. Blurring the issue. Don't let him distract you, Greaves. Charge him for Philomena Wise."

"You've already done that."

"I withdraw that charge. It's your case."

"You withdraw? But, Mr. Filey—think. Such a splendid theory shouldn't go to waste. D'you want me to prepare a case for the DPP, even when I've got no faith in it?" Greaves was calm. The more he said, the more moderate and ponderous his voice became.

"I'll help you with it, for Chrissake!" Then Filey abuptly controlled himself. His voice moderated. "Let's get him inside, then we can argue about it."

Filey had his back to Greaves and was facing us, so that it was perhaps only I who could detect the satisfaction on Filey's face. I would've said he'd been defeated in his intentions, but apparently not. I was beginning to realise that this scene was as false as the one he'd played with me in Dorothy Mann's office. He'd been after something, and it appeared he'd got it. It was just that I couldn't imagine what it might be.

Greaves scratched the side of his nose with his pipe stem. "I'd have said yours has precedence, you know. After all, yours was the death of a police officer. After you, Mr. Filey."

Filey turned to him, annoyed by this persistence. "I don't want him. Didn't you hear me? I've got Carl Packer."

"But if we leave him free, he'll be on to the Sunday papers, seeing who'll make the biggest bid. Can you just imagine it! I KILLED A COPPER AND GOT AWAY WITH IT. They pay well, you know."

"But he won't be free to do that, will he!" said Filey heavily. "Not if you arrest him for killing Philomena Wise."

"Oh, I can't do that." Greaves shook his head shaggily. "You see, it's not finished. I've only got a small team, and we haven't completed our enquiries. Somebody might just have seen him leave the scarf in the phone booth. What a lot of fools we'd look . . ." He left it hanging there, and tried drawing on his cold pipe. His face was very serious, having worked its way there during his speech.

Filey was breathing deeply through his nose. "Then you don't intend to detain him?"

"There's nowhere he can run to."

For a few moments Filey stared blindly into Greaves's bland face, then he stalked quickly past him, past the police cars, and out into the street.

Art gabbled, "Me! What about me?"

"Nothing about you, son. We'll get round to you later, but don't try to go anywhere. Otherwise I'll play safe and put you in custody. Do I make myself clear?" Then he nodded to the two constables and ambled away towards his car.

Lucy and I released Art's arms. He still seemed dazed. Then slowly his legs gave way and he went down on his knees and put his hands over his face. I could see his shoulders shaking.

Lucy said softly, "Look after him, Paul." She meant keep an eye on him.

I nodded. Her eyes flashed at me, then she walked away after her boss. I watched her go. There was a spring to her step, and knowing I was watching she put a swing to her bottom. I bent and put a hand beneath Art's arm.

"It's past opening time. Let's see if we can get a drink."

He struggled shakily to his feet, wiping the back of his free hand across his lips. "Where?" he croaked.

"The hotel. Where we had lunch. Come on. We're making an exhibition of ourselves here."

I hadn't before noticed, but now I saw that the seemingly deserted village had spawned a multitude of heads, which stuck up above the two side walls and the roadside one. Theatre in the square, so to speak. There were faces, too, at the upper windows of the hotel.

"Let's go, Art."

"Yeah. Sure." He shook my hand off, and together we walked out, and the populace, robbed of an exciting suicide, drifted away before us.

Art wasn't saying anything. From time to time he juddered, though it could have been from cold. I paused at the entrance to the hotel's car-park, which was a narrow opening beside the building and came to an abrupt halt at the rear, where it faced a vertical wall of rock. Backed in and parked there, at the far end, was Dorothy's Fiat two-seater.

We walked into the lobby. What had been deserted when we first visited now buzzed with excited chatter, which stopped as we entered. They rustled aside, feet shuffling. We were the heroes of the hour. The manager was present, managing not quite to bow.

"Is the bar open?" I asked.

"Certainly, sir. To your right, through there."

The bar was not only open, it was bouncing with custom. Strained nerves were being soothed, and hearty voices were engaged in a replay, like football fans reorganising fact. At our entrance the voices gradually faded, and there was a listening silence. Now they had access to the truth. I didn't need to raise my voice.

"A brandy for my friend, and a dry ginger ale for me." I reckoned I was going to need all my wits in full running order.

We took our drinks to a corner table. When it became clear that nothing exciting was going to happen, the attention drifted away from us. I drank. Art downed half his brandy, and choked.

"What's this stuff?" he asked, obviously never having encountered it before.

"Brandy. Medicinal."

"Yeah? I bet." But his voice was stronger, and already the colour was flowing to his cheeks and the end of his nose.

"All right if I leave you for a minute?" I asked.

"It's just off the lobby. I noticed."

"Not that. Somebody I want a word with. Okay?"

"Sure. Take your time." His wits had recovered sufficiently to enable him to realise he was in an ideal situation for free drinks. He flicked me a grin. "I'm fine now."

He hadn't yet realised that his position was still unresolved. Greaves, whatever Filey's attitude might be, would not be able to ignore Art's admission of having killed Ted Adamson. For now, he might be prepared to leave Art hanging, but eventually, when he had more time, he would have Art in, and have a few very serious words with him. Art's movements were not going to be as free as Greaves had suggested. Sure, he was fine now. Let him believe it would continue.

And I was beginning to see some direction to Filey's efforts. He knew exactly what he was doing. The pressure he'd been applying need not have been aimed at Art.

So I left him. Dot—I was becoming used to the name—not being in the bar, was most likely to be in the lounge. I hunted it out, half a glass of medicinal Canada Dry in my fist, and there she was, on a red plush corner seat with a coffee tray on the table before her. She was alone. I went across and, without permission, altered that.

"Heh there!" I said. "How are things with you?"

The chair I drew forward was no more comfortable than the Hepplewhite at the Wise's.

FIFTEEN

I had spoken cheerfully, though in fact she didn't appear to be at the peak of her form. Her face was pinched with strain—or weeping.

"Paul," she said shortly, merely acknowledging my presence. "I'm glad you found me." But she didn't sound pleased.

"I spotted your car. Are you staying here now?"

"Temporarily. I couldn't stand it any more at the house."

"But you were a friend of their daughter."

"Hardly that." She shook her head, but with too much emphasis.

She was not relaxing. I tried to think of an amusing remark to lighten the gloom, but nothing came.

"I wanted to see you," she went on. "There's something I have to tell you."

"I had an idea there might be."

Her eyes seemed startled for a moment. "How could you know . . ."

"Things that've been said, attitudes, allusions."

"What on earth are you talking about?" she demanded, more acid in her voice than I deserved, I thought.

"You must have seen. And maybe heard, I'd have thought. What went on outside," I prompted. "In the car-park. If you didn't see, you're about the only one around here."

"I saw and I heard. But it wasn't that."

"Filey took it too far. He's too anxious to make his arrests."

She moved her shoulders slightly. "Yes, I saw it from my window upstairs. I had it open, so I heard snatches. As the wind caught it, you know. Filey's a fool. He always did push too hard. But, Paul, do listen please. That isn't important."

I had never seen her face so grave, even worried. There were lines on her forehead that were new to me, and she certainly hadn't taken much trouble with her hair.

"Not important! You must've missed most of it. Art was definitely telling the truth about the scarf, and that means—"

"Paul," she said firmly. "Please stop jabbering and listen. I want to tell you something else."

"Oh? Say on."

She flinched at the hint of flippancy, but it involved no more than a corner of her lips. She wasn't in the mood.

"Paul, I wanted to tell you that I'm getting away from all this as soon as I can. Away from here. Away—anywhere."

And that was it. Nothing to add, nothing to be taken away. I thought about it, sipping my drink.

There was now no valid intention, in the minds of either of us, to travel together to America. But was she simply running away? If so, from what? What I could see in her face could well be a suppressed fear.

I looked up, to find her eyes on me. "Will they let you leave?"

She shrugged, grimacing. "I'm not about to ask for permission. Nobody needs me here. Paul—I've got to get away."

I looked at her from beneath lowered eyelids. "Away from what?"

"Not from you, Paul." She allowed herself a small moue of amusement. "Don't flatter yourself."

"I don't. I've never been good at frightening women."

She bit her lower lip, a comment suppressed. I gave it a few moments, but she seemed to have said all she intended.

"Then it's as well I caught you," I went on. "You see, there's something I'm sure you can tell me."

"If I can help you, you know I will." This was on a give-and-take level, and she was clearly relieved I'd changed the subject.

"It's just that you and Philomena had become friends, sort of, and if she'd confided in anybody I'm sure it would've been you."

"Not necessarily." A shutter was lowering. "I've already told you all I know."

"I mean, you spent hours, days you told me, persuading her to give evidence at Packer's trial . . ."

"Even so—"

". . . and you'd have had her confidence then. So when it all cropped up once more, I thought she might have confided in you again."

Her fine, beautifully shaped chin was tucked in, as though to avoid a blow. "There was nothing for her to confide." She was quietly stubborn.

"There was certainly something she'd got to worry about, and make a decision on. I've already told you what Packer wanted her to do, and you'll have heard Art Torrance admitting that he killed Ted Adamson. Don't make the mistake of dismissing that as hysteria, because it wasn't. So Philomena, who must've known the truth, would have had some decision-taking on the menu. She would probably need help. You were available. So—who better to turn to than you?"

"Why me?" She was looking down at her empty cup, playing for time.

"Why you? Because you were the one who persuaded her to give evidence in the first place."

The hand she had rested on the table clenched. "I persuaded her to give evidence . . ." She shook her head. Then, "Not what evidence she should give."

I forced on with it. "But now—more recently—she'd have had to decide what evidence to retract. For that she'd need your advice, Dot, as a professional. As an ex-policewoman."

Her voice caught in her throat. "I don't know what you mean."

"Of course you damned-well do. If she'd gone to the police to retract her story . . . for heaven's sake, don't you see! There's a world of difference between her saying, 'Carl Packer didn't do it, but I don't know who did,' and her saying, 'Carl Packer didn't do it, it was Arthur Torrance.' Surely you see that!"

She was staring at me as though I'd gone insane. "I don't see . . ." she began softly, but she allowed it to tail away, her eyes searching my face.

"And I hoped," I said gently, "that she might have confided in you. It'd be a great help if you happen to know what she decided."

I was convinced it held the answer to her death.

Her voice was more confident when she saw what I was asking. "She didn't ask my advice, Paul, and she didn't say what she'd decided to do. You've got to realise, this was an older and much more mature young woman than the one who got mixed up in that warehouse robbery. She wasn't going to ask anybody—she made up her own mind. All she said was that she was going out to meet Art at the bus stop."

"No hint?"

She would go no further, but just sat there, shaking her head. I got to my feet and leaned across the table, and put a finger under her chin. When her head came up I kissed her gently on the lips. They were cold.

"Good luck, then," I said quietly.

Then I walked out quickly and went to dig Art from the bar, and found him laughing with a crowd of oldies at the table. Britain's great white hope, that was Art, because he'd sent a couple of coppers packing and in disarray. They didn't consider that he'd made a public admission of despatching one policeman even more finally.

I took him out and stuffed him in the car, and drove him back to Mrs. Druggett's. A small car fell in behind me and kept station all the way.

"Get inside and stay there," I told him briskly.

"What you so crabby about?"

"Nothing. Do as I say and don't argue."

He got out and slammed the door, nearly hard enough to take it out the other side. The small car remained, tucked in beside the church wall, as I drove back to The George.

Lucy Rice was sitting in the bar, which was almost empty of customers at that time. She rose to her feet.

"Where is he?"

"I left him at Mrs. Druggett's," I said, keeping my voice neutral.

"Mr. Greaves put young Geoff Freeman on . . ."

I plunked down on the bench along the back wall, suddenly realising how exhausted I felt. "He's there, don't worry. Art's shot his last bolt, and now he's waiting for the attack."

She came and sat beside me. "You sound as bitter as Filey."

"Sorry. Just tired."

"Get you a drink?" George asked, but I shook my head.

"You do realise," said Lucy, "that it can't be left as it is. You're on his side, that's what it is. You heard what he said—"

I interrupted. "I'm not on his side. Say that he has my sympathy. For some reason, he trusts me."

"There's nothing you can do for him," she told me severely. "Why don't you let it lie, Paul? Greaves knows what he's doing."

"Sure he does."

"Paul!" she said sharply. "He made an admission. He said it was he who shot the policeman. We'll have to have him in and make the admission into a confession, and the whole case will have to be reopened."

I sighed. "I'm quite aware of the situation. Art knows how he stands. To tell you the truth, I reckon he'll almost welcome it. The whole thing's been too heavy for him to carry around."

"Hmm!" Then she grinned, and the lightning flashed from her eyes. "You moved fast. I couldn't have got to him in time." The normal solemnity took over again.

"He's a grand lad, is Art." I shrugged. "Even his wall-scrambling was a fake. He didn't try very hard."

"You're a cynic."

"I reckon so. They train you in it, at Gartree."

She got to her feet, smoothing her slacks as though she'd forgot-

ten she wasn't wearing a skirt. Seeing me struggling up, she made
a little gesture. I subsided. I liked the way she could convey so
much with a gesture, in the flicker of a smile, in the movement of
her eyes, the lift of her chin. It was masterful—mistressful?—un-
derstatement. The impression was that there was so much left un-
deployed, which it would be interesting to explore.

"And you?" she asked. "What now?"

"I'm going to get some rest."

"And after that?"

"There's something that's got to be settled, and then—"

"I told you—Greaves has got it in hand."

"Something personal."

"Oh!" She looked round. "I'll leave you to get on with your resting, then."

She went out, pausing to whisper something to her brother. I
waited until she was well clear, then followed, meeting George in
the passageway. He said he'd give me a shout when they had an
evening meal ready for me, but I told him not to trouble. It didn't
matter, I told him. I was having difficulty deciding what really did
matter.

Even now I couldn't understand what Dorothy was doing. If she
was leaving, there could no longer be any need to hide anything
from me. Yet this, I was convinced, was what she was doing. She
knew something, or she suspected something, but it was not to be
shared with me. Yet she was terrified, of that I was certain. That
was why she dared not speak. If she'd allowed me to share the
knowledge, I could have shared the danger.

I kicked off my shoes and lay down on the bed. Not to sleep. I
was waiting, my brain chasing its tail and denying me any relaxation. I waited as the room darkened, and when the setting sun
blushed on the ceiling I slipped down and left by the rear door,
quietly and unobtrusively. Nothing would happen until after dark
I reckoned.

I got the car started and drifted it out on to the street, then
headed for the Port Sumbury road. The whole frontage of Seagulls
was a rank of lighted windows, but I drove on past. She wasn't
there any more. The road was quiet, and I saw no other traffic.
Without making a show of it, I swung into the car-park and drew
to a halt in the deeper shade of the shed. Two other vehicles were
parked on the far side. They appeared to be empty.

Hugging what cover there was, I went first to check that her Fiat
was still in the recess beside the hotel. It was. There was a side
door that I hadn't previously noticed, but on returning to the car-
park I discovered that from the shed I could see part of it in the

light from a low-power wall light. I could also see all the hotel's frontage, and there could be no way out at the back because the building was cut into the hill behind. It didn't matter that I couldn't see her car from the shed. When I perched on the wall, my back was just too far from the shed to be able to lean against it. I sat with my legs hanging free. Then I was still, and I waited, and became part of the same shadowed mass.

Gradually the cold from the rock surface penetrated through my slacks. The top of the wall was uneven, and I began to ache. I thought that one of my feet had died and dropped off. The sun had now sunk behind the lowering hill, and I waited. Another car drew in, and the owner walked past behind me. I was motionless, and he didn't see me. Yes, I decided, Dorothy had been afraid of something. Everything was moving too fast, now. The momentum could engulf her. And I waited.

Cars were beginning to come into the park, and their occupants to walk away towards the Stormy Petrel. Lights were on in most of the rooms fronting the hotel, but as I didn't know which was her room it didn't help me. The tide was apparently going out. What had been a boom was becoming a shish and a gurgle. I found myself nodding and jerked myself awake.

Behind the obscured glass in the top half of the side door a light came on. It opened. It closed. I slid from the wall and tried to run silently across the street, but I'd been right about my foot. I nearly staggered on to my face and pain shot up my right thigh. Forcing myself, I slowed to a limp, and reached the opening to the hotel's car-park.

She was just unlocking the door to her car, and I was forming her name on my lips (my hesitation caused by the fact that I couldn't remember what name I was now calling her) when a shape moved ahead of me, and then was between us.

"Dorothy!"

It was Filey's voice, but it was not the tone I knew. It was softer, quiet and calm, but all the same she jerked round sharply, and her response was tense and explosive.

"What the hell d'you want?"

"You know what." I'd never heard him so smoothly confident. "Don't be a fool, Dorothy, you know I've got to be certain." He moved closer to her. I now had difficulty in hearing, and edged inside the entrance. "She would've told you. What did she intend to do?"

She lifted her head. "She?" Her voice held contempt. "I suppose you mean Philomena. What does it matter now, anyway?"

"It matters. Torrance has admitted he killed Ted Adamson. You must have heard."

"Will you stand away from my car, please."

I thought I saw his left hand shoot out and take her arm. There was a hiss of indrawn breath. I slid closer.

"What did she intend?" His voice whipped the air.

"She wouldn't say."

"What did she tell you, Dorothy?" he insisted. "It matters."

"Perhaps she was going to tell the truth, Filey." I could detect that she now had difficulty in maintaining the contempt. Her voice was uneven with pain. "You know damn well I persuaded her to give evidence at the trial, but it was you who told her what evidence to give."

"That's a damned lie." He shook her angrily. "You of all people."

"You're hurting me!" With her free left hand she was fumbling for her shoulder-bag. I thought she intended to hit him with it. "I'm warning you—"

Then he struck her. I saw his right hand go over and catch her on the side of the jaw. At the same time he released her arm. She fell across the bonnet sideways, and he stood back. Slowly she slid down to the hard concrete surface, where she lay, her face in the square of light cast from the side door, lying on her side with her mouth open and bleeding, eyes open, and her whole body twitching in an enormous effort to reach her shoulder-bag, which was lying beside her head.

He looked down at her, then he drew back his foot. She was staring at it.

I had been moving from the moment his fist was raised, but time had become distorted. I seemed to be moving slowly, but the blow, her slide from the bonnet, her fall to the ground, all these had been so fast. I was roaring in mad fury as I charged, but he was not distracted. His foot was still moving when I took him with my shoulder down into his side, took him and swept him forward, over the low bonnet of the car, over the squat roof, and over the short tail. We landed together between the car and the vertical rock wall.

I was on top of him, he gasping for breath, legs working, arms flying in an attempt to slow me, head butting into my face. But I was possessed by an uncontrollable fury that I knew and recognised. No pain or blow was going to distract me. It was the same fury with which I'd dragged my father from my mother, and clamped my fingers on his throat. As I did now, snarling and spitting, and digging in the fingers that had killed before.

There was a pounding of blood in my head and a roaring in my ears. Nothing existed but Filey's choking face beneath me. There was a veil between me and reality, behind that veil there were shouts, through it reaching hands, though all this was tangled in the web. Until a voice cut through it.

"Paul! That's enough. Stop it at once." It was Lucy's voice, her lips close to my ear, her face against mine.

Slowly the pressure in my head retreated. I watched, rather than willed, as my fingers relaxed. Then they were free of him and I lifted my hands, fouled by contact with his skin. Pressure was now on my shoulders. I was rolled free, tumbled beside the car, and lifted so that I was sitting on the ground with my back against the rear wheel, and wondering who was sobbing into those same hands.

Lucy crouched beside me. "It's all right, Paul," she whispered. "It's over."

My hands, soothed by the tears, now seemed soft.

I heard Greaves snapping out orders. "Get back to the car. An ambulance, and quickly. Lucy, see to Miss Mann. Is he alive, Parkes?"

"Alive, sir. In a bad way, though."

I couldn't see her, the other side of the car, but I recognised Dorothy's voice. "I'm all right. Leave me. What about him?"

"Which him?" Greaves asked.

"D'you think I care for Filey," she snapped, viciously enough to indicate he hadn't inflicted too much damage.

Greaves told her I was fine, and there was no more sound from her. Then it was a period of waiting, while everything set itself into official routine. The ambulance came. Filey, who was now croaking obscenities, was helped in, with a laconic, "He'll live," from one of the men. They examined Dorothy's face. We still had not looked at each other, not eye to eye. She was said to have a split lip and a loose tooth. Filey had paid his debt—a tooth for a tooth. She asked if she could go back to her room, and Greaves gave his permission.

Then they got me to my feet. The shakes had gone. There was nothing wrong with me except that my hands ached, from finger-tips to elbows.

They walked me across to the car-park, to one of the two cars I'd noticed on my arrival. The other car had chased off, following the ambulance. All I had to contend with was Greaves, with Lucy's support. At that time Lucy was supporting me physically. I didn't really need her hand to my arm, but the comfort was welcome.

They put me in the car, on the back seat, with Greaves beside me. Lucy sat behind the wheel, twisted round so that she could watch us.

"Now," said Greaves. "Kindly explain what happened. And you'd better make it good, otherwise I'm taking you in for criminal assault on a police officer."

In the pursuit of his official duties? Hardly. I sighed wearily. It was as though I'd reached the end of a long journey, but it wasn't just the journey that'd finished. I had set out hopefully to save the life of Philomena Wise. This I had now done. Not, perhaps, the real one, but my Phil's. And in doing so I was left with nothing. There was an emptiness in my life, and future vistas were not yet taking shape.

Seeing Greaves produce his pipe, I wound down a window, then I told him what he needed to know.

SIXTEEN

"I don't think you could call it criminal assault," I said. "Something more like self-defence or justifiable, I'd have thought." I met blank lack of belief. "When you're defending somebody else," I explained. That fact had helped me with my trial.

"Suppose you leave me to sort out the law," Greaves said placidly. "Just explain."

"He'd raised his foot, she was helpless, and it was aimed at her head. He intended to kill her."

He grimaced. "You made that split-second decision?"

"It was all the time I had."

"You seem to make a lot of these abrupt decisions. Explain why he would want to harm her." He wasn't giving an inch. Calm and decisive.

"Because she knew too much about his past activities, and when Art Torrance stuck his neck out and admitted he'd killed the copper, it put Filey dead in trouble."

There was a pause. Greaves glanced at Lucy. I did too. There was nothing encouraging in her expression.

"How did it do that?" demanded Greaves at last. "And"—he

pointed the pipe stem at me, right between the eyes—"try to talk sense this time."

"I've always—"

"Say it!" he barked.

"I suppose you know about the warehouse raid . . ."

"Of course."

"Art was the only one of that lot—five of 'em I think—who wasn't wearing gloves. He's admitted he fired the gun. So why weren't his fingerprints on it? Answer me that one."

"I don't answer your questions, you answer mine. Get that straight, right now. If you think you know the reason, say it."

Lucy, twisted in the driver's seat, pouted at me. I took a breath. "Filey wiped the gun clean. He knew Art'd fired it, but he wanted Carl Packer for that. He wanted to put him away for a long time. So Filey cleaned the gun, then he got at Philomena Wise—once Dorothy had persuaded her to give evidence—and told her to point out Packer as the gunman. Because of this Dorothy hated Filey for landing Philomena in danger from Packer. And Filey knew Dorothy realised he'd done it."

Said like that, stripped of all motivation and down to the bare details, it sounded very empty. I'd have liked more time . . .

"Tell me . . ." Greaves was shaking his head, his jowls flying as he assembled his attitude. "Tell me, do you read much romantic fiction? Was that all they could find you in the prison library? I've never heard such a load of rubbish—"

"It's true, damn it."

"Don't argue with me, Manson. I'm warning you."

Lucy cleared her throat. "May I say something, sir?"

He inclined his head. "If you can make sense of it, by all means."

"Well . . . surely the possible truth of what Mr. Manson has said isn't really the point. If he *thought* it was true, if he had reason to believe Mr. Filey was about to kick her head in, surely *that's* what matters. Sir," she added as an afterthought.

I smiled at her. She didn't smile back. It was Greaves who did so, a wolfish grin. "But that isn't what matters to me. Manson made a murderous attack. What you said, Sergeant, is for the defence to bring up in court."

I was silent. Greaves opened his window to shake his pipe outside. Lucy watched him with grim anticipation, while Greaves made up his mind.

"I'll need to speak to Mr. Filey, of course. Later, I'll get along to the hospital. But in the meantime, it's clear I'll have to have a word with Dorothy Mann."

"Yes," I agreed. "You do that. She'll tell you—"

"Be quiet! I shall speak to her. We'll see if there's anything other than wild imagination in what you've told us."

I had my hand on the door catch. "Yes. We'll see then, and you can just—"

"You, Mr. Manson, will see nothing. The sergeant and I will go over there now. You will remain here. You'll sit where you are now, and not move. I've got men who can persuade you if you've got other ideas. You will sit, and you will wait. Do you understand?"

"Of course." I couldn't get much force into it.

"I'm very pleased to hear it. Come along, Sergeant. She'll have had time to clean herself up by now."

They got out of the car. Not even glancing back, Greaves being so certain of the strength of my surveillance, they walked across to the hotel. I waited. Looking round, I could see no sign of large, rugged coppers. But, having no intention of doing anything provoking, I had no difficulty in sitting back, closing my eyes, and trying to relax. Ridiculously, I fell asleep, jerking awake as the car door opened. Greaves slid in beside me, Lucy again climbing in behind the wheel.

For some moments Greaves didn't speak. His face wasn't moving around now, but was set rather more grimly than I liked to see. At last he marshalled his words.

"Miss Mann has told us that she thought Mr. Filey was about to kick her head in."

"Just what I told you!"

"She has claimed that he's hated her ever since the warehouse job. She remains adamant that he conned Philomena into pointing out Carl Packer at the trial. And she says Filey did this by offering Arthur Torrance's freedom from prosecution on the murder charge."

He'd said this in a toneless voice, giving me no clues as to his reaction. I helped him along. "Exactly what I said."

"Oh no! Oh no it's not. You said Mr. Filey interfered with the evidence."

"And so he did. He cleaned—"

"I got the impression," he went on, raising his voice, "that Miss Mann is as obsessed as you are about it. No . . . the other way round. What *you* say is what she's fed you." He held up his huge palm. "And if you interrupt again I'll have your mouth plastered over. Listen for once. You've got yourself involved in this, and you've taken it on yourself to go round questioning people. It's your right to do that. Not to demand answers, but to ask. I can't stop you talking, more's the pity, but you seem to have accepted that everything you've heard from everybody has to be the plain truth. No, damn you, shut your mouth. I believe that Miss Mann is no longer in a condition to think logically on anything. Arthur Torrance is a born liar and clever with it. Carl Packer would say *anything* to get out of Gartree. And Douglas French! My God, you can't tell me he was sane. All these, you've listened to and believed. So now . . . I've had enough of it. When I've had a word with Mr. Filey—we'll see. If he cares to lay charges against you, then you'll find yourself inside again. Do I make myself clear? That's a question, so answer it."

I licked my dry lips. In contrast to his normal attitude, Greaves in a nasty mood was impressive. I didn't dare to look at Lucy.

"All I can say is that I agree I've spoken to all those people you've mentioned. But not like a policeman, like an ex-Gartree resident, Mr. Greaves, and I'm quite convinced I heard the truth."

"Hah!" he barked in disgust.

"But *you,*" I said, trying to sound more forceful, "you're going to take the word of Filey."

"I most certainly am."

"I've spoken to him, too," I said quietly.

"And what does *that* mean?"

"If anybody's psychotic, it's him."

"Watch what you say!"

"Watch it, be damned. I can't make anything worse than it is. Assume there was something in it, what Filey did over the warehouse robbery."

"I'll assume nothing of the sort."

"Then I will. It all follows from that. Filey came here, just after Art did. Filey had his spies out. Philomena was going to make a decision on Frenchie's offer. If what she decided to do included anything about Filey, then he'd have been in trouble. But she died. Frenchie might have known her decision, and was only waiting for her to pass it on to Art. So Frenchie presented a danger, and he died. Dorothy was close to Philomena. She could have known the truth, as told to her by Philomena. So she had to die. She would have died, only I happened to be there. And you intend to take the word of such a man!"

"I don't believe it!" Greaves whispered to his pipe.

"I didn't expect—"

"Lucy," he said, "have you been taking this down?"

"No, sir."

"It's just as well. Our Mr. Paul Manson must be crazy. Or so ridiculously naïve that it's a wonder he's still walking around." He returned his attention to me. "And you will not be walking around for much longer, believe me. I can put theories together just as well as you, you know. And I can say you came here from Carl Packer to kill Philomena Wise, and that you did so. You argued with Douglas French, who'd also come along to do the job, and you put *him* away with a chunk of rock. You knew that Mr. Filey suspected all this, so you seized on an opportunity, when he and Miss Mann were disputing something between themselves, in order to attack him, and to kill him too. It's in your blood, Manson. A killer instinct."

The skin of my face felt tight and drawn. He was watching me with what I thought might be a slight smile. "You don't believe a word of that."

"Enough of it to put you away in a cell for safe keeping."

"It's bloody absurd!"

"Not nearly as nonsensical as the ideas you've been throwing around."

"Dorothy confirms he was going to kick her head in. You said that."

"She could change her mind."

"I've got to see her!" I cried, feeling panic rising in me.

"I thought you'd say—"

"You've got no right to stop me—"

He spoke casually. "She asked to see you."

"She . . . asked . . ."

"When I told her I was going to take you in, that was what she asked."

"Well then . . ."

"I told her you could be seen in your cell at the station."

"For God's sake . . ."

"But I'm an impatient man," he said placidly. "You may do it now." The folds of his face were now so much relaxed that I was suspicious.

"And you'll let me do that?"

"Certainly. But Sergeant Rice will be with you. *This* will have to be recorded. I think Miss Mann wants to tell you there'll be no help coming from her direction."

My mind hunted for stability. He was trying something on, and I couldn't see what it was. "More likely," I fumbled, "she wants to thank me for saving her life."

He shrugged, spreading his hands. "Wouldn't that be nice! Lucy, you know what to do. Oh, and Manson, if you intend to try anything funny involving Sergeant Rice—don't. Just don't."

Unable to answer him, I struggled with the door catch and almost fell out of the door.

Greaves, I tried to convince myself, didn't believe his stupid theory against me, otherwise he wouldn't have given me this chance. No, he expected something to emerge when we met, but how could that be if Lucy was with me? He was playing games with me, pushing the pieces around and hoping for checkmate. I was his black knight.

Then Lucy was at my elbow, and together we crossed the road, not glancing at each other, not speaking. She led me through the lobby, already knowing which was Dorothy's room. I tramped at her elbow, up the wide, marble-treaded staircase. The flock wallpaper was shiny at shoulder level, the red carpet runner worn thin. Lucy had now fallen back behind me. It was my visit. Lucy was my attendant shadow. She indicated which door.

"This is it."

I knocked. Dorothy didn't call out to ask who it was, but the door moved to the pressure of my knuckles. I put my shoulder against it and walked in.

She had a large room with a bay window, overlooking the yacht basin. The furnishings were heavy and old, the bed large and high from the floor. It was possible to be able to sit on it comfortably, and she had been doing so, but now she'd fallen sideways to her left, away from me, her head resting on her left arm, which was spread on the coverlet. Her right arm was hanging towards the floor, the fingers lax. Beneath her hand was lying the small automatic pistol I'd last seen in her office at Killingham. Her shoulder-bag was a yard away on the floor, lying open with its contents scattered.

It might have taken a long while to absorb this picture, or a split second. Still believing wildly that she could be asleep, I moved slowly into the room until I could look down at her. There was a small, angry hole in her right temple. Very little blood. I whispered thanks that there was very little blood, but that was before I looked at the bedcover, beyond her head.

I turned, retching drily. Lucy moved past me into the room. I ran from there, ran into the wall opposite, staggered, then leaned against it, gulping in air. Lucy was shaking my arm. "Get Greaves. Quickly, Paul!" Her face swam in front of me, the blood drained from it.

Slowly my head cleared. "Get Greaves!" I had to force myself into movement and found myself fumbling down the stairs sideways, both hands sliding along the marble balustrade. In the lobby I was only yards from the open air, clean and fresh air. I thrust myself through the door. Get Greaves, she'd said. I stood at the head of the steps, the sea air cutting at me, catching my breath.

Below me, standing on the pavement with his fists on his hips and his feet braced apart, was Inspector Filey.

"So there you are," he said hoarsely.

I stood, swaying. He wasn't real. He was in hospital, so he couldn't be real. Nothing was real. I opened my mouth, but couldn't speak.

Then he'd run up the steps and grabbed my arms, and was shaking me. "What is it? What is it, Manson?" he croaked.

"Upstairs," I whispered.

He stared into my face for a moment, then he released me and ran into the lobby. Slowly I sat down on the top step and buried my face in my hands.

SEVENTEEN

"Did you touch anything?" said Lucy.

"What?"

"When you went into her room—did you touch anything?" She jerked at my arm.

I raised my head from between my knees. We were in the lounge, alone, sitting in the corner on one of the wall benches, our knees touching because we were at right angles to each other. There was a table in front of us, on it a glass of brandy. I recalled that she'd fetched it for me, but I'd been unable to touch it, afraid of aggravating the nausea.

"I don't think so," I said, my voice seeming to be miles away. "You were there—you must've seen."

"Try some brandy. Your brain's slipped out of gear."

I tried to smile at her, but only half of my mouth seemed to be working. She'd had experience, and was very much less affected by the death than I was. I took a sip of brandy. It felt good, so I took another.

"Does it matter what I touched?"

Her eyes were shaded, and she did not look at me directly. "It's too early to say what matters. Think. Try to remember. Did you touch anything? I'd got other things to do than look at you."

I knew that I needed every tiny cell of my brain working at full stretch, and welcomed the warm flow of blood the brandy had provoked. The question was a tester, so I gave it my full attention. She was trying to help me.

"The door was open a crack. Yes. I knocked. Remember? Just knuckles. It swung open a bit more. The rest . . . I put my shoulder to it and we just walked in. And looked. And came out again."

"Good."

"You're thinking about fingerprints?"

"Fingermarks, we call 'em. Yes. It could be a question of elimination."

I groaned. "Why? I'd have thought it was all too bloody obvious."

"Nothing's taken as obvious in a sudden and violent death." She was shaking her head when I looked at her. In sorrow for me? "Oh, Paul, you know so little of what goes on. There's a routine, a procedure. It has to be like that, then nothing's missed. All down as evidence, solid, undisputable, on record. That's in case anything gets challenged in court."

I reckoned she was talking just in order to give me time to recover. "Why're you telling me this?"

"Because very soon Mr. Greaves and Mr. Filey will be down here to put a few questions to you, and I don't want you coming out again with a load of nonsense, such as we got in the car a little while ago."

I stared at her, startled. Her voice had been stern and inflexible.

"It wasn't nonsense."

"Hah!" She chopped what might have been a laugh into a sharper bark of contempt. "If you only knew! It was all Mr. Greaves and I could do to prevent ourselves from laughing out loud. All right, don't look so offended. You'll get the chance of asking Mr. Filey yourself. I reckon you've got five minutes or so to pull yourself together, Paul."

Like that, was it? Even Lucy now! "I wouldn't have thought they could spare time for a useless nothing like me."

She didn't say anything. When I glanced at her she was smiling down at her hands. I could tell it was a smile, from the side. One corner of her mouth was twitching.

"Oh, but you're important, Paul. Believe me." She twisted so that she could face me more squarely, her knees firmly against mine now. "They'll be standing out in the corridor, up there, discussing things. You, perhaps. The SOCO's in charge."

"Sockoh?"

"Scene of Crimes Officer. It's Sergeant Forbes. It's his job to take charge, tell the technical lot what he wants doing, and make sure it's all done by the book. He wouldn't allow any paltry Inspectors across the threshold. Do you understand what I'm telling you, Paul?"

"No."

"Oh—for heaven's sake pull yourself together. You've been basing all your ideas on a complete misunderstanding of what happens when a serious crime occurs. Admit it, you're completely ignorant."

"All I know about it is being taken in and charged, and all that."

"There you are then."

There I was where? She was warning me. Don't stick your neck out, Paul. Which—I was now being informed brusquely—I'd been doing far too eagerly. I got to my feet, just to stretch my legs. My brain was working again, and I was just checking the rest of me.

Lucy watched me as I wandered round the lounge, idly looking at the prints of old fighting vessels on the walls, flexing my knees, rotating my arms.

"Wondering whether you can run fast enough?" asked Lucy gently.

"How long'll they be?"

"Don't know. I can't go and give them orders."

I moved across and stood in front of her, baffled that she'd been able to ride to easily through a scene of violence. She could force herself into objectivity. It wasn't a dead person, it was a case. "D'you like your work, Lucy?"

Smiling openly now, she said, "You meet a few interesting people. From time to time."

Before I could pursue this, she looked past my shoulder. "Here they are now."

I turned. Greaves, unsmiling, stood just inside the doorway. Filey, strangely smiling, was at his shoulder, carrying two thirds of a pint of beer in his fist. From time to time he was taking a sip from this, to lubricate his throat. They both stopped and stared at me. I was tensed, poised for action which might well be anything. When Filey spoke, I could tell the lubrication was working.

"Any trouble, Sergeant?"

"None at all, Inspector."

"A pity. I was looking forward . . ." He raised his glass and sipped.

"He's ready to talk," said Lucy.

"He'd better be. Sit down, Manson. Over there." There was still very little power in his voice.

Filey was carefully separating me from Lucy by urging me to

take a seat in the middle of one of the side benches. This left Lucy
alone at the table, and when I glanced at her I saw she'd produced
her notebook, and everything I said was going to be in there. For
posterity.

Greaves asked me if I wanted anything to drink. I shook my
head, and led off before anybody could take the initiative.

"I thought you'd gone to hospital, Mr. Filey."

"Nobody puts me into a hospital bed, laddie. I could stand and I
could walk, so I got out and walked back."

"I'm glad you're all right."

He raised his eyebrows. "Are you? You surprise me. Let's get on
with it. Mr. Greaves?" he asked politely. He was all brisk officialdom, and nothing was going to distract him from that.

Greaves was too busy fouling the lounge with his pipe. This he
waved. "Go ahead."

Filey looked round, located a loose chair, and yanked it across.
He sat facing me, his beer on the floor beside him. I could see the
bruises on his throat.

"I'm told you've had access to information that we'd never get.
Is that correct?"

As there was now no force in his attitude, I felt I could reply in a
friendly tone. "People in a certain section of society tend to confide. It's my apprenticeship that does it."

This, I realised, was a much more reasonable Filey than I'd previously encountered. Gone was the flip aggressiveness. We were
down to the nitty-gritty, and there was now no part in it for false
exhibitionism. My voice had wavered. My defensive mechanism
had been poised to leap in the wrong direction. He confirmed this.

"I can understand that. And amongst all this special information, do you know of anything that would account for Dorothy
Mann's suicide? You realise I don't usually *ask* for facts when I'm
dealing with—"

I saw it as a smooth trap. "Suicide?" I burst out. "Oh, come on,
Mr. Filey!"

"Dealing with bloody amateurs," he completed.

"Smile when you say that, Mr. Filey."

He realised I'd been ahead of him. He smiled, not pleasantly,
exposing his missing right molar, or whatever it was.

"There—you see," I said in triumph. "It's your right tooth you
lost. And Dorothy Mann did that. So she was left-handed, unless
she came at you from behind."

Filey looked round at Greaves. "Is there *any* point in talking to
him?" he complained. "Knows it all, he does." He whirled on me.
"Of course she was left-handed. Do you take us for idiots! The gun

was beneath her right hand, with her fingerprints on it, if you want to know. Rigged. As obvious as that blasted smirk on your face."

"So why did you try to trap me?"

At this point Greaves interposed his own sober voice. "We'll get along much better, Mr. Manson, if you shake off a bit of this persecution complex of yours. Quite frankly, I think it's something that Gartree's left you with. But we don't want it now. Nobody's trying to trip you up. That's for the book writers. So she was killed. We'll start with that. Do you know who would want to kill her?"

"Apart from Mr. Filey, d'you mean?"

"Oh, Paul . . ." Lucy whispered.

But Filey gestured her to silence. He hadn't taken his eyes from me, and his expression was one of curiosity and interest.

"This had better be good, Manson. On what you say depends the question of whether or not we take you in for criminal assault. On me. And don't . . ." He held up his hand. "Don't, please, give me any of that tripe you gave Mr. Greaves in the car. I'm asking you: why did you attack me, and nearly sodding-well kill me?"

Did he really believe he could bluff his way out of it? "Because you attacked *her*. You'd have killed her."

"Dorothy Mann being more important to you than I am?"

"You could say that."

He sipped at his beer, put it down again. A little of his old frivolity crept in. "Then will you tell poor little unimportant me what I did that you saw as an attack."

"Good God! You hit her in the face so hard you nearly shot her over the car."

"Because," he said pleasantly, "she was a lying bitch, who was trying to ruin my career. Yes, I hit her. I owed her that much." And he smiled without humour, displaying the gap. "There was also the fact that I had to keep an eye on that shoulder-bag."

I should have been warned by his deceptive calm—but no. "All the same," I plunged in, "you raised your foot. You were going to kick her head in. Don't tell me that was another debt you wanted to pay!"

For a moment he held my eyes, then he turned to speak over his shoulder to Greaves. In that second's pause, I realised just how silent the room had become. And how cold.

"How often," he asked Greaves, "d'you get witnesses interrogating you? Oh, he's a good un, this one." He turned back to me, his eyes snapping. "What I owe *you*, Manson, isn't answers, but you can have this one. I was trying to kick her shoulder-bag out of her reach. Not her head. Where d'you think that pistol was, you stupid clown! I knew she'd got it. D'you imagine I didn't have her office watched! She was seen to return there. I got in and found that her gun and passport were gone. And before you ask—we checked, and no gun was registered to her. She'd obtained it illegally."

He'd yanked the carpet right from under my feet. For a moment my head swam. Now I didn't know where I was, and in which direction my loyalties should have been.

I realised they were both watching me with critical concentration. They were waiting for my next move, ready to pounce. "All the same . . ." I said weakly. I glanced towards Lucy. She was frowning, but nevertheless she nodded in encouragement.

Greaves spoke kindly, as he would to a poor broken old man.

"Suppose you tell Mr. Filey what you know about the warehouse job, as you've heard it from Arthur Torrance and Dorothy Mann."

He didn't add the obvious: always bearing in mind that you can't accept one word she's told you as being true.

So I told it all, and in spite of Filey's fixed stare and Greaves's cool consideration of my face, I felt my self-confidence stirring. Having to put it all together, dovetailing the two accounts, really set my brain pounding away, and because it all seemed to fit together so satisfactorily my voice began to firm up. The fact that Filey didn't interrupt led me to believe I wasn't putting a foot wrong anywhere. When I reached the end, which was the point where Philomena identified Carl Packer in court as the gunman, I simply stopped and waited for Filey's outburst.

But strangely he was silent, and seemed to be mulling it over. Greaves cleared his throat. At last Filey spoke.

"That's interesting. You say Dorothy actually claimed I'd got at Miss Wise—as you put it—and persuaded her to identify Carl Packer. But Dorothy would've had no reason to say that. Not to you. None that I can see. I thought it was she who'd done that."

He looked round to Greaves. "It took me completely by surprise in court. My guess all along was Art Torrance. But we'd got the gun and there were no prints on it, and Art was the only one with no gloves, so I didn't—"

"You're a liar," I burst out. "You cleaned the gun yourself."

At this outburst—a residue from my original intention to protect Dorothy—there was a sudden, shocked silence.

Then Greaves murmured, "That's enough of that, Manson." And Lucy whispered, "I warned you, Paul."

But Filey seemed unoffended, even pleased I'd given him the opening. "No, let me. The poor man doesn't know what he's saying. I could not have touched that gun, Manson. Nobody in the police team could've done that. They were all out on the chase, and I was in my car, ordering up the back-up team and contacting the Scene of Crimes Officer. There'd been a killing, Manson. It would not have been possible for any police officer to have got near that gun."

"Well somebody did. Art told me he shot Ted Adamson. And he wasn't wearing gloves. It was a pure reflex action of fear, if you want to know. So *somebody* must've wiped that gun clean, Mr. Filey."

His eyes were shining, his face set in a painful, twisted smile. "Guess who," he suggested softly. "I didn't realise it myself until Torrance admitted he'd shot Ted Adamson. *Then* it became obvious. Nobody needed to persuade the stupid girl . . ." He left it there for me to visualise.

I strained for a mental image, and got it. "Oh, Lord," I groaned. "Of course."

"Well?"

"You were where, Mr. Filey, in your car?"

He cocked an eyebrow at me, challenging me to carry it on. "Round the corner." He was forcing me into saying it in my own words, then I wouldn't be able to dispute its validity.

"And your team was chasing around," I said eagerly. "Art told me he tried to lead the chase away from Philomena, but she was still there to be picked up when you all came back. Why hadn't she driven quietly away? It was because she'd been busy. Is that what you mean? She'd seen Art shoot the policeman. She'd be in shock for a minute or two, I'd expect, then she saw what she had to do, and she sneaked across to the warehouse and cleaned the gun, and then returned to her car—and got caught."

Filey leaned back in his chair and slapped his knees. "Well, well —what would we have done without him! What d'you think, Mr. Greaves?"

Greaves looked startled that he'd been consulted. "I'm sure that's what you had in mind."

Filey's mind was darting around. He almost bounced in his seat. "It was a thought. Hell, I've let myself be distracted by Dorothy. That little devil, Philomena! She faked the evidence, and when she found out she was expected to point a finger, she picked on Packer. Christ! Packer of all people! Get on the wrong side of Packer . . ."

"Can I say something?" I asked.

They stared at me. Filey minimally nodded, so I went on. "It's just that I'm not so certain Philomena was as scatter-brained as everybody seems to think. Listen to Art, and you get the impression of a right hellcat, in for anything. Talk to her mother and you get an ungrateful little chit with no morals. But I'm beginning to have some sort of sympathy with her, I think she was brighter than everybody realises. Plucky with it, too. Art was everything to her. He's got a way with him, you know. But I don't think she went along with Art's ideas on what was a night out on the town. She saw something in him, and all women go for potential. I believe she considered Packer and his mob were leading Art in the wrong direction. She saw a chance of separating Art from all that —by putting Packer away for a long while. She couldn't save Art from a year inside Winson Green, but when he came out . . . he hadn't changed one iota. He told me she'd gone off him, though he didn't like to admit it. She was disappointed. It was a kind of challenge, and she as good as told him—change your ways, or I'll look elsewhere. Perhaps towards Australia. Maybe she tossed that at Art. His last chance. That's how *he* saw it, anyway."

Filey took a swallow of his beer, as though it'd been he who'd talked himself dry. "I'll have to admit you've heard things I've never even guessed at. Art a prize! Strange, that." He poised his head, considering it.

Lucy put in, "He'd have gone far. Could have . . ." Then she blushed. "Sorry, sir."

Filey tried to grin at her. "And . . . Dorothy." He shook his head. "That was what our disagreement was all about, me thinking she'd persuaded Philomena to name Packer."

"Why would she do that?" I asked quickly. "What'd Dorothy gain?"

Filey laughed harshly. "Gain? Well, it made a more important case for us, catching a bigger fish. It'd reflect on her, and she was aiming for promotion. Damn it all, I'd got her all wrong."

"And she you?" I made this sound doubtful, but as soon as I got the words out I realised there could be no doubt at all. Nothing else would explain their mutual hatred and distrust, because each of them would have realised one basic fact: whoever might have persuaded Philomena to point her finger at Packer would automatically have persuaded her to sign her own death warrant. Each had blamed the other, but only Dorothy had been in a position to do anything about it.

But there was more to it than that. I realised, with a surge of contrition, that I had never really understood. She would have known that Packer would assume that Dorothy herself had been the one to direct Philomena's evidence. He would surely have had his feelers out, so that Dorothy had found herself in personal danger as well as having to support a responsibility for Philomena's own safety.

Filey hadn't answered my question. Something had occurred to him. His expression was for a moment outside his control.

"And now I'll never get a chance to apologise," he murmured. "Oh hell—the trouble that Wise girl's caused!"

Caused for Dorothy, particularly. She'd been a woman of great courage, with no thought of flight. She had waited for the danger to come to her, had even assumed Philomena's name, but not only in an attempt to hide her own identity. It had been a ruse to combine both personalities into one—one target instead of two. Why else had she named her agency WISEMANN?

"Yes," agreed Greaves, "a lot of trouble. And I'm not even sure it's finished."

That thought produced a solemn gap in the proceedings. Again I had a chance to glance across at Lucy, who did not meet my eyes this time. She was concentrating on her notebook, head down, probably catching up on a few of her loops and curlicues. I noticed some of my brandy was left and went across to fetch it. Bending over her I whispered, "How'm I doing, Lucy?"

She looked up, disapproval shading her eyes to deep, dark blue. "Don't get cocky, Paul. Mr. Filey's not finished with you yet." Then she lowered her head again.

Somewhat chastened, but determined to establish a remnant of my confidence, I returned with my glass to face Filey again.

He looked up from a contemplation of his feet. "Yes," he said, as though no interval had occurred. "She'd got me all wrong. I don't rig evidence, Manson. I don't prime witnesses. I play it straight."

"Such as that scene in the car-park?"

He sighed. "I always fancied Art as the gunman, and I was hoping to push him into making a mistake. I knew Dorothy was at the hotel."

"But Art didn't kill Philomena."

Greaves loomed at Filey's shoulder. Now we were talking about his case—cases, if you included Dorothy's death. Greaves was no longer going to take a back seat.

"Manson, we're willing to concede you've got information that could be useful to us. You've made your point. Now, keeping in mind that all you've heard need not have been the truth, let's have your thoughts on Miss Wise. And you can start with your last remark. Art couldn't have killed her, you said. Is this based on what *he* told you? Because if it is, you can forget it."

I thought about that. It was based on some sort of crazy logic, which itself was based on one significant gesture, which I hadn't up to that time considered deeply enough. And now, with Dorothy dead, I was the only one who knew about it.

"It's nothing to do with what Art said," I told him. "Well . . . what he said convinced me, but there's a confirmation. I think."

"You *think!*" said Filey, leaning back and slapping his knees. "This *is* a change. You always know."

"I haven't had time to work out exactly what it means. Look, I'll tell you, and you can both help me out."

Greaves appeared amused. "I'm sure Mr. Filey will join me in being honoured to assist you in your thoughts, Manson."

"Indeed!" said Filey.

Then they looked at each other and laughed themselves silly. It was not encouraging. I waited until they were silent.

"All right. Forget it, then."

"No, no." Filey was abruptly serious. "This is something else you know, isn't it, Manson?"

"Dorothy knew, I think. But she wouldn't tell me anything."

"That," murmured Greaves, "might have been the reason she died."

I'd been thinking that. "It was something she saw."

"And how the hell can you base anything—"

I cut off Filey's outburst. "If you'll just let me tell it in sequence. Look, I've got to talk myself into it. Okay?"

"Let him say it," Greaves decided. "It saves us thinking up questions. Lucy, I hope your pencil's sharp."

"Sharp and poised," she said.

It was clear that nobody was taking me seriously. "Can we at least agree that Philomena's death had to be related in some way to the warehouse robbery?"

They turned their faces in order to consult silently. They nodded to each other. I didn't wait for them to nod to me, but plunged straight on.

"Right. And I know Frenchie came here to offer Philomena money for her to change her story. I got that from Packer in circumstances that convinced me. Now just think about that. Assume Frenchie had managed to contact her. She hadn't made a decision about it right up to the evening of her party, and her death. Dorothy said she thought she finally made up her mind, but Philomena wouldn't say what she'd decided to do. And everybody was waiting to see what it was going to be. It meant a lot to several people, you know."

Lucy said, "Can you go a bit slower?"

"Who?" demanded Greaves. "Who are these interested parties you mentioned?"

"To start with, there was Art. Prime interest there. Then there was Frenchie. He'd want his answer, and perhaps if it was no thank you, he'd been given instructions to kill her. And dear old Grant Felton, he'd be interested. He was waiting to get engaged to her, and his woman was going out to meet another man. He wouldn't be pleased. Dorothy herself . . . oh, she'd be interested, you can bet. You could say she was intimately involved."

"True," agreed Filey.

"In exactly the same way as you, Mr. Filey."

"Now don't get *too* clever, my friend."

"Don't tell me you wouldn't be interested if a major case of yours got overturned, and Packer released."

"Put it like that—"

"And if you weren't interested, how come you arrived in this district at just the right time?"

"That'll be enough of that," Greaves interrupted. "Mr. Filey's interest was official. I'm saying no more. Just watch your tongue, that's all."

"Very well. For the sake of argument, shall we say that's five people, all interested in Philomena's decision. Yet she'd only made it at the last possible moment—just before she left the house. So you get the picture of five people lurking in the wood, all waiting to hear the important words she was going to say to Art. He was certainly going to be the first to hear them."

"I can't say I get such a picture," Greaves observed. "Don't get too flowery. Keep to facts."

"All the same, it all rested on what she said to Art, if she got the chance, and nobody knows what it would've been because she didn't get the chance."

"So why're you wasting our time?" asked Filey in disgust.

"Because I think I know what she'd decided. Something Dorothy said, though she might not have understood its significance."

"And you do?" Filey was back on his old form, sneering.

"I do. Think so, I mean. Dorothy told me that Philomena left the house wearing nothing over her head. There was mist coming in from the sea, and she'd had her hair done. So Dorothy ran after her down the drive, calling her name, and taking a nylon headsquare with her."

"Is the man insane?" Filey asked the row of pictures above my head.

"Lucy?" I asked.

"What is it?"

"You heard me, I'm sure. You'll have it down in your little book. Is that valid?"

"Well, yes—I'd say so."

"Good. Make sure *that* goes down. Where was I?"

"Dorothy running down the drive," Lucy reminded me.

"Right. And Philomena stopped to take the headsquare from her, then walked on a few yards and dropped it at the side of the road. Can you just see it?"

They were staring blankly at me. In the end, Greaves muttered, "So she decided she didn't want it. Manson, you're reaching. Talk sense."

"I told you I'm beginning to understand our Miss Wise. She was a bright girl, and with a sense of fun. You'll need to understand that this headsquare was a present from Grant Felton, part of a joke he'd thought up. The headsquare first, then show her the BMW convertible he'd got for her, the headsquare to protect her hair when she's blinding along at ninety. She wasn't supposed to know about the car—a surprise, that was. But you can't tell me she didn't know! Of course she did. She simply went along with the joke. What he'd aimed for was her disappointment over the headsquare, followed by the delight over the car. But—and Dorothy told me this—Philomena had her own bit of fun with Grant. She accepted the headsquare in a grave and stately way, instead of pouting at him."

"Is this getting us anywhere?" asked Greaves impatiently, while Filey bored at me with his eyes and said nothing.

"It's getting *me* somewhere. My first idea on it was that she dropped the headsquare because she was a bit disappointed. But now I see she wasn't, because she knew about the car. So . . . why *did* she drop it like that? Because, I'm thinking now, she'd just made her decision. If it was either way, she'd still have needed the headsquare to protect her hair-do. If she was intending to return to the party, she wouldn't want her hair in a mess. If she was intending to throw in her lot with Art, surely she'd want to look her best for him. So the dropping of the headsquare had to have an entirely special significance.

"She walked a few yards," I went on, trying desperately to get through to them, "then she did it like this." I picked up my empty brandy glass and held it out, my arm extended horizontally, gripping the stem delicately between forefinger and thumb with my little finger poised in a genteel way. Then I let it fall to the carpet. "Like that," I said. "It was a gesture of rejection. There was contempt in it. She was rejecting everything that was now behind her."

I stopped. Nothing. No expressions of admiration or rejection. A poised pencil and a raised face from Lucy. There was a blank lack of enthusiasm on Filey's thin face, and bland emptiness as Greaves lit his pipe again. Then Lucy stuck her pencil between her teeth to control her tongue, and nodded, her eyes shining. To her, the gesture was complete.

"Don't you see!" I cried, leaning sideways to retrieve the glass. "She was, I believe, simply walking away from her family—and frankly I couldn't see anything to hold her there—and away from Grant Felton and his bloody sheep and his car and his engagement ring. What she hoped to do then, I don't know. She wasn't the practical type. Maybe she was depending on Art. Maybe she hoped to help Packer to get released, and get her money. Whatever it was going to be, it was going to be with Art Torrance, so she was not about to drop him in it."

Greaves and Filey looked at each other, nodded, and Greaves said for both of them, "Carry on."

"You accept, then, that she intended to throw in her lot with Art, so that he'd have no motive for killing her?"

"We accept that."

"Then you're right slap bang face to face with the fact that the fawn silk scarf was in the telephone booth after she was dead."

"It's always been obvious," said Filey heavily, "that there had to be a substitution, the scarf for something else."

"Something? Such as what? Not hands. That'd show very special bruises. Am I right there?"

"Not with hands," agreed Greaves. "But now . . . you've introduced a nylon headsquare into the picture."

"It couldn't have been that. Dorothy told me that she picked it up and took it back to the house."

"Ye gods!" said Filey, bouncing to his feet. "Are we still going to accept what Dorothy Mann said?"

He turned to address Greaves, and paused. A constable, uniformed but hatless, was speaking to Greaves.

"The chief super's arrived, sir."

"All right. Tell him we're in here . . ."

But the chief superintendent was already there, a bull of a man, bustling in with a heavy tread of authority, his dark and baleful eyes at once aimed at me.

"Ah . . . Greaves. Getting along with it, are we? Fine, fine."

"We're coping, sir."

"Got somebody already, I see."

"Mr. Manson's helping us with our enquiries."

"Helping!" I heard Filey whisper in disgust. Then he turned his head and quaintly winked at me.

"Very well," said the chief super. "Let me know if you need my help. I'll just pop upstairs and see what's going on."

"Sergeant Forbes is in charge," said Greaves.

The chief super nodded, impaled me again with his eyes, then stumped out.

This interlude had given me a short break, and at the same time convinced me that I was now in a situation in which much heavier guns than Greaves and Filey could soon be levelled at me. In half a minute that man had impressed on me his force and inflexibility. Did I say the room was cold? Suddenly, I was sweating. The chief super had been in uniform. It had resurrected the Gartree atmosphere of repression.

Filey resumed his seat. "Well?"

I moistened my lips. "I can't remember what I was saying."

Lucy said, "Dorothy Mann told you she'd taken the headsquare back to the house. Mr. Filey questioned the truth of this."

I struggled to recapture the form of my thinking. "Somebody could've seen it, on a table in the hall. Somebody could've seen her, in person, in the house and around the place . . ."

"You're groping," said Filey thinly. We were no longer progressing in a straight line. "Nobody saw anybody. They were all making themselves clean and beautiful for the party. Except for Grant Felton, and he'd shut himself in with the car."

"All right then." I took a deep breath. "You're going to argue that Dorothy picked up the headsquare and followed Philomena with it. But why should she *do* that? Her decision must have been instantaneous, at the moment she picked up the headsquare and held it in her hands. And all that'd happened to alter the situation was Philomena's dropping it on the ground. But what else could it have told Dorothy? If it meant anything at all to her, that is. It was that Philomena was rejecting Felton and throwing her future into Art's hands—that's what. And *that* couldn't have harmed Dorothy. It may have even pleased her. It'd be an end to all the trouble, because someone else would be taking over the problem."

"I'm not sure of that," said Filey uncomfortably.

"She might even have seen in it the possibility that Philomena intended to tell the truth of what happened at that warehouse . . ."

"Ah!" murmured Filey.

". . . which Dorothy would see as trouble for you, Mr. Filey, and freedom for herself."

"Very well." Greaves gestured as Filey seemed about to pounce in. "But you've just eliminated the headsquare as a possible murder weapon."

"Better that way. It blurs the issue."

"And you hope to clarify it?"

"I'm eliminating suspects."

"All you've got left is Frenchie—"

"And Mr. Filey, here," I said sharply, stubbornly.

Filey moved. I held up a hand. "Give me a sec', I'm still eliminating. We're left with somebody who knew she was going to meet Art, and who was interested in hearing what she was going to say to him. That somebody might well have been waiting at that patch of woodland, in order to intercept her and ask her what that was. Right? It's just possible."

I was losing their confidence. I pressed on. "But we know now that she was going to tell Art it was him and her together, and to hell with everybody else. Except perhaps Packer. If Frenchie had met her, that's what she'd have told him—that she was going to do her best to get Packer free. So Frenchie would have no grouse. And the same goes for you, Mr. Filey—always supposing, of course, that you didn't do any evidence rigging . . ." I held up my palm. "No, no. You're the one who knows. If you didn't rig things, then you'd have no reason to kill her. So it's your turn. Does that clear you?"

Filey laughed easily. He reached forward and slapped my knee. "It clears me." The slap had been more forceful than absolutely necessary.

"But only if you accept that I'm right about Philomena's intentions."

"And he expects me to argue about it!" Filey leaned back to appeal to Greaves, who spared him a distorted grin.

"Which means Art was telling the exact truth, his movements and the silk scarf and the telephone booth," I said gloomily. "Somehow, you've got to get that scarf—"

"Somehow," said Filey, vastly satisfied with the situation, *"you've* got to get that scarf from A to B."

"Me?"

"You've just eliminated everybody but yourself."

"Have I?"

"Everything you've said has been based on what you claim to be privileged information. It wouldn't be said to us, and you know it. If it was ever said at all. You came out of Gartree, hunting for Philomena Wise. There's only you to say there was an offer of money involved. You came to kill her. You vied with Frenchie in this, and killed him. You were also paid to kill Dorothy Mann—"

"Now wait a minute!"

"You've had your say. Now shut up. Packer believed Miss Mann primed Philomena over the evidence. She feared for her own life.

Why the hell d'you think she took on Philomena's identity? Ah! I see you've already thought of that—or you already knew. Aubrey Wise was paying her—yes, we've got to accept that. But she took it on, two people in one identity. Whoever was hunted out first, she'd be waiting. And she'd got herself an illegal weapon. And you, Paul Manson, contacted her when you'd recently come from Gartree."

"There was more to it—"

"And you now base these theories of yours on what *she* told you! Don't you see, you fool, she'd never have confided anything important to you."

"I believed what she told me."

"Because it's so damned convenient for you. Oh . . . this lovely story of five suspects and a dropped headsquare. But no mention of the sixth suspect, I notice. That's you, Manson."

"It's not so!" I shouted.

"You're a liar, Manson. A proven and demonstrated strangler, who strangled again."

I almost choked to get it out. He was waiting, his eyes gleaming, his lips compressed into what could have been a triumphant smile.

"She was not strangled with the hands, Filey."

"Pff!" he said, dismissing it.

"Ask yourself why not."

There was a pause, into which Lucy whispered, "Slower . . . slower."

"You can't have it both ways." I raised my voice. "You can't say I'm a strangler with my hands—because of my father and because of yourself—and claim that's proof I killed Philomena, because she *wasn't* strangled by two hands."

There was more silence. Into it, the chief superintendent's voice rasped, "What the hell's going on here?" He stalked into the room.

Filey was on his feet. "Sir."

"If you can't control the situation, have him back at the station, Greaves. I'm not having this sort of thing in a public place."

"No!" I croaked. "A minute . . ."

"Everything's under control, sir," said Greaves, his voice neutral. "Mr. Manson was just about to clear up a few points. Weren't you?" he asked me.

I didn't know what the hell I'd been about to do. Faced by three unresponsive faces, two of them openly antagonistic, I felt completely overwhelmed.

"Come on, man," snapped the chief super. "Get on with whatever it was. We haven't got all night."

"I was going to ask Mr. Filey why he thought Miss Wise wasn't strangled with the hands."

"And you know?" Filey demanded.

Plunging in desperately I croaked, "Yes. I know."

EIGHTEEN

I had, indeed, sketched out a scenario in my mind, but it was far from being finished. I spoke directly to the chief super, because I was afraid I'd have to back-track over all the rest, just to clue him in.

"I've been telling Mr. Greaves and Mr. Filey that Philomena Wise . . ."

"Why're we talking about that?" he demanded. "That's Dorothy Mann upstairs."

"Sir." Greaves attracted his attention. "If we could just hear this last bit, I'll put it all together for you later."

"Hrrmph!" He clearly wasn't happy, but I knew he saw in front of him a suspect about to crack, and he wasn't far from wrong. And he wasn't about to cradle me into any sort of confidence. "Then say it," he snapped, "and let's get on with it."

"Philomena Wise made a gesture, dropping a scarf in the road. It meant she'd come to a decision. That would've been obvious to anyone who saw it, because Dorothy'd just run after her waving the headsquare and calling her name."

"Does this make sense, Greaves?"

"Yes, sir. If you'd please listen," said Greaves, gently polite.

I caught his eye, and went on while I had the chance. "The decision that Philomena was to be killed must have come at the moment that headsquare was dropped. So I suppose you could say it wasn't a premeditated murder. In that event, there would be no question of wasting time hunting for a suitable weapon. There would be anger, you see, and I can tell you that a person's natural choice is his own pair of hands. But a silk scarf was used to disguise the weapon, and quite a bit of work was involved with that —all because the obvious weapon couldn't have been used. The question is—why wasn't it? There's one person who wouldn't have dared to use his hands, because he would have left behind him a very personal mark. Grant Felton has got no more than a stump instead of a left thumb."

I paused, taking deep breaths, waiting for comment, but there was nothing. That was encouraging—it meant they were at least listening.

"Go on," said Greaves.

"Dorothy ran down the drive calling Philomena's name. At that time, Felton was in the garage, polishing the car. He could hardly have failed to hear. What would he do but go out on to the terraced drive to see what was going on? He would know she was intending to meet Art. She would've told him that much—in fact, she'd be defiant about it. So, from that terrace he would look down and see her drop the headsquare, and he would know, without any possibility of doubt, what she meant by it. She was rejecting *him*, and going to Art. Permanently."

"Does this make any sense to you, Greaves?" demanded the chief super, his patience stretched tight.

"Very much so, sir. Indeed."

"Then let's have it. Manson, is it? Hurry it up, man."

This, I had to guess, was to assert his authority. I continued, but now not in so much of a hurry. He could be damned.

"This character—Felton—he's very much of a macho type. Thinks he's God's gift to womankind. He just couldn't let her do that, not reject Grant Felton for a penniless, thieving young lout. He'd kill her first, before he let her make such a fool of him. I can see him, standing there, wating for Dorothy to get clear, and realising he didn't dare use his hands. But he didn't need to. He'd got the means right there. Not the headsquare—he'd got his cleaning rags, strips torn from a sheet. He snapped one at me. Wet." I held up my still-swollen left hand. "So he went after her with one of those, and from that moment it was all premeditated. He caught her up, and no doubt demanded to know what she thought she was going to do. She probably told him to get back to his sheep . . . and he strangled her with his cleaning rag."

I was talking myself hoarse. Filey realised, and reached down for his near-empty glass of near-flat beer, and offered it. I gulped at it.

"And the silk scarf?" Greaves asked quietly.

"Coming to it. Felton, as I see it, would've realised, then, that he'd made a bit of a mess of it. The cleaning rag, if he left it, would lead straight back to him, but at least it hadn't made any marks peculiar to him, as his hands would. Maybe he took it away with him straightaway. In any event, he had to give a thought to Art. Such as . . . where exactly was he at that time? It'd be around seven o'clock. Art might've started to walk to meet her, and could've seen . . . well, anything. So he'd have to locate Art, and I reckon there'd already be thoughts creeping into his thick skull on how he could incriminate him. Then, if Felton hurried to the meeting place he'd see Art there. Don't forget, he'd never met Art, but the fact that a young man was hanging around the bus stop and carrying something that was obviously a birthday present—that would identify him."

I paused in order to finish off Filey's beer. This time it tasted terrible. Now it was obvious that I'd impressed them. There were no comments. They waited.

"He saw Art dash off to the phone booth, followed him, saw him run from it—and noticed he'd left the present behind. Now . . . *there* was a decent bit of luck for Felton. He'd have dragged her body into the trees before he left her, so when he saw Art dashing off in the direction of the house, he knew Art would run straight past. So what could be easier than to leave the present beside her body! No—even better than that—open it first, to make it look as though she'd opened it herself. So he did that, and, joy upon joys, it was a silk scarf. Ideal. He could leave the wrapping, which'd even got Art's name on the gift tag. Then all he'd got to do was tie the scarf round her neck and get back to the house as quickly as possible, nip into the garage—and wait to be fetched out by Dorothy when things began to fly apart. In fact, she locked him in, to stop him interfering."

I stopped. To me it seemed valid and logical, everything fitting into the time scale. But there was no enthusiasm. Oh yes, Lucy looked across at me and smiled. But the others—no. I knew what was stopping them.

Greaves said it for me. "All this—the whole thing—is based on one blasted gesture. A dropped headsquare."

"It's a matter of meaning," I explained. "F'rinstance, if I do that"—I jerked up two fingers at him—"then you know exactly what I mean. Make it one finger, and it means something else. I can see you get the point. So I'm saying that Felton knew exactly what the dropped headsquare meant. He'd been in the garage, sulking. She'd no doubt told him she was meeting Art at the bus stop. He thought that this meeting was going to put an end to it all —this stupid thing between Philomena and Art. So he had to allow it to go ahead, but he wasn't going to let himself be *seen*, nervous and impatient and infuriated. No . . . he went and hid himself away with the car. That rejected headsquare would have been a personal insult—"

Greaves cut in with sharp impatience. "All right." He put up his hand. "That's enough. You've made your point." He looked to the chief superintendent for agreement. "We'll go and see him. Ask him a few things."

"I'd say so," agreed the chief super. "And at once, before it cools off. One point. This headsquare he keeps burbling about—has anybody seen it? Does it exist? Where would it be now, I wonder?"

Eyes were on me. "The last I saw of it, it was on a table in that entrance hall of theirs. Where Dorothy said she dropped it when she'd rescued it from the road."

"Very well." The chief super seemed to have taken charge. "We'll go along there now. Two cars and no fuss, Greaves. It's nearly midnight. Might have to knock 'em up. Right? Let's get moving, then." He led the way out, leaving the death of Dorothy behind him.

Filey looked at me sternly. "You," he said. "Come with us."

"You don't need me."

"No? You're forgetting something, aren't you. This is all based on something you say Dorothy told you. Of course we'll need you, if only to keep an eye on you. On your feet."

Lucy was already tidying her stuff away, and looked very efficient. She took my arm, as though I might be under arrest, and marched me outside. Uniformed officers seemed to be standing around everywhere, wearing their hands out saluting. Two cars were at the kerb. Across by the car-park there was a shadowy mass of locals, who were quite prepared to sacrifice sleep for sensation.

We loaded ourselves in, Filey, Greaves, and the chief super in the leading car, Lucy with me in the following one, each with a driver, very correct in their driving. There were no flashers, no sirens. We drifted quietly along the road back to Seagulls.

"Well?" I asked cautiously. Lucy and I were virtually alone at last, but I didn't know whether she was now the strict guardian of the law or a friend.

"It's far from well, Paul, as you must know."

"Surely nobody believes—"

"Since you've been around, people have been dying left and right, all over the place."

"You surely can't be saying . . ." I looked sideways at her, but it was too dark to detect any expression. Yet her voice had been sufficiently daunting to change my course. "What's going to happen now?"

Relaxing into safer officialdom she was able to speak more

freely. "We shall interview Grant Felton. *You* will be silent, Paul. I hope you understand that. We shall hope to find the headsquare, but I don't see what *that* will prove. Only that you haven't invented it. Oh . . . I see we're here. Remember what I said, and speak only when you're spoken to."

I nodded, though she probably didn't see it. We were turning in at the entrance to Seagulls, climbing quietly to the dark frontage of the house. The cars stopped side by side opposite the entrance door, facing along the parking terrace. There was no sign of life in the building.

We got out, leaving the two drivers sitting quietly behind their wheels. The three senior men stood in a small huddle, whispering together. That they'd been so circumspect in their approach, and were still being so, hinted that they saw a certain amount of truth in my theory. And yet—and my spirits sagged at the thought— Grant Felton needed only to deny everything with sufficient conviction and they couldn't do a thing.

Greaves turned and gestured to me, as Filey walked towards the car they had used. Greaves spoke quietly. "The table you mentioned, is this the hall you meant?"

I nodded. Answered softly. "Yes."

Filey returned, carrying a torch. "Show us where," he said, and he handed me the torch.

Inside, I'd have known exactly where. From outside, it wasn't so easy to decide. Slowly, I walked along, flicking the torch light in through the windows. About two thirds of the way along I stopped.

"Look."

The nylon headsquare still lay there, untidily, on the table, on top of a couple of magazines.

The chief super nodded. It now existed. We prowled back to the door. Lucy touched my elbow, and drew me back into the shadows. Greaves pressed the bell-push. We heard nothing. It was so silent that I thought I could hear the sea. Looking back, I could see the moon reflected in it, smearing it.

He rang again, and lights went on. We waited. There was the clatter of a released chain and the door opened. Aubrey Wise, in pyjamas and dressing-gown, the light behind him caught in his tousled hair, stood peering out.

"What on earth . . ."

"We're police officers, sir," Greaves said, his voice gravely quiet. "You'll remember me, of course. We'd like to speak to Mr. Felton, if we could. Grant Felton." He was playing it very cool.

"I can't see . . . understand . . ." Sleep fuddled him.

"A few words."

"But he's not here."

"Not?" Even in that one word there was a lift of interest in Greaves's voice. "You mean he's left?"

"That is so. Packed and left."

"When was this, sir?"

"An hour ago."

Filey and Greaves glanced at each other. If I'd been them, and there'd been a shooting at Port Sumbury, I'd have put a road-block at the end of the road. There was no other way out. That had surely been a couple of hours before.

"He had his own car, did he, Mr. Wise?"

"You could say that. He'd be using the BMW, I assume." There was a certain acidity in Wise's voice. He was coming out of his daze. Clearly, there had been some acrimony involved in Felton's abrupt departure. "Do you mind telling me what this is all about, Inspector."

"We're investigating a shooting incident in Port Sumbury."

Aubrey Wise drew in his breath sharply. "And . . . and . . . who?"

"Dorothy Mann, sir, I'm sorry to say."

"Oh, my God, another! Is there to be no end . . . you're surely not implying that Grant—"

"We shan't know, sir, until we've spoken to him. There's one other point, though. We can't take anything from your house without your permission . . ." He left it hanging.

"What? What?"

"The headsquare, Mr. Wise. On that table along the hall."

"Are you mad?"

"If we may."

"For heaven's sake, take what you like! This is ridiculous . . ."

Smiling thinly at him, Filey slid past into the hall, and came back dangling the headsquare by one corner between two fingers. "Thank you," he said.

"And if that's all!" Aubrey snapped.

"I think so, sir," murmured Greaves, and they stood back.

Say this for Aubrey Wise, his manners won over his anger. He closed the door with barely a sound. The three men went into a huddle again, their heads together.

"Now what?" I asked Lucy softly.

"Be quiet."

I tried to hear what they were saying, but only odd phrases crept through. ". . . can't have got away," from Greaves. ". . . lying

low," from Filey. And a deep grumbling impatience from the chief
super. It went on for ages. I cleared my throat.

"Is it all right if I make a suggestion?"

They turned and stared at me. Then they moved in on me. This
was perhaps something else that I knew and they didn't. "What?"
demanded Greaves.

"If I was Felton, I'd realise you would have the road blocked. I'd
tuck myself away in the car somewhere . . . and wait until it's
clear."

"Where?"

"The garage," I suggested. After all, he'd haunted it for days.

They peered about them into the darkness.

"The garages are round the side. The BMW was in one of them,
the last time I saw it." My hand still hurt.

"We'd better take a look," said Filey.

"May I?" I asked politely.

The three heads were close to mine now. "Why you?" whispered
Greaves, aware of the possibility.

"He might not have heard what's going on. If he sees me, he
might think I'm alone. You don't want trouble, I'm sure. Right?
There's a chance I could get him to say something. If he sees you
lot, he'll say nothing."

"I don't like this," said the chief super. "We'll simply go and pick
him up, if he's there, and stop messing about."

"Sir," I said. "If I could . . . look, it's his word against mine. I'd
like a fair shot at it. There's something that might provoke him."

Filey beat me to it. Smiling mockingly, as far as I could tell, he
held up the headsquare by its corner. "This?"

I nodded. Filey glanced at the chief super. This was definitely
unprofessional procedure I was suggesting. But, in a way, it was
part of my own defence. The moonlight glanced across his eyes
and the line of his jaw. I'd swear he smiled. Maybe cynically.

"Let him make a fool of himself, Filey. What can we lose?"

Filey offered me the headsquare, saying nothing.

"Can I handle it?"

"By its corner only. There could be traces . . ."

I took it tenderly. This was the only clue, this and its meaning.
"If I need help, I'll shout."

"We'll be there before then."

I grinned at Lucy, though she might not have detected it. Then I
walked out past the end of the building, the headsquare dangling
from my right hand, my eyes switching immediately to the row of
garages. Back there, in the heavier shadow, it was impossible to
detect whether the doors were all closed. The BMW had been in

the end one, closest to the house. I stared at the patch of shadow, and thought I could detect just a glint of reflection from chrome or headlamp glass. Felton had perhaps polished too well. I stopped, ten yards away. Now I was certain the car was in there, its nose facing out. That meant, I realised, that he'd used it since I'd been there last. A trip to Port Sumbury, no doubt.

"Grant," I said, trying to keep the quaver from my voice. "It's Paul Manson. I've got something to show you."

Silence.

"I know you're there."

Then the headlights came on, full mains. It was like a physical blow, and nothing else existed but the glare. I narrowed my eyes, but it wouldn't ease. There was actual pain, a shot of agony inside my head. Even, I felt, it was too powerful to shout through. But all the same, I shouted.

"Remember this?"

I held out the headsquare at full arm stretch, finger and thumb still holding the corner, and then released it. It fluttered down, but before it hit the ground the engine flared into life. He must have started it in gear with the clutch held out, because at once the tyres screamed and the lights weaved, then sprang at me. In blind terror, I dived to my left, and felt something catch my heel, spinning me back towards the guard wall at the rear. I fell, turning and rolling, and saw the lights swing across the low parapet, knew he was turning, tail sliding on the smooth surface because he'd got too much power on, towards the front of the house. There were shouts above the roar of the engine, and I rolled again. I lifted my head. He was nearly head on towards the two parked cars, his lights catching one door flying open, one startled and frantic face behind a windscreen.

Then he tried to turn away from them, and overcorrected. The rear wheels broke away and he spun, the tail side-swiped the wall, and then the car was over, pitching tail down then nose down, and over the edge of the parapet.

On hands and knees, one of them painful, I scrambled forward to the wall and lifted myself to peer over the top. I was in time to see the car bounce to a halt on the road below, canted so that the headlights, still proudly searching, were flaring into the sky. Only in the sudden silence did I realise the extent of the noise its descent had made.

There was no fire. They ran down the drive, followed by the two cars. Lucy ran to me. I thought she seemed weaker than I was.

"Oh, you fool, you fool . . ." she kept saying.

I tried to smile, sitting there on the top of the wall. "You must admit, I certainly got a reaction." The right one, too.

Later, much later because I was in no hurry to find out, I heard that Grant Felton had not been wearing his seat-belt, and had suffered serious injuries. He died in hospital without saying a word. But in the garage they found a length torn from a sheet, which was creased in such a way that it could well have been flung round a neck, a slim feminine neck, and tied. They were also able to prove, I heard much later, from the skin of Felton's right hand, that he'd recently fired a gun.

The headsquare told them nothing. It had said enough already.

NINETEEN

We were in the bar at The George, Lucy and I. She was no longer required to keep an eye on me, because statements had been taken and signed and I was free to leave. It was three-thirty in the morning. The remnants of sandwiches were on the table before us, empty glasses, and a nylon headsquare that nobody seemed to want.

It is at this time that a person's life-force is supposed to be at its lowest ebb. At this time the police are liable to pounce with an arrest warrant, certain that you'll be fuddled and confused, unable to defend yourself either physically or verbally. Lucy sat with me. My defences were way down. Vaguely, I realised that there was now no need for her official presence, but I said nothing. My bed seemed far distant in the future. All I wanted was to sit there, my muscles setting stiffly, my aches and pains assembling themselves to assault me if I moved.

Lucy spoke softly. "You won't be in any hurry to leave the district."

I mulled this over. Had it been a statement, a question, a suggestion? "Greaves said he'd finished with me."

"He has, yes." She caught my quick glance. Light winked in her eyes. Then she was very solemn. "What will you do?"

"When I leave?" I shrugged. There was nothing certain about

that, either. I forced my mind to consider it. "Back to the U.S.A., I expect. Yes. There's some unfinished research, just this side of the Rockies. My notes . . . I'll have to catch up . . . it's been years. Four years." Lost time, rejected time, precious time when I'd been learning nothing. No. That wasn't quite correct. I'd learned a lot. I shook my head . . . shaking the memory free. "Yes, I'd better get back to my research."

"It sounds interesting."

But now, because I'd already envisaged it in a special form, though with a blurred image rather than with its now sudden brilliant clarity, I knew I didn't want to go alone.

"I might find it's different now," I said with pitiful inadequacy, because suddenly her response had become vitally important to me.

She gave me her best solemn pout, and her eyes again caught the light. "Because you'll be lonely, with all that great big sky?"

"Not quite that. Alone—yes. Not with the right companion." I hesitated. "Will you?"

"I'll give it a thought." There was no hesitation. So she had.

"Yes," I said. "Do that." Why was I talking like an idiot? "It'll take a good month to arrange. I'll call in on the way."

She laughed, something I'd not heard before, a tinkling sound that picked at my nerves excitingly. "Not quite on your way."

"It'd be worth the diversion," I decided. "It's rough, though. A big Cherokee, and supplies for a couple of months. Camping out under the stars."

"I've never tried that."

"Coyotes and snakes."

"Ooh!"

I grinned at her expression. Into one word she'd compressed the very essence of mockery and faked fear, while her eyes came alight with challenge. And I, like a fool who couldn't control his impulses, picked it up and tossed it back. "I need you with me, Lucy."

She got to her feet. "A month is the length of notice they expect." Then she kissed her fingers and reached over to touch me on the end of the nose, and walked towards the door, taking the headsquare with her.

With the door open, she paused and glanced back, a provocative glance, raised her hand with the headsquare between finger and thumb, and dropped it to the floor.

I stared at it, at the closed door. There was another meaning to that same gesture, the dropped handkerchief inviting the gallant retrieval of it and its return. The same gesture, but oh what a different meaning to it!

I'd based everything on my interpretation, and as it turned out I'd been correct. It was only now she told me I could've been wrong.

I went quickly and picked it up, but I was too late to hand it back. The car engine awoke in the night outside, and faded away.

That night I got about four hours of dead sleep, had an extended breakfast, then drove over to Mrs. Druggett's. She sounded annoyed.

"They've taken him off! Poor lad—what could they want with him?"

I didn't tell her, and left her to cherish her illusions.

At the station all was quiet and sleepy, the aftermath of concentrated effort. Greaves said I could see Art, but be careful what I told him. I was, apparently, *persona* slightly *grata*. But, by this time, there would be little I could say to Art that I hadn't said already, except goodbye. Greaves got a constable to take me to the cells.

Art bounced to his feet from the sterile bed. "What's going on, Paul?"

His cockiness was in tatters, but he tried to draw it round himself. I tried a warm smile. "When Greaves has got the time he'll want a statement from you. All that stuff you said in the car-park. Then it'll take its course, and you'll be tried for the murder of Ted Adamson."

He was pugging at me, protruding his lips. "That'll do that bastard Filey, anyway."

"I wouldn't be too certain about that."

"An' they'll get him for killin' Phillie, too."

"No, Art."

"Sure to. She was gonna land him in it."

"Sorry, Art, but he didn't do it."

Then I told him how and why Grant had done it, and halfway through he sat down again.

"That Aussie bastard!"

"She was going to try to get Packer's money, and set up house with you, Art."

He blushed, then abruptly covered his face with his hands. I waited. At last he looked up, his eyes like beads.

"But they'll get Filey for Frenchie?" he asked hopefully.

"No, Art. Let me say this, you idiot. Felton also killed Dorothy. Yes, Dorothy Mann, whose office we searched. She was keeping close to him, and he was beginning to believe she knew more about his actions than he fancied. She'd seen the dropped headsquare, you see." I explained about the headsquare, and he seemed to get it at once.

He nodded. "Sure. The old two fingers, she gave him."

"So in the end Felton's nerve went, and he shot Dorothy with that gun—"

"The one outa her office?"

"That very one."

He nodded over that, and gave it some thought. "But they'll still get Filey for Frenchie?" You could tell he didn't like Filey.

I shook my head at him. "It's not on, you know, Art. It wasn't Filey. Just look at the motives we've got for the death of Frenchie. He'd followed you here—oh yes, he had. I thought otherwise at one time, but not now. You were the obvious connection with Phillie. And you'd know he was on your heels, but you wouldn't know exactly what it was about, only that he must've come from Packer. Then, when she died you had to assume Frenchie had come for that, in spite of the fact that strangling wasn't in his line. So that when the opportunity came, and Frenchie was short of one knife and quite a lot of blood, then you grabbed your chance. And a chunk of rock. Isn't that so, Art?"

He stared at me with stubborn rejection, for once at a loss for words.

"No proof, of course," I went on blithely. "There's not even any evidence that you were in Port Sumbury that evening."

"So why the hell're you wastin' my time?" he demanded.

"I was going to suggest you ought to admit to that, too, when you see Greaves."

"You crazy or somethin'?"

"Not really. You said almost the same thing yourself: two for the price of one. Two sentences running together, then you'd be clean when you come out. Older, but clean. And who knows, when they sentence you for Frenchie they might take into the account that you've removed a blight on society, and give you a negative sentence, to be served concurrently. Sort of knock a few years off the sentence for Ted Adamson, as a mark of public approval."

For a moment he was sullen, then he grinned, his face lighting up. "You're a right clown, Paul Manson. You know that!"

I slapped him on the shoulder and left him to his decisions. Then I drove to The George, to tell them I would be calling in at a later date to take Lucy to the U.S.A.

I got the impression they already knew. Who else would she rush to with the news? "I'll leave her this headsquare," I said. "She'll know what it means."

George grunted. "I'll have your bill ready when you come."

"Why not now?"

"We'll have to have a going-away party. I'll expect you to pay for that."

"All right with me. Credit card?"

"Cash, matey, cash."

"By that time," I told him, "all my spending money will be in U.S. dollars."

Still with a straight face, he said, "U.S., eh? Then we'd better make it an early Thanksgiving party."

I didn't ask him for whose departure he'd be giving thanks.

CENTRAL 8795